LoveChild

LoveChild

Herbert Williams

For my wife Dorothy
Unstinting in her support and
encouragement of my work

First impression: 2011

© Herbert Williams & Y Lolfa Cyf., 2011

In any edition of the work, the publisher will acknowledge
the author as the owner of the full copyright.

Cover design: Chris Iliff

The publisher acknowledges the support of the Welsh Books Council

ISBN: 9 781 84771 307 0

Published and printed in Wales
on paper from well maintained forests by
Y Lolfa Cyf., Talybont, Ceredigion SY24 5HE
e-mail ylolfa@ylolfa.com
website www.ylolfa.com
tel 01970 832 304

1

S TEVE WAS MORE than usually restless that night. It was Smythe's fault: the man was an idiot. They'd had to change the front page splash in double-quick time because of an air crash in Jersey and he had panicked, literally panicked. He'd flapped around like a bishop in a brothel while Steve and Scottie had done the necessary. The man simply wasn't up to it. Night editor? Give me morphia, as Jos's Aunt Cecy would say.

The result was that Steve got home soon after 3 a.m. with a thumping head and the night's big stories bumping around in his brain like angry dodgems. Even a Scotch and water had failed to soothe him and when at last he crawled into bed he lay awake, thinking of that useless prat Smythe and how he'd only got the job by brown-nosing the right people. Sending him to Hanoi might be the answer. With a bit of luck the Yanks might drop a bomb on his head, now they were doing their best to further world peace by blasting North Vietnam into Kingdom Come.

Beside him, Jocelyn slept like a baby. She was so used to him coming in at all hours that she didn't twitch an eyelid. Well, it was just as well. If she got her rag off over things like that he wouldn't stand a chance.

The big stories (the air crash, the adultery of an Old Etonian cited in a divorce petition, Harold Wilson's latest bombastic speech to businessmen) eventually stopped bumping into one another, and Steve slept fitfully until a little after eleven. By then the traffic on Putney Hill had long been an undercurrent to his dreams, a flattened-out buzz that remained when the dreams were dispersed and he was fully awake.

Steve Lewis was a man of middling years, just turned thirty-seven and with a waistline notably thicker than it had been when he had first come up to Fleet Street from Wales. A receding hairline had robbed him of the waves he had been so proud of in his youth, but in some respects he was better-looking, the nose which had once seemed too prominent harmonising more easily with the firmer features of maturity and his lips, once almost too feminine in their fullness, being narrower and paler than hitherto. He seemed a man at ease with himself, but as he scanned the front page of the *Daily Comet* he frowned slightly, thinking that perhaps the splash headline he had put on the story of the air crash wasn't quite as good as he had imagined the night before. Well, it was gone now and that was the nature of the beast: the stories they'd sweated over had already been skimmed through on the Tube or the bus and were halfway to being consigned to the rubbish bin.

He let the paper lie in his lap and sipped his coffee slowly. He came to life gradually, his head still gummy with the semi-consciousness that passed for sleep, his body sticky and stale. When he had finished his coffee he'd shower and shave, freshening up for another day in a life which in many ways was fulfilled, but in which he left many a door in his mind firmly shut for fear of what lay the other side.

As usual, Jos had left the morning's mail on the coffee table. He riffled through it desultorily. A bill from the Gas Board; an invitation to renew his long-expired membership of a book club; a postcard from their friends Bill and Avis, on holiday in Majorca; a letter from the secretary of the tennis club, reminding them of the annual meeting a week hence.

Putting all this aside, his eyes met those of his nine-year-old son Simon, whose earnest bespectacled face looked out at him from a small gilt frame on the sideboard. Jos did not particularly like this snap; she thought it made him look too serious. But he *was* a serious child, and none the worse for that, mused Steve.

Jos would be collecting him from school at half past three, after her own foreshortened day's teaching. They would be together, the three of them, until Steve set out for another night's subbing on the *Comet*. Returning in the early hours, a new set of stories would be bumping around in his brain. Jos would again sleep on, scarcely stirring as he slid in beside her. He might hear her leave with Simon just before half past eight; he might not. But this time next morning he would again be sitting alone, slowly adjusting to another day. It was not a bad life.

They lived in a 1930s semi with mock-Tudor gables and a narrow drive barely wide enough to squeeze a car up. They had extended the once-tiny kitchen into the garden but it was still so narrow that two people couldn't pass one another without a brush with intimacy. He stood in the doorway to chat as she cooked for herself and Simon, Steve having had a pub lunch at the George, washed down by a pint or two of Younger's.

He was struck anew by the fairness of her eyelashes and the way she appeared detached from her mundane task as she stood at the electric stove. In his eyes there had always been something in her of the medieval lady, outwardly chaste but inwardly raging for the knight in shining armour to pierce her defences. She would have been surprised to know this, for Steve was a man who, for all his passion and openness in many ways, revealed only so much of himself as he wished (revealing different things to different people). Slowly she had come to realise this, and with the realisation had come a sense of hurt that, for a while, had threatened her commitment to their marriage.

'Bill and Avis seem to be enjoying themselves,' he said cheerily.

'Yes. Can't understand why.'

'Oh? Why shouldn't they?'

'Place looks ghastly. All those jerry-built hotels made out of Lego.'

'They aren't staying in them though, are they? They've gone self-catering.'

'More fool them. Paying through the nose, I expect.'

He was determined not to be put down.

'I quite like the idea of Majorca,' he confessed. 'Robert Graves lives there, you know.'

'Does he now?'

'Chopin lived there too. With George Sand.'

'Well, maybe Bill and Avis will pay them a visit.'

Turning, she gave him a brittle smile.

'I see Jack's hustling us to the annual meeting,' she said later, just before he set off for his shift on the sub-editors' desk. 'You off that night?'

''Fraid not.'

'Pity. I'd like to go there.'

'Nothing stopping you, is there?'

She glanced at Simon meaningfully.

'I'll be all right, Mum,' the boy said reassuringly.

'Don't be silly.'

'I can go to Aunt Evelyn's.' Jocelyn didn't answer. 'I like it there,' Simon persisted.

'It may not be convenient.'

'Oh, Mum. Please.'

Steve smiled. 'You like their new colour telly, don't you?'

'Can we get one, Dad?' Simon asked eagerly.

'Some day maybe.'

Simon pulled a tell-me-another face.

'Can't you get a night off for once?' Jocelyn asked.

Steve looked pained with her irritation. 'I am off. I'm off on Friday that week.'

'Can't you change with someone then?'

'I could. But I don't like doing that too often.'

She gave him a glance that said *you love that paper more than me*. She had actually said it to him once.

'It's only a tennis club meeting, for God's sake,' he exploded.

'Only,' she repeated sarcastically. 'Everything's *only*.'

Simon looked from one to the other unhappily.

'I'll see what I can do,' said Steve woodenly.

'Don't break your neck.'

The strange thing about the *Daily Comet* was that, although Fleet Street's most up-to-date paper (or so it claimed), it was housed in an ancient building with askew, Dickensian corridors and laborious stone stairways. The editorial offices were on the second floor, a storey above the composing room where the printers pursued their ancient, inky trade amid the clatter of Linotype machines and farther still from the thunder of the huge presses on the ground floor that spewed out the finished product. Communication was by means of the compressed air tube that sucked down the subedited copy and blew back the proofs, or by stairs up which generations of hacks had puffed their way to fitness or an early grave. Some day, the management promised, they would have a new building. Some day, the cynical hacks silently retorted, pigs might fly.

This greasy temple to Mercury was called Presswood House, after the Presswood brothers who had established their newspaper empire in the first half of the twentieth century. Charles and Michael Presswood had started life modestly enough as the sons of an open-cast coal prospector in the south Wales town of Aberdare, and to the astonishment of their father (who rated neither of them highly) had achieved great wealth and social status by the acquisition of a comfortable nest of provincial papers. Charles was now Lord Presswood of Cynon, an absentee peer who put in only an occasional appearance at the Palace of Westminster. His brother had recently gone to his grave as Sir Michael Preswood, a bon viveur with an excellent taste in claret and an insatiable urge for nubile young women. The *Daily Comet* was the jewel in their somewhat tawdry crown, its unexpected success winning them plaudits for their commercial astuteness. Any praise, however, was more properly due to the swashbuckling journalism of Gus Chapple, the editor who had revived the ailing *Daily World* and transformed it into the *Comet*, which to everyone's surprise had in the space of a few years overtaken the *Mirror* as the biggest-selling national. The decision to appoint him (happily rubber-stamped by the Presswoods, who were sensible enough not to interfere in matters about which they knew very little) had been that of Gerry James, group editor of Presswood Newspapers. James, like the Presswoods, had his roots in Wales, nourished not by open-cast mining but by the scholarly awareness of his headmaster father Ceredig

James, MA, who while admiring his son's success, wished it had been achieved in a field of endeavour more rarefied than daily journalism.

Smythe, the night editor, was closeted with Chapple when Steve took his place on the subeditors' table just after six. Scottie, the chief sub, was plainly off colour. He barely gave Steve a glance and snapped edgily at the copy taster, Phil Dixon, over a story about a White Russian princess that Dixon felt had human interest.

'Bollocks to that. No-one knows what a White Russian is these days, for Chrissake.'

'They're interested in Russians,' said Dixon defensively.

'Only if they're spies. Is she a spy?'

'No, of course not.'

'There's no *of course* about it. Every Russian's a bloody spy so far as our readers are concerned. Don't you know your own paper?'

'I know it as well as you.'

'That'll be the day.'

'So you're not going to run this?'

'It might make a filler.'

'A filler! Jesus.'

Steve treated himself to a small, private smile. Scottie and Dixon were a double act surpassed only by Scottie and Smythe. He reflected, not for the first time, that the comedy of a newspaper office was far funnier than anything on telly, Hancock excepted. His ruminations were abruptly despatched by a cry of 'Steve' from Scottie. He looked up, just in time to catch the tightly-folded sheets of copy paper flung at him by Scottie. It was a down page story about sharks off the coast of Cornwall, destined for page five of the first edition, Cornwall-bound before midnight.

As he cut the story back, he felt a stab of frustration and irritation. He would never get used to subbing, which he privately dismissed as 'shoving silly bits of paper around'. He still missed the thrill of the chase, the sheer adventure of a reporter's life in Fleet Street. He'd been up there with the best, getting into the Profumo story with a memorable piece on Stephen Ward just before the poor bastard was hounded to death. It was illness that had forced him out of the big time, the dicky heart that had plagued him ever since his boyhood rheumatic fever. 'Don't want to lose you, boy,' Gus Chapple had said, flashing him his showy smile. 'Have a spell subbing. Do you good – and us.' Steve was grateful to the Chief, but now he was itching to be back on the road. He missed not only the excitement but the camaraderie of the pack, the piss-taking and boozing which were as intrinsic a part of the hack's life as deadlines and smooth talk. Cooking up a clever headline was bugger-all beside that.

Just after nine, Steve looked cautiously around. Scottie, his face paler than ever beneath that auburn Highland thatch, had been whisked away for a quick, between-editions conflab with night editor Smythe. Dixon, his sidekick, was gloomily sifting through news agency copy, his tomb-black hair as lifeless as much of the stuff he was reading. Po-faced Stan Dewey, oldest sub on the desk, was steadily working through the Briefs, paring them down to the bone with grim tenacity. Some of the other subs had already sidled out, jackets straddling their chairs as 'proof' that they hadn't gone very far. One or two had even left half-smoked cigarettes smouldering in ash-trays. No-one was deceived. Nonchalantly, Steve pushed back his chair. Dixon looked up. 'Where do you think *you're* going?' he rasped.

'To the library. Checking something,' Steve coolly replied.

'Like hell you are. Look, this boozing lark's gone too far. It's got to stop.'

'Why not come over for one yourself? I'll buy you one.'

'Fat chance. I'm too bloody busy for that malarkey.'

'Bring you one back then, shall I?'

'Sod off. And don't be too long about it, either.'

Steve grinned, strolled out, took the lift to the ground floor and crossed the road to the Dog and Duck, the Comet's watering hole – every paper had one. He avoided the swill of subs at the bar to join a noisier group – his old mates, the reporters. 'Hi, Steve, what're you having?' 'Don't worry, I'll get my own.' 'Bugger off, what is it?' There was only time for a quick one, a second pint taking too long and befuddling the brain. Even so, he was back later than the rest and Dixon treated him to one of his famously long, cool looks.

It was quieter than the night before. They were reduced to a page one lead about Frank Cousins quitting his post as transport workers' boss and their Fleet Street rivals – their first editions arriving soon after ten – had nothing better. Steve, suddenly tired, began to look forward to going-home time.

Just before half past eleven Dixon's phone rang. 'Who? Is it a personal call? If so…' He glared accusingly at Steve. 'For you. An old mate with a good story. So he says.'

'Who is it?'

'Didn't get his name. Get rid of him. I'm busy.'

Steve hurried across. A thin voice said, 'Steve? Is that you? Bill Merrick here. Remember me?'

'Who? Sorry…' The line was bad. Steve jammed a finger in his right ear.

'Merrick. Bill Merrick. We worked on the *County Dispatch* together. In Glanaber.'

'*Bill.* Of course I remember. How are you?'

'Oh, so-so.' The line crackled. 'Look, I've got a good story for you. An exclusive. How much do you think your paper might…' The rest of the sentence was lost.

'What's that? I can't hear you.'

'For God's sake,' fumed Dixon.

'Sorry, Bill, you're coming and going. It's a bad line. Look, I'll call you back in the morning. What's your number?'

'Nobody else has got on to this yet.' The words were suddenly clear and Steve had a vivid mental picture of Bill Merrick, ginger-thatched, mackerel-eyed, glaring at him across the reporters' desk of the *County Dispatch*. 'I tell you it's a scoop. How much will you pay me for it?'

'I can't say, Bill, just like that. Look, I'll call you back in the morning. I can't talk to you now.'

'You'll be sorry if you don't, Steve.'

'Thank Christ for that,' muttered Dixon, as Steve went back to his place. 'Tell your pals not to call you this time of night. We're too bloody busy for that.'

'He's not a pal.'

'What?'

Steve let it pass. So did Dixon.

'Copy down,' called out Scottie, the chief sub.

A rather elderly copy boy (the term was loosely used), took the sheets of paper from Scottie's upraised hand, and shoved it down the hungry tube for setting.

The next edition of the *Comet* was swiftly taking shape.

2

WHY HAD BILL called him? They had never really been pals. In fact, quite the opposite. They had practically had a fight in the office. Steve remembered, with embarrassment, the stupid scuffling in the reporters' room that had ended with them both sprawled on the floor of the *County Dispatch* with Brenda Marsden – the editorial secretary who'd had the hots for him – prancing about in a panic.

He remembered so much else, but did not wish to. All that was behind him. It had happened fifteen years ago, but seemed more like a lifetime.

Bugger Bill Merrick! Couldn't he just ignore him? No, he could not.

He showered, shaved, read the note left him by Jos:

I'll be late home today because I have to take Simon to the dentist, remember? Give me a call if you can. Love, Jos xxx

The face he saw suddenly was not that of his wife. It was the face of a girl with chestnut hair and a proud expression, and she was saying things about him he did not wish to hear.

It was going on for midday before Steve got around to ringing his old colleague. The call went unanswered for so long that he was about to give up when a voice said crisply, 'Glanaber 2714.'

'That you, Bill? Steve here.'

'Morning Steve. I was hoping you'd ring.'

'Sorry I couldn't talk much last night – it was pretty hectic.'

'So I gather. Well, do you want this story or don't you?'

'It depends what it is.'

'I'll want some money for it. I told you.' The voice was flat, unfriendly to the point of hostility; Bill obviously hadn't changed.

'I can't say anything about that till I know what the story is, can I? You know that, Bill.' To his annoyance, Steve detected a note of pleading in his voice. What was wrong with him? He was the Fleet Street success, Bill the failure, the stay-at-home Glanaber hack too scared, or too dozy, to try his luck away from that sleepy, lotus-eating town in the far west of Wales.

'I'm not writing it up myself,' said Bill implacably. 'All I'm doing is giving you the tip-off. If you don't want it I'll try the *Mirror*. Or the *Mail*.'

'You've got to give me some kind of a clue, Bill.'

'All right then. Does the name Jill Manders mean anything to you?'

'The film star?'

'Of course. And Haydn Lucas?'

'Who?'

'The principal. Glanaber Uni.'

'Don't know him.'

'You ought to. He was in the news a lot last year. Your own paper attacked him.'

'What for?'

'Calling for import controls on people coming into Wales.'

'Oh yes, I remember now.' Steve smiled. 'Pretty daft thing to say, wasn't it? Man in his position?'

'He wasn't principal then. He became so last autumn.'

'I see. Well, what's the story, Bill?'

'What's it worth?'

'Oh, I don't know… two hundred maybe. If it's good enough.'

'Two hundred? That's all? You must be joking.'

'What were you expecting then, Bill?'

'At least a thousand. Possibly two.'

'Come off it. This isn't Profumo, is it?'

'It's something very like it.'

'Really?'

Dead silence.

'Bill? You still there?'

'Yes, but I'm not sure how long. I think I'll try the Mirror.'

'Wait!' The name Jill Manders rose huge in Steve's mind. What if there *was* something big here. A sex angle? 'What's Jill Manders got to do with it, Bill?'

'Ah-ha! So you're biting now, are you?'

'I might be. What's the story?'

'Let's see the colour of your money first, Stephen.'

He took a risk. 'We might go up to five hundred for a tip-off. If it's big enough.'

'A thousand.'

'No. Five hundred. I can't go more than that, Bill.'

'Well… that's a starter, I suppose.'

'It's probably a finisher.'

'We'll see about that. I'll tell you so much. They're linked.'

'What are?'

'*They* are. The film star and the principal.'

'To what extent?'

'A great extent.'

'You mean they're having an affair?'

A pause. 'Yes.'

The old thrill of the chase coursed through Steve's blood.

'And he's principal of the college?'

'It's a big story, Steve,' said Bill excitedly. 'They're…'

'What?'

'I can't tell you more. Come down with the money.'

'Who knows about this, Bill?'

'Everyone here. You know Glanaber.'

'But the press… hasn't the *Dispatch* done a story?'

'No.'

'Why not? You're working there, aren't you?'

'Not any longer.'

'Why not?'

'Never mind. The point is, they're not running this. You know what the management's like. They're scared of their own shadow. And there are other considerations.'

'Such as?'

'Printing contracts.'

'Oh. I see.' Thank God he had got out of that dump while he could.

'Come down here, Steve. As quick as you can. I tell you, it's a scoop for the Comet. The story's yours.'

Steve thought swiftly. 'Trouble is, Bill, I'm not reporting just now. I'm on the subs desk.'

'I know that. Your wife told me. Terrible shame that, Steve, man like you. Why…'

'Never mind,' he interrupted, 'I think I could swing it. Look, leave it with me, Bill. Thanks for the tip-off.'

'You won't forget now – your promise?'

'Of course not. Look, I've got to get moving on this. I'll be in touch.'

He put down the phone. Glanaber, he thought. A scoop. In bloody *Glanaber*. Christ.

Again he thought of the girl. With chestnut-coloured hair. Lying beneath him. In her parents' house.

Annette.

He was a little soldier, he really was, thought Jocelyn, and then corrected herself impatiently. No, not a soldier. He was a little *hero*. She glanced proudly at Simon, sitting beside her in the dentist's waiting room. Of course dentists were far better than they used to be, but all the same... Some kids still did anything to avoid going. But Simon had always been fine with Mr Woods... never any trouble. And Woods *was* a fine dentist. Not young, mind. But quite avuncular, with his jovial pink face and laughing eyes. The sort of man you could trust. Simon trusted him anyway.

The boy was reading *The Eagle*. It wasn't bad, as comics go, in Jocelyn's estimation. She disapproved of comics generally: their obsession with war, either those past or (even worse) projected for the future, was disgusting. How would the world ever grow out of wars if kids were forever being told they were inevitable? She had put an absolute ban on anything militaristic in the house; no toy soldiers, sailors or airmen for Simon. He had seemed not to mind, to be quite happy with what he was given. But he couldn't help being tainted; war was in the papers, on the TV news – especially now, with those stupid Americans fighting a ridiculous war in Vietnam. And it had such support, even in Britain! Couldn't people see it was all cooked up by the Pentagon and their pals in the arms industries? Oh, people were so foolish!

'Simon? Your turn now!' The dental nurse with the garish lipstick turned her bright smile and friendly eyes on the boy. He put down his comic immediately.

'Shall I come in with you, darling?'

Simon shook his head determinedly, as Jocelyn knew he would, and strode to the door of the surgery. The nurse flickered a sympathetic smile at Jocelyn. When the door closed behind Simon, a woman opposite Jocelyn said admiringly, 'Brave little boy you've got there. Catch mine doing that, and he's a lot older.'

Jocelyn smiled appreciatively, yet resented the woman's intrusion. She did not quite know why. She knew Simon was brave, and deserved this woman's admiration. If she had analysed her feelings further, she might have concluded that her son's stiff-upper-lip made her feel ineffective; that she really would have *preferred* him to need her enough to want her to accompany him into the surgery. But she simply pushed back her impatience, and coolly read (or pretended to read) an article in the woman's magazine she had picked up from the table in the waiting room. When Simon came out a minute later, having had the injection that preceded the filling, the woman swept past her as if deeply offended.

'OK, darling? Soon be over now. Mouth feels a bit funny, I suppose?'

Simon nodded. 'Mr Woods said it would. It's just all stiffening up.'

'We'll get you something nice on the way home. Something special.'

'That's all right, Mum.'

Something special. What on earth did she mean? The boy wouldn't feel like eating anything much. It was just something to say, to show that she cared, that she *did* admire him. He was a bit like his father – remote in an odd, impersonal way. You never knew really what either of them was thinking.

When Simon went back in for the filling, Jocelyn thought ahead to the weekend. Could she persuade Steve to stay overnight with her parents in Guildford? They were spending Saturday with them anyway, but rather than go back to Putney in the evening she would prefer to stretch their visit into Sunday. Even after ten years of marriage, she missed her leisurely Sunday mornings with her mother: not doing anything special, just pottering about and chatting. But she feared Steve would have none of it. He would make the excuse that he was working Sunday evening, even though he didn't have to leave for work till after five – well after five on Sunday, in fact, with the roads swept clear of their weekday congestion. The reason was obvious, though never stated. He did not really like her parents. Oh, he tolerated them and was never unfriendly, but after the first couple of years, when he had put on a bit of a show, he had never reached out to them as they had to him. That was how she thought of it: reaching out. You either reached out to someone, or you stood back. Steve was standing back; and not only from her parents. Acknowledging this, she felt a chill inside her, so deep and so raw that it made her shiver.

3

'CAN'T SOMEONE ELSE go? Why's it got to be you?'
'Because I've got contacts there. I know the place.
It used to be my patch.'

Looking at his earnest, persuasive face, his shining eyes,
she recognised all the old symptoms. He was on to a story.
Nothing would stop him.

She had returned home to find him, surprisingly, still
there, not doing a subbing shift at the office. At first she
feared he'd been taken ill again, but only for the most fleeting
of moments. It had all come out in a rush – the call from
Glanaber, his response to it, his immediate phone call to the
news editor, the way the paper had instantly put him back on
the road to cover this scoop.

'But you can't go tonight, Steve.'

'I must.'

'But that's ridiculous – what's the urgency?'

'You know, Jos – I can't sit on this. I've got to get down
there right away.'

'And what about us?' To her horror, she heard her voice
shaking.

'What?'

'Where do we come in your reckoning – Simon and me?
Not very far, is it, Steve?'

'Jos! Don't be like that. Don't be silly.'

Scarcely believing she had said this, he put his arm round
her. She shook him off.

'Don't patronise me, Steve. I don't want it.'

'I didn't think I was,' he said stiffly.

She knew he was in the right; that's what made it so awful. He *had* to go. He was a reporter – one of the best on the paper, only temporarily shunted on to the subs' desk by the illness that had weakened him. He was rarin' to go. She could see it.

'I was hoping we'd go to Mum and Dad's this weekend.'

'Well, you can still go. There's nothing to stop you.'

'Thank you very much. That's very kind of you.'

'For Christ's sake, Jos!' he exploded. 'Don't be so unreasonable.'

'Yes, I am, aren't I? I'd just like to see more of my husband. Very unreasonable.'

'It's my job, Jos.'

'Don't I know it. Working all night and now haring off to some godforsaken hole in Wales.'

'I'm on a story, Jos. A big one. If I don't get it someone else will.'

'Oh, to hell with them all! I'm sick of the whole business.'

Simon came down from upstairs. He looked from one to the other.

'What's wrong, Mum?'

'Oh, nothing. Dad's got to go away, that's all. I wasn't expecting it.'

'Where are you going, Dad?'

'To Glanaber,' Steve said cheerfully. 'There's a story I've got to cover. Sorry about that, Simon – I won't be away long though.'

'Oh,' said the boy reproachfully. Young though he was, he knew that 'Glanaber' wasn't simply the name of a town, but a word that could make both his parents unhappy, in ways he did not understand.

'Will you be eating before you go?' asked Jocelyn, exasperated.

'No. I haven't got time. I should be on my way by now really. I stayed here till you came home.'

'How very thoughtful of you. Well, you'd better be going, I suppose. Have you packed your things?'

'Yes.'

'I suppose you've made a mess of it, as usual. And left something behind that you'll need.'

Steve bit his tongue, seeing the unhappiness on Simon's face at this parental squabble.

'I'll ring you when I get there. It'll take me a few hours.'

'Don't suppose you know how long you'll be away?'

'Haven't a clue, love,' he replied cheerfully.

He was so bloody *happy,* she thought angrily. To be away from her, or to be on a story again? Both, she suspected, but the exact proportions she didn't like to imagine.

When he had gone, she did all the usual things: ate a meal with Simon, helped him with his homework, played three games of draughts with him, of which he won all three, read him a bedtime story and then patted downstairs to look at the telly alone. It was an evening like any other, except that her husband wasn't subbing at the *Comet* but driving to the town in the far west of Wales that had once been his home. She had been there only once with him and hated it. The small town, huddled between, on the one side, a hill curiously topped with a stone pillar and, on the other, a crumbling cliff that looked to her like a gigantic coal tip, had something so alien about it that she could not bear to be there more than a few days. The nit-picking faults she found with it – the grittiness of the sand, the poor quality of the seaside entertainments, the Welsh conversations she overheard ('And why shouldn't they speak Welsh?' Steve had enquired. 'It's their own language, for God's sake.') – were attempts to rationalise something purely instinctive. It was the *soul* of the town that repelled her, steeped as it was in a history dark and misshapen and unknowable. In which, she suspected – a suspicion she kept as deep below the surface of her consciousness as possible – it resembled her husband.

The new Triumph Herald, he would say with his tongue more than half in his cheek, was his pride and joy. The corny phrase would normally grate on him, but when applied to his car it was perfectly apt. It was the first brand-new car he had ever bought; the step up from the second-hand market seemed a significant event in his life. They had gone around the showrooms together, he and Jos, delighting in the sheer fun of it like children. She had left the mechanical assessment to him, flattering his maleness in the assumption that she could not be expected to understand anything like that (and in truth she knew very little about it, even less than he did), confining herself to such issues as comfort and safety and colour. They had both gone for this model, not least for its appearance. It looked so purposeful and smart, with its green-and-cream trim: boot and bonnet cream, like the upper parts of the doors and wings, the rest of it lime green. It was a smart little car, quite fast, and easy to park. 'You can turn it on a sixpence,' the salesman had said repeatedly ('But who would want to?' he had thought). It was due to the high wheel arches, the man had expansively explained. 'The front wheels will turn almost ninety degrees,' he insisted, demonstrating. 'You see? You can edge it into tiny parking spaces – hardly any longer than the car!' He had made the point especially to Jocelyn, confirming her impression that although he would trust Steve anywhere with this car, he wouldn't trust *her* an inch. Buying the car had been a happy day for them both, their happiest for ages, for there were difficulties in the marriage neither of them openly acknowledged. They had been together nearly ten years and, they insisted, were fine. It was what she always told her mother – 'We're fine, Mum, don't worry' – whenever that astute woman raised doubts on that score. And they *were* OK, mainly. They'd had their sticky moments, especially with Steve being in the job he was in, but that was inevitable. Wasn't it?

The green-and-cream pride and joy responded to his every touch with what appeared to be human sympathy. He was through High Wycombe in no time, then bounding along the Oxford bypass and taking the honey-coloured Cotswold towns and villages in his stride. Witney, Burford, Stow-on-the-Wold, Broadway... then Evesham, Worcester and Leominster, and along the A44 into Wales. The milometer ticked along pleasantly, adding sixpence to his pocket with every twitch of a number. Two hundred and twenty miles to Glanaber, give or take a few miles – no, make it two hundred and fifty each way, nobody would know any different at the *Comet* – two hundred and sixty maybe, could he push it that far? Why not? Fleet Street knew more about the backside of the moon than the geography of Wales. 'Could you slip up to Bangor?' news editors would ask their Cardiff-based reporters. 'Slip up,' indeed! As soon 'slip up' Mount Everest in a dodgem. Twice two-sixty was five-twenty, five hundred and twenty miles at sixpence a mile was... something pretty massive, he mused, forgoing the mental arithmetic to concentrate on his driving.

He settled himself more comfortably behind the wheel, filled with a sense of well-being. He could hardly believe he'd swung this with the office – subs were subs and reporters were reporters, and they hated each other like poison. Only the huge credit he'd amassed as a newsman had enabled him to make a successful pitch for the job – that, and his knowledge of this freaky dump in the far west of Wales. 'I know everyone there,' he boasted. 'They're a funny lot. They won't say a word to anyone they don't like – I know how to get them talking.' All the same, it had been touch and go. The newsdesk was still fuming.

The undulating border country, where the shift from England to Wales was marked only by a 'Welcome to Wales' sign half hidden by hawthorn branches ruffed with blossom, gave way to the steeper hills of Radnor Forest. It was years since he'd been in these parts, but Glanaber and all that had happened in it fourteen years before still haunted him. It was not only eagerness to cover what could be a very juicy story that had made him so keen to swallow the bait dangled by Bill Merrick. He wanted to see the town again, to walk the prom and breathe that incomparable air... And perhaps stumble on people who had played a big part in his life one turbulent summer? He saw a pert face, heard a high female voice, felt a thrill of anticipation, and gripped the wheel more firmly.

'Lewis,' he repeated crisply. 'Steve Lewis.'

'Lewis... let me see now...'

The man at the hotel's reception desk had a crumpled look, as if he'd been pressed between the pages of a very large book. Steve had a feeling that he'd seen him before; it was a feeling he would have many times in the next few days.

The man was running his finger down a list of names, with deliberate helplessness, it seemed to Steve. His thin, blotchy hair, neither grey nor black but an unhealthy mixture

27

of both, his prematurely wrinkled face and dusty grey suit, all spoke of some kind of inner collapse, a defeatism that found redress in this insulting inability to find confirmation of the reservation.

'I rang this afternoon,' said Steve impatiently. 'I booked a single room, en-suite.'

'I'm afraid we have no en-suite rooms left, sir. They were all taken some time ago.' His weak, breathy voice gave Steve the eerie impression that somehow it was made out of cardboard.

'I booked one this afternoon, I tell you. I rang from London. A woman answered. She definitely booked me in, I tell you.'

'Really, sir?' the man murmured disbelievingly, head bent, eyes obscured as he continued his infuriating, futile search.

'Well, if you can't find it I'll go somewhere else.'

'Oh, just a moment, sir. I think this might be it. Mr Lewis of Gladstone Road, Putney?'

'Yes,' said Steve coldly.

'I'm terribly sorry, sir. The records were a little confused. Room 23. Overlooking the bay, sir.' He smiled ingratiatingly. Steve was sure he had met him before, but could not place him.

'Well, can I have the key then?'

'The key, sir. Of course. I hope you'll enjoy your stay, sir.'

'Thank you.'

'Would you like some help with your luggage, sir?'

'No thank you. I'll manage.'

The man's excessive politeness, surely an obscure form of insult, grated on Steve. He hauled his suitcase to the lift, which clanked slowly and noisily down. The second-floor carpet was scuffed and faded. The Prince of Wales Hotel, Glanaber's seafront palace in its glory days as the Brighton of Wales, had obviously gone down in the world.

In his younger days as a reporter on the local rag, he had never imagined the day might come when he would actually book in there. It had been a place for *them* – nabob tourists with more money than sense, business types who lit cigars with fivers, and the kind of native upper-crust who came into the category of *crachach*, that well-heeled and influential lot who were the nearest thing to a Welsh Establishment. Why had he chosen to come here, instead of finding somewhere simpler? The answer came readily. Because it was easier (or should have been) just to ring up in advance. Because he needed the comfort. Because it was on expenses.

It was getting on for half past ten, the street lamps shedding their ghostly light over an empty prom. The sea swished and snickered on the gritty shore. Standing at the window, curtains drawn back and room lights off, he stared out and pondered. He remembered his yearning to get away from this godforsaken hole… and now he was back, if only temporarily. How long would this job take? Would it even be a story? Bill Merrick could be woefully, miserably wrong. Yet he had sounded confident enough. Miserable git though he was, Bill was journalist enough to know what made a national story and what didn't.

Thinking of the possibilities, Steve felt a touch of the old excitement. He knew nothing of the college principal Haydn Lucas, but Jill Manders was a big name all right. The sexiest – and most accomplished – British film star in the business was always good copy. Her move to Wales about a year ago had been splashed all over the papers. Why had she gone there? Was she dropping out of the big time? She had answered all questions with aplomb, and posed for pictures in her renovated old cottage – a genuine Welsh longhouse, he recalled her insisting, as if this alone were explanation enough for her move from Hampstead. She was just over her marriage to an actor with a drink problem as huge as his talent, vowing to clean up her life amid the fresh air of the Welsh hills and the gorgeous simplicity of the locals. Oh yes, she'd been full of it... but what was she up to now, shagging a Welsh academic in Glanaber? Was it true? If so, would he get the story? Self-doubt seized his stomach. He shook his head fiercely. Of course he would. He would have to.

4

ANNETTE ALLAN ONLY had half an ear for what Robert was saying because she was intrigued by what her husband was doing in the garden.

'Well, can we, Mum?' the boy repeated patiently.

'Can we what, darling?' she asked absently, squeezing the dishcloth as she stared through the picture window in the kitchen.

'Go to Ocean Park. Geraint's going. And Roger. All my friends are.'

'Mm.' What on earth were those shrubs he was planting? And why hadn't he told her about them?

'*Can* we?' Disbelief widened his eyes. 'Today?'

'What?' Annette snapped back into the moment.

'Can we go there today, Mum? *Please*,' he pleaded.

'Go where?'

'To Ocean Park.'

'Of course not. I've told you before.'

'But you just said, Mum,' the boy wailed. 'You promised.'

'I did no such thing.'

'You *did*, Mum, you *did*.'

'Well. I didn't know what you were saying. I was looking at your father.'

'That's not fair.' The boy stood his ground, outrage filling his sturdy seven-year-old figure.

'I'm sorry, pet.' Annette, penitent, suddenly realised the extent to which she had unwittingly misled her younger child. 'But you know what we think of those places. They're dangerous.'

'No they're not. You ask Brian John. He's been there, and his dad's a policeman. There's nothing wrong with them, Mum. Honest.'

'Well, we're not going. We'll do something else instead.' She flashed him a bright smile. 'We'll think of something in a minute, right?'

'No, I don't want to go *nowhere!*' he cried vehemently, and stormed upstairs.

Annette sighed. She wasn't really a good mother. She didn't listen enough, was too self-absorbed. Or so her own mother had always told her.

She dismissed Robert from her mind as she went into the garden. Nigel was on his hands and knees, furiously digging a hole with a trowel.

'What's all this?' asked Annette.

He looked up, smiling. 'Do you like them?'

'I don't know. What are they?'

He named them.

'Becoming ambitious, aren't we? You'll be entering the flower show next.'

'I don't think so.' He caught on to something in Annette's expression. 'You don't mind, do you?'

'Not in the least. But you might have told me.'

'Darling! I've upset you. I'm sorry. It was just an impulse buy. I was passing the garden centre yesterday and just popped in for a look. I thought I'd surprise you.'

'No you didn't. You didn't think of me at all. You just went in and did it.'

'They'll look good though, won't they?'

'I daresay they will. Since you're such an expert.'

She was half-chaffing, half-serious. It was her way. He knew it.

He pulled a face, playing up to her.

'Maybe I *will* enter the flower show at that. I might surprise you.'

'Nothing you do surprises me, Nigel.'

He smiled, pleased. But he knew she didn't really mean it. He was the most predictable of men, usually. But she liked to make him out to be more adventurous than he really was. It pleased her to do this, and it pleased him to go along with it.

Nigel began scuffing the soil again, making space for another plant. His head nodded slightly as he worked so that, grotesquely, he reminded Annette of a pigeon. The image made her smile inwardly, because he was a most unbirdlike man. Broad-shouldered, strong-backed, he exuded an air of purpose as he went about any physical task. But a casual observer, standing beside Annette as she looked down on him, would have been surprised had he glanced up, revealing a face that seemed at odds with the stocky frame. There was a softness in the features, and a thoughtfulness in his deep brown eyes, that spoke of qualities that did not naturally go with the animal body. Something other than the pigeon-like nodding amused his wife at that moment, and this was the fact that his rough gardening trousers were being held up by a pair of braces rather than a belt. They were the braces he wore with his dark grey office suit, but she did not ask him to explain their unexpected promotion this Saturday morning. Instead she said, 'Got anything in mind today?'

'No. Have you?' he replied, firming the earth down around the newly-planted shrub.

'Not especially. Rob has though.'

'Oh? What's that?'

'Ocean Park.'

'Not again! Doesn't give in, does he?'

'Don't suppose he ever will.'

'What did you tell him?' Nigel asked, standing up.

'Same as usual.'

'Don't suppose he thought much of that.'

'He said Roger's going, and Geraint, and that beastly Brian John.'

'He didn't say beastly, did he?'

'No. I did.'

'Bloody place. Should never have been allowed there. Shouldn't have had planning permission.'

'Well.' Annette shrugged. 'It's there now, worse luck.'

'*Pleasure parks*,' said Nigel derisively. 'Death traps, that's what they are. The standard of inspection is dismal.'

'Try telling that to the kids,' said Annette dryly.

Nigel trod the earth down carefully around the shrubs and picked up the old newspaper he had been kneeling on. 'There you are,' he said succinctly. 'Job done.'

They walked back to the house together. They made a good-looking couple, in their middle to late thirties. Nigel was an inch or so shorter than Annette, his black hair peppered with the merest sprinkling of grey. His swarthy skin and solid build made him more obviously Welsh in appearance than his wife, who had kept the rich chestnut hair of her youth but not the slimness of those days. Maturity had broadened her hips and robbed her breasts of the uptilting pertness that had endorsed the sprightliness of her personality. She was still, though, an attractive figure, walking with the grace of one confident in herself and at ease with her place in the world. Rob was sulking in his bedroom but his ten-year-old sister Joanne was downstairs, looking her Saturday morning best in a flowery dress.

'Going somewhere?' asked Annette casually.

'Yes. Shopping with Enfys and her mum. I told you.'

'So you did. What're you going to buy?'

'Depends how much you give me,' Joanne said cheekily.

'Oh! Two and six, OK?'

'Could you make it a pound?'

'A pound! You think I'm made of money.'

'Please, Mum. I want to buy that T-shirt I was telling you about.'

'All right then. If it suits you.'

'It does. Auntie Doreen says.'

'Oh, *Auntie* now, is it?'

'She told me to call her that,' replied Joanne defensively.

'Did she now,' said Annette, with an irony not lost on her daughter. 'Well, that must be all right then.'

Joanne flushed. She had her mother's fair complexion, and – to her horror – the freckles which Annette had long lost.

'Will you be home for lunch?' Annette asked.

'No. They've asked me back there.'

'Right. Just so long as I know.'

'You and Dad going out?'

'Not very far, I don't suppose.'

'Rob says you're taking him to Ocean Park.'

'Did he now? That's the first I've heard of it.'

'He says you promised.'

'Well, he's wrong, isn't he?'

After Joanne had left, kissing her mother goodbye, Annette felt a stab of guilt, feeling she had been hard on her. Why shouldn't Enfys's mother call herself Auntie Doreen? Everyone in Glanaber was auntie or uncle to half the neighbourhood.

Her irony had been directed not at her daughter but at Doreen Scofield, a woman for whom she felt a deep distaste. She was into everything, that woman – town forums, cinema club, county history society, parent-teachers association… She was close to being a model wife and mother, and Annette felt that she herself was neither. Her daughter Enfys looked like following the same path, and for the life of her Annette could not understand what Joanne saw in her. But, she thought resignedly, the girl had to make her own friends, and so long as they weren't thieves or vandals she couldn't very well interfere.

The silence upstairs was suspicious. Was Robert still sulking? Annette found him sitting on his bed, scuffing one shoe against the other and looking sullen.

'Well, bright eyes,' Annette said cheerfully. 'You coming to join us?'

The boy shrugged.

'Can't stay here all day, you know. It's lovely out. Would you like to ask Bryn around?'

Rob shook his head.

'Look,' said his mother gently, sitting beside him. 'I know you're disappointed about going to – that place. But it's really for the best. We don't think those rides are safe.'

'Yes they are – I know they are!'

'But there've been accidents, darling. There was one at Blackpool – '

'I don't care!'

'Well, we do. We care a lot. We don't want you hurt.'

'You're just mean.'

'Mean? You call us mean?'

Annette sounded querulous and knew it. 'Look,' she said briskly. 'Let's go swimming. You'd like that, wouldn't you?'

'Dunno.'

She sensed a breakthrough.

'Maybe Mike would like to come. Shall we ask him?'

A silence, then: 'I don't mind.'

'There then!'

Downstairs, Annette found Nigel in his study, scanning a brief. 'What on earth are you doing? It's Saturday.'

He was still wearing his gardening trousers and the dark green braces looked more absurd than ever. 'I'm just looking through something. I won't be long.'

'You shouldn't be bringing stuff home like this. You work hard enough as it is.'

'Don't worry. I'm perfectly happy.'

'Well, I'm not.' She looked over his shoulder at the document he was scanning. '*Davies v Matthews*,' she read aloud. 'Sounds like a prize fight.'

'It is in a way. Us against them.'

'Who's us?'

'Davies.'

'Do you think we'll win?'

'Should do. But you can never tell.'

'I'm taking Rob to the College Baths. You coming?'

'Oh. Got over the sulks then, has he?'

'Just about. You'll come then, yes?'

'I don't think so, darling. If you don't mind, I'd rather get on with this for a while.'

'But what's so urgent about it? Can't it wait?' Her voice, always high-pitched, became stratospheric, to her own annoyance.

'I'm sorry, Annette.' He turned to face her. 'You know what it's like these days, with Edgar as he is. I've got a bigger workload. I've got to keep up with things.'

'You'll be keeping down with things if you're not careful!' flashed Annette. She gestured at the floor. 'You'll be down there – with the worms!'

Nigel smiled again. 'Don't be so melodramatic, darling. It's not as bad as that.'

'Oh, isn't it. I'm not so sure.'

'Look,' he said patiently. 'It'll be better when Stella comes back. We'll be back to normal then.'

'Normal! There's no such thing as normal in that office. There never was, even when I was there.'

He thought of joking, 'especially when you were there,' but thought better of it.

'I'm sorry, love. But I'll be free in a couple of hours. You go and enjoy yourselves. We can go out somewhere this afternoon, right?'

'I don't know if Jo will be back by then,' clipped Annette. 'She's with *Auntie* Doreen.'

'Who?' asked Nigel but his wife, retreating, didn't answer.

In the early hours of that Saturday, Steve, lying half awake, heard a plaintive and mournful sound. That aching cry of a bird he could not name, holding in its dying fall much of the sorrows of the world, drew from the recesses of his soul grief long buried. He thought of his dead father, the dead baby he had sired, his dead love affair with the baby's mother. How was Annette? What was she doing? He had heard nothing of her since his mother had left the town to return to the south Wales she loved. And why should he know anything? Why bother his head with her now? She belonged to a past he had outgrown, along with the *County Dispatch* and all it stood for, the parish-pump inconsequence of its news stories, the lick-spittle kow-towing to advertisers and businesses that meant it stood aside from the biggest stories on its doorstep because of a printing contract. Pathetic!

Awake now, he sat up in bed. The bird, whatever it was (curlew? sandpiper? he hadn't a clue) had gone now. He thrust the old memories back where they'd come from. He was sorry now he'd volunteered for the job. The sooner it was done and he was out of this place the better. He didn't want to see anyone he knew. He didn't care about a single soul there.

Bill Merrick had moved to a new estate at the top of the hill on the road to Machynlleth. All the streets were Heol this or Bryn that (and this was something new, he reflected, the total Welshification of Glanaber), and all the houses looked alike. He found a passing regret for the incipient standardisation of a town which, for all its faults, had numbered a jumble of architectural styles among its virtues.

He found the particular Heol where Bill lived without too much bother. The estate was open plan, the front lawns shorn and spruce. A next-door-but-one neighbour, cutting his grass, gave him a glance and looked away. A greeting died on Steve's tongue. So something else had changed: the neighbourliness that meant that even strangers had a word for each other, even if it was only in the all-purpose 'Awright?'

Bill answered the door. Steve, taken by surprise by how old he looked, took a second or two to recover.

'Come in, Steve. So you found us all right. Betty's resting.' Quietly he added, 'She's none too well, I'm afraid.'

The living-room was tidy to the point of anonymity, with new G-plan furniture, bland reproduction paintings and scarcely a book in sight. 'Make yourself at home,' offered Bill. 'Coffee or tea?'

'Coffee, please.'

The Bill Merrick he remembered had been smart and vaguely gentrified, with tweedy suits and fly-fisherman's hats and an air of being above the common herd. Now he wore a dull yellow cardigan, brown carpet slippers and green corduroy trousers. His ginger thatch had thinned out and declined miserably into muddy grey, and his pale mackerel eyes had dulled into insignificance. Something of his old arrogance, however, remained in his cool tone of voice, touched with a hint of the sardonic.

'I'm glad you were able to come yourself. I was afraid you wouldn't be able to, when I found you were subbing.'

He only half-listened to Steve's explanation of how he had been temporarily drafted to the subs' desk to avoid the scurrying life of a tabloid reporter after his illness and operation.

'Well, I'm not kidding you. This is a big one. Worth a lot of money.'

Steve shifted uneasily in his chair, not wishing to become involved in an argument about payment.

'What's the story then, Bill?'

'I told you. Haydn Lucas and Jill Manders are having an affair.'

'How long's it been going on?'

'Not long. Couple of months possibly. Who can tell?'

'Are they living together?'

'Not all the time. Sometimes she's in her own place. He goes there. Other times she's with him in the principal's house.'

'Here? In Glanaber?'

'Precisely.'

'Where's the house then, Bill?'

'Where it's always been. In Brynpadarn Road.'

The name 'Brynpadarn' brought back memories of Ivor, the carpenter Annette had been going out with at one time. A strange feeling passed through him, a sense of unreality.

'Of course,' Bill added coldly, 'you didn't have much to do with college matters, did you? I used to cover those.'

Steve forced back a grin. It was a sad case of attempted one-upmanship, a small-town hick's reminder that at one time he had lorded it over the junior reporter saddled with town council meetings and magistrates' courts.

'All this is just rumour, I suppose,' Steve said brusquely, needled by the older man's put-down. 'There may be nothing in it.'

Bill smiled faintly. 'There's a good deal in it. If you don't want it, I'll give it to somebody else.'

'I've got it now though, haven't I? I can just go ahead and do the story.'

'You need contacts. Proof. Quotes. I've got those already. You'd be starting from scratch.'

The two men exchanged a long look. They hadn't exactly been the best of mates in the past. They'd actually come to blows once, or as near as dammit. Steve stifled the memory, saying casually: 'I'm still amazed it hasn't come out yet. Who's editing the *Dispatch* now?'

'Sam Evans.'

'You're kidding! Christ. They must have been desperate.' Sam had been sports editor in Steve's time on the paper, a lank, pathetic hack scared of his own shadow. 'Why didn't they make you editor, Bill?'

'That's not a question you should be directing to me, is it?' said Bill stiffly.

'When did old Meredith retire then?'

'Seven or eight years ago. I can't remember exactly.'

'Who took charge then?'

'Ronnie Banks.'

'Ronnie!' The slew-eyed news editor, scrabbling through the week's pickings from half-soaked village correspondents in his cubbyhole office. 'Was he any good at it?'

'You knew Ronnie. And before you say any more, he's dead now. Died in harness of a heart attack.'

So Bill had been passed over twice. No wonder he was so bitter.

'Poor bugger,' Steve returned belatedly. 'Anyway, about this story… you're quite sure there's been nothing about it in the paper?'

'Absolutely. Not a word. And unlikely to be, either.'

'That's pathetic.'

Bill shrugged. Steve sipped his coffee thoughtfully. 'Look…' he began, but was interrupted by a cry from the other room. Bill rattled his cup back in its saucer. ''Scuse me a minute,' he muttered.

In the next room, the voices of Bill and his wife were too indistinct to be heard properly. After a minute or two, Bill returned.

'Sorry about that. I'm afraid Betty needs a lot of attention.'

'What's wrong with her then, Bill?'

'Leukaemia. It's a terrible illness.'

'I know – that's awful.'

'I'm hoping to get her treatment in America. They can't do anything over here.' He looked at Steve directly. 'That's why I'm hoping your paper will come up with something decent. Five hundred isn't enough.'

'It's what they usually pay for this sort of tip-off, Bill.'

'It's not just a tip-off I'm giving you. It's solid information. Contacts in the college and elsewhere. It's a big story, Steve. You know it.'

'What's the reaction of the college likely to be?'

'What do you think?' asked Bill, that faintly cynical smile playing about his lips again.

'Will they fire him?'

'They might. Anything's possible. Anyway that doesn't affect the story, does it? Jill's latest fling is what sells papers, I imagine.'

Steve, in a moment of pity for a man he had never liked, had a sudden, sharp realisation of what a success Bill Merrick might have been in the Street, had he not wasted his talents on a useless rag in the far west of Wales. And why had he done this? Because he wanted to stay a big fish in a small pool? Because he loved the town too much? The man was a mystery.

'I'd like your co-operation,' said Steve. 'I've got to get this story fast. I'll have a word with the newsdesk, see if they'll come up with more cash. At the moment five hundred's the limit.'

'Thanks, boy. I appreciate that,' said Bill, with a mateyness he had never before shown Steve.

'But you'd still be a long way short, wouldn't you? Even twice that wouldn't get you the treatment in the States.'

'It would be a start though, wouldn't it? I'm launching a campaign in the town to raise funds. People are very good like that.'

'Well,' responded Steve, feeling slightly ashamed without quite knowing why. 'Good luck with it. Now, help me with a run-down of the situation, will you?'

5

JOCELYN WOULD NEVER have admitted it, even to herself, but driving to Guildford in her bright red Mini, with only Simon for company, she felt a sense of relief. For a start, it meant she could stay overnight and spend Sunday with her parents, instead of rushing back to Putney. And next morning, if the day was fine she could take a stroll with Mum, then help her prepare the Sunday roast. Dad, of course, would be in the garden all morning, teaching the weeds a lesson – with Simon lending a hand, or sloping off to the park to watch football with his pal Mark. All in all, it looked like being a nice, relaxing weekend.

'When will Dad be back, Mum?' Simon asked suddenly from the back seat.

'I don't know. It depends how things go, I suppose.'

'He hasn't been away for a long time, has he? Why's he got to go now?'

'I don't know, I'm sure.' She added, 'I suppose they think he's the right man for the job. Being Welsh and all that.'

Jocelyn glanced in the driving mirror. What was going through his head?

'He used to be away a lot, didn't he?' ventured Simon. 'When I was little.'

'Yes, he did, pet. But he was a reporter then. He's not now.'

'I know. He's a subeditor, isn't he, Mum?' said Simon importantly.

'Yes, but I don't know for how long. He much prefers being out on the road, I'm afraid.'

Afraid? The boy noted the word but said nothing. He was playing battleships with pen and paper, without his mother knowing.

Jos drove on through the Surrey countryside. The mix-and-match of tidy woodland and well-groomed fields was entirely to her taste. So were the trimly ordered villages, where privacy and the quiet pursuit of comfort plainly held the keys to the good life. She would love to be living here – it would be good for Simon's health, too – but, she conceded, it could be a lot worse. They could be somewhere in Wales, with the rain tipping down and everyone babbling in Welsh. She was suddenly touched by guilt: shouldn't she be worrying more about Steve's state of health? She'd made sure he had taken his tablets with him, but all the same… He could easily have a setback, with all the strain of chasing this story. *Story!* She hated the word.

'Gone to Wales?' said her mother, puckering her brow. 'What on earth for?'

Jos explained. Laura Wiltshire listened, not too sympathetically. 'Well,' she said at last, 'I only hope it won't be too much for him. Couldn't he have refused to go?'

'Refused? You must be joking. It's right up his street. He couldn't wait to get away.'

Her father did his best to sound sorry, but in her heart of hearts Jos admitted they all felt happy to be on their own for a change. All, that is, save Simon.

Jos felt a stab of guilt. But it was none too sharp.

Annette sat on the edge of the pool, dabbling her feet in the water, watching Rob and Mike splashing around – Mike far more energetically than Rob. Mike's fair head bobbed up and down as he flailed his arms in a stroke of his own invention, a cross between the crawl and a dog paddle. Rob stuck soberly to the breaststroke his father had taught him, his steady progress sharply contrasting with the violent motions of his friend.

'Careful now!' warned Annette, as Mike veered course. 'Don't go out of your depth!' She raised her voice above the clamour of the kids, and the lifeguard standing on the opposite side of the pool gave her a keen, appreciative glance. She felt his eyes on her, but did not respond. A married woman in Glanaber had to be careful. Instinctively she raised her hands to her head, lifting her wet hair away from her shoulders and then letting it fall back again. The droplets of water, glistening in the spring sunshine that flooded through the glass behind her, gave her chestnut hair an added gloss. Her very air of nonchalance spoke eloquently of her self-awareness, and the lifeguard, at least ten years her junior, smiled to himself as his keen eyes took in her still shapely breasts above the midriff she was struggling to keep in shape. Her blue, one-piece swimsuit clung too tightly in places, but as she slid into the pool again she made an attractive figure. Playfully she splashed water over Mike as he stood in the shallow end, and he responded zestfully until, sensing the lifeguard's sardonic attention, she said sharply, 'That's it, Mike. Sorry. Got carried away, I'm afraid.'

Afterwards they sat in the cafeteria overlooking the pool. The boys noisily sucked up Coca-Cola through straws, while Annette sipped a black coffee. A man sat alone a few tables away, idly reading a paper. His cheeks were hollow, highly coloured, his nose broad, his forehead narrow. It would have been an unprepossessing face were it not for the gentleness of his eyes. Caught staring at him, she flushed. He smiled. She smiled back. The swift acknowledgement of each other's existence held no embarrassment, for they knew each other by sight – it was the way things were in Glanaber.

Walking back to the car, the boys scampering ahead, Annette paused to enjoy the view over the town. It was familiar enough, but she was suddenly overwhelmed by a sense of strangeness, almost exile. She felt she was living an alternative life, that this view was the backdrop to a play in which she had been wrongly cast.

The boys clambered into the back of her spruce little Austin A35. As she drove the short distance home, the sense of strangeness slowly passed – overlaid, like so much else, by the unrelenting reality of the present.

'It's no good going there this afternoon,' Bill insisted. 'He won't be in. He's gone down to Swansea for a meeting.'

'Hell. Are you sure about that?'

'Sure as eggs. They'll all be there – it's a big academic thing.' He saw Steve's face. 'Don't worry – he'll be back by tomorrow. He's having a lift home tonight.'

'How do you know?'

Bill stroked his nose with a forefinger, wiseacre-style. 'Contacts.' He was enjoying this.

'Hope you're right. I've got a photographer coming down tonight.'

'You didn't bring one with you?'

'No. He's coming down from Manchester. It's their territory, remember? You used to do enough linage for them.'

It was something of a dig, a reminder that like the rest of the *County Dispatch* reporters, Bill Merrick hadn't been loath to make a few bob by ringing up the northern editions of the dailies with stories before they went in their own paper.

'So did you, if I remember rightly,' said Bill, unabashed.

'Will he talk, do you think – the principal?'

'I haven't got a clue. You'll have to doorstep him, won't you?'

Steve, bristling at Bill's manner – snide and faintly silly, his reference to 'door stepping' thrown in just to prove he was well up with Fleet Street lingo – said nothing.

'You could start off by going to see his wife,' Bill suggested. 'She'll give you some good quotes.'

'You reckon?'

'I should say. Talk the hind leg off a donkey. Ring her from here if you like.'

'Where's she living?'

'With her mother, in Nant-goch.' Bill paused, catching Steve's blank look before adding, 'Road to Devil's Bridge.'

'What's she like then?'

'Rosie?' Bill smiled thinly. 'You'll soon find out.'

'Her name's Rosie?'

'Yes. You sound surprised.'

'Not the sort of name you expect from a Welsh Nat's wife.'

'Doesn't mean to say she's one.'

'Why did she move out? I mean – rather than him.'

'He's the principal. The house belongs to the college.'

'Does that matter?'

Bill gave him the long, amused look of a man who knows everything gazing at somebody floundering.

'I still can't understand the *Dispatch* not running a line on this,' said Steve tersely. 'It's got a damn cheek, calling itself a newspaper.'

'Nothing new in that, is there, Stephen? It's why you left, isn't it?'

Steve shrugged. He felt like a hooked fish being played by an angler.

'Another coffee?' invited Bill.

'No thanks. I'll be on my way.' He stood up, then said quietly, 'I'm really sorry about Betty. I'll do what I can, Bill.'

'I know you will.' Bill suddenly looked old again. 'Thanks.'

Nant-goch. He vaguely remembered the name. It was one of those villages up in the hills where local correspondents, paid a fiver a year if they were lucky, had avidly penned snippets about whist drives and WI meetings and chapel outings ('they returned home tired but happy, and a good time was had by all') during his days as a cub reporter on the paper. Sometimes old 'Scoop' Matthews had made sorties into the territory, to stir up lazy correspondents and nose out news himself, and there had even been times (best forgotten) when he too had been sent to these outposts. He had generally scraped up some tittle-tattle and spent the rest of his time in the pub before catching the bus back to town: no Triumph Herald in those days. What had become of Scoop Matthews? Briefly, he felt ashamed for not having asked. Perhaps he too had 'passed away', like all the people whose obituaries he had respectfully penned: nobody simply died, in Scoop's book. It had been another life, lived not by the man he was now but a younger, more vulnerable person, caught between love for the girl he had intended to marry and an older, more knowledgeable woman who had taught him far more than he needed to know.

Steve stretched out his legs, surveying the passing scene. The prom looked much the same, though there were fewer people walking it this Saturday morning than he'd expected. Perhaps they had other things to do these days; but what? It was a calm, dull day, the sea barely frothing at the mouth as it lipped the dark brown shoreline. The air, though, had that heady tang he always associated with the town, so bracing and light that it was like breathing the essence of champagne. Should he have stayed here after all, those fourteen years ago, quenching the ambition that had goaded him into leaving for London? He would have succeeded Gwyn Meredith as editor of the *County Dispatch*; the job had been practically promised him. But how would he have coped with all the small-town pettiness? And would he have had even a sniff of the story of the Professor and the Sex Symbol, with printing contracts in the balance? Like hell he would. And there'd have been no by-lines in the Street for him then. No Stephen Ward scoop splashed over the front page of the Comet. No dash to Dallas after the Kennedy assassination. No snide stories about the absurd Signora Mussolini making her singing debut back in '60. But any amount of stuff about rates increases and water in the milk and mayoral parades and beauty contests. And thieving postmen. One of the doors he kept rigidly closed in his mind flung open and he stood up abruptly.

He went to the bookshop where his pal Dafydd used to work but found Dafydd long gone and the shop sadly altered. So instead he bought an Ordnance Survey map in W. H. Smith's and pored over it in the car. He had a snack in the Pelican Café and then set off for Nant-goch. Might as well get some quotes from the wronged wife before doing the big stuff next day.

Driving through Pen-bryn on the main road south out of town, he all but stopped to take a look at the council house where his girlfriend Annette used to live. She surely wouldn't be there now, but her parents might; Ted and Lorna Morris were the type to put down roots and stay, unless prised out by some unforeseen disaster. Where Annette was now, God only knew. He'd lost touch with Glanaber when his mother moved back to south Wales, after his father's death. She could be anywhere, though he suspected she was still somewhere in town. Married or single, what was it to him? He was perfectly happy with Jos, thank you very much. *Perfectly* happy, he assured himself vigorously. He'd have to ring her up later, for a chat with her and Simon. Wouldn't be surprised if she stayed in Guildford overnight, now he wasn't there. Well, why shouldn't she? It was perfectly natural, wasn't it? All the same, a shiver of irritation stirred him up as he thought of her father prattling on about bugger-all... But, fair play, her mother wasn't bad.

These not entirely pleasant thoughts saw him safely through Pen-bryn and on to the high road to Devil's Bridge, the beauty spot twelve miles out which fed on unlikely legend and the thunder of the Mynach waterfalls. The day had shrugged off the morning gloom and bright sunshine burnished the fresh green of the roadside hedges. To his left, between gaps in the hedges and trees, the broad valley east of the town could be glimpsed, the main road well out of sight on the valley floor. The road he was on climbed steadily into wild hill country so different in atmosphere from that of the university town he had left that he felt he had crossed an invisible frontier. He could not remember coming this way before. The few times he had been to Devil's Bridge it had been on the *Lein Fach*, the narrow-gauge railway whose trains made their slow, hissing way along a narrow shelf with steep drops to one side and bends so acute that the guard at the back could almost shake hands with the driver. He had not realised Nant-goch was so far out, and when he got there he would have missed it were it not for the road sign half hidden by a tangle of nettles. He braked and drove slowly past a disused chapel, a squat terrace of single-storey cottages, a smart new bungalow and a larger house where a bald man was working in the garden. Beyond the house the village petered out in a clutch of corrugated-iron sheds. Steve parked the car. The bald man looked up.

'Excuse me. Do you know of a house called Ger-y-bont?'

'Wha'?' Baldy returned blankly.

'Ger-y-bont,' repeated Steve, pronouncing the word precisely. 'It's somewhere round here. You know it?'

'Jerry what?'

'Bont. Ger… y… bont.'

'Never 'eard of it, mate. I'll ask me missus though. 'Ang on.'

Missus emerged of her own accord, giving Steve a suspicious look.

'Oh, there you are,' Baldy greeted her cheerfully. 'Ever 'eard of an 'ouse called – what is it now?'

'I 'eard 'im,' Missus said, in the same Brummiespeak as Baldy. 'What you want with them then?'

'I just want to see them, that's all.'

'Awright, don't boite me 'ead off. Only troying to 'elp. See that phone box up the road there?'

'Yes,' said Steve, forcing an emollient smile.

'Well, you go past that, take the first road to the roight, then go left and it's on the…' She flapped her hands in different directions. 'Roight and soide,' she concluded triumphantly.

'Right. Thanks very much. Sorry to bother you.'

'That's awright. Funny people, moind. Old lady's deaf as a post. Welsh as they come.'

'Is she now? How amazing. What's she doing living here?'

The house was on the left: a stone-built cottage with plum-coloured front door and plain brass knocker. He rat-tat-tatted. Silence. He tried again, more forcefully.

'I'm coming, I'm coming,' came a peevish voice from within. The door shot open. 'What d'you knock like that for?' a small woman with a sharp look demanded. 'I'm not deaf, you know.'

'I'm sorry,' Steve lamely replied. 'Is Mrs Lucas in?'

'Who's asking?'

'The name's Lewis. Steve Lewis. Of the *Daily Comet*. I'd just like a word with her, please.' He produced his off-the-peg winning smile.

Her tone changed. 'Reporter, are you?'

'Yes.'

'Why didn't you say? Come on in, lad.'

She shut the door firmly. 'Go on, go on in,' she said impatiently, waving him into the living-room. It was dark, low-ceilinged, cluttered, with heavily-framed photographs of bonneted Victorian ladies and their moustachioed gentlemen hanging on the wall above a worse-for-wear upright piano. An ancient Bakelite radio stood on a round-topped bamboo table in a corner. There was an odour, not unpleasant, hard to place: as if a respectable slice of the past had been corked up and the stopper removed.

'Sit down by there,' the woman demanded, pointing. 'Now, before she comes back. She's not going back to him – that's settled. He's a lying little toad and not worth tuppence, but he'll pay through the nose for this, you see if I'm wrong. What you going to put in your paper then, lad?'

'I don't know. I haven't spoken to anyone yet.'

'You haven't seen him and that tart then?'

'What tart's that?' Steve asked innocently.

'That actress bitch, of course. That's what you're doing here, init? Writing about her and my son-in-law, stupid bugger that he is?'

'Why, what're they doing then? Having an affair, are they?'

'That's what they call it now, is it? I can think of other things…' She breathed quickly, eyes glistening, a small, eager field mouse of a woman. 'What you want to know then, eh? Tell me now, quick – before Rosie gets back.'

'Well,' he said quickly, 'how did it happen? It all seems so strange – man like him taking up with a film star.'

'I'll tell you what – she dropped her knickers fast, that's what. Right little tart she is. And he's so stupid – Haydn. Stupid as they come. All brains and no common sense. Faugh!'

'How long's it been going on then?'

'How long? God knows. Long enough – that's why she come back here to live. Couldn't take no more. Can't blame her, can you? Brought up well, my daughter. If her father was still alive…'

She stopped abruptly as the front door opened. Rosie Lucas was tall, statuesque even, plain in features but with immediate presence. Her jaw was rounded but a little too prominent, her eyes keen behind rimless glasses. She carried a bunch of wild flowers in her right hand. 'I see we have guests,' she said, after giving Steve an unhurried look. 'Are you going to introduce me, mother?'

'This gen'leman's from the paper. He's doin'...'
Courage failing her, the old woman looked helplessly at
Steve.

'The name's Lewis,' Steve said genially. 'Steve Lewis.
Of the *Daily Comet*.'

'Really?' said Rosie coolly. 'How impressive. Would
you excuse me for a moment, Mr Lewis? I have to attend
to these little beauties.'

She brushed past him, closer than she need have done,
giving Steve an unexpected sexual frisson. A tap was
turned on in the kitchen. The old woman gave Steve a
wild, encouraging look, smiling maniacally and nodding
vigorously to emphasise a point inadequately made.

'I'm not in the habit of pillaging the hedgerows,' said
Rosie, returning, 'but I simply couldn't resist them. Will
you forgive me, Mr Lewis? I know you have high standards
on the *Comet* – although it's a paper I don't often read.'

'Of course. They look very nice,' Steve said.

'Do sit down, though I can't imagine why you dropped
in like this without any warning. Aren't you in the habit
of making proper arrangements?'

'I'm sorry about that, Mrs Lucas, but it's a question of
time. You see, we're doing something on your husband
and I'd really like your side of the story.'

She frowned. 'Doing something? What, precisely?'

'Well – his relationship with Jill Manders.'

'Relationship? What on earth are you talking about?'

Behind her, seated now on an ancient sofa draped with
a faded antimacassar, her mother continued to pull bizarre,
ineffectual faces at Steve.

'Well, to put it bluntly – his affair with the lady.'

Rosie smiled. 'You're wasting your time. Somebody's

having you on. He's not having a relationship with anyone – leave alone – what did you say her name was?'

'Jill Manders. Mrs Lucas…'

'I *believe* I've heard of her – but she's very much a third-rater, isn't she? My husband wouldn't have anything to do with her. Now, if that's all you have to say, would you mind getting along? I'm afraid your car's blocking the lane. The farmers…'

'The farmers can wait. I'm giving you a fair chance, Mrs Lucas. We're running this story, whatever you say.'

Her face convulsed with sudden anger. 'Then run it. And we'll sue your rotten paper for every penny it's got. Now – get out of here, you rotten little guttersnipe.'

Steve drove away, more than a little too fast. He'd got the quote he wanted – '*she's very much a third-rater*' – but at what cost? Of being a rotten little guttersnipe?

6

SOMETHING WAS BOTHERING Annette. It had been on her mind for some time, thrust into the background, but now it was assuming greater dominance. Her son's words that morning came back to her now, 'Can we go there today, Mum?' *There*. Ocean Park. And her inevitable answer, 'Of course not.' Because Nigel forbade it.

She leaned her head back, closed her eyes. They would have to face up to this soon; they couldn't go on avoiding it. It wasn't fair to Rob. '*All my friends are going... Ask Brian John. His father's a policeman.*' If a policeman's son could go there, why couldn't he? It was a fair question.

He was looking at *Dr Who* now, sitting on the floor, hands clasped around his knees. His favourite position for watching telly. He loved Dr Who... the Tardis, the Daleks... everything. His sister purported to hate it. 'Kids' stuff,' she scoffed, from all the eminence of her three-year seniority. *Juke Box Jury* was more her style – it had been on just before. Nigel had no time for it, but he didn't mind *Dr Who*. Where was he now – back in his study again? She'd have to go and drag him out; he'd be killing himself.

She thought back to the morning at the baths. Rob and Mike swimming, one dark head, one fair. The man reading the paper in the cafeteria later, someone she sometimes spotted on the prom, walking jerkily, arms swinging stiffly like a marionette. Who was he? Did it matter? Her thoughts focussed on the paper he'd been reading, the *Daily Comet*, and the special significance it held for her. Steve, her old boyfriend. The man she had nearly married. Again she had the strange, disorienting feeling that she was not where she ought to be, that the life she was living was an alternative to the one that had been planned for her. But planned by who, or what? An unpleasant memory assaulted her, the tearing out of a page from her diary, the page bearing the date of the wedding she had decided she could not go through with. She had been quite clear about it at the time, but that tearing out of the page seemed now something abominable, as if she had slapped Steve in the face.

She opened her eyes and went quickly to the study. Nigel was sitting at his desk, reading.

'*Dr Who*'s on,' she said. 'Aren't you going to watch it with Rob? It's the start of a new series.'

'Oh, right.' He snapped the book shut. 'I didn't know what time it was.'

She looked at the title. A slim volume by a man she'd never heard of. 'Any good?'

'Yes, it's OK,' he replied, off-hand.

'What are they about?'

'Oh, all sorts of things.' He pushed his chair back.

Flicking through the pages, a word or two caught her eye. '*Cariad*,' she read out. 'Love poems, are they?'

'Some of them, yes.'

'Write some for me,' she teased. 'In Welsh.'

'I don't write poetry, do I? Anyway, you wouldn't be able to understand them.'

'You could translate them. Wait a minute.'

'What?' He paused in the doorway.

'I want a word with you about something.'

'Oh?'

'Rob. We upset him this morning.'

'How come?'

'Ocean Park. We stopped him going.'

He made a flat, sweeping gesture with his hand. 'You know why.'

'Yes, but he doesn't. We'll have to tell him, Nigel.'

'Why?'

'It's not fair to him if we don't. Nor to us. He just thinks we're meanies.'

'Let him think what he likes. It's nothing to do with him.'

'Of course it's to do with him. Why do you say that, Nigel?'

'Nobody told *me* why I couldn't do things. I just did as I was told.' He was looking dark, thunderous, his brown eyes smoky and dangerous.

'Oh. So that makes it right, does it?'

'It doesn't make it wrong. Children should be seen.'

'And not heard? Oh, come on, darling. You don't mean that.'

He said nothing, but she sensed the tightly-wound spring inside him give way a little.

'We don't have to say much,' Annette persisted. 'Just give him some idea, that's all.'

'I'm not sure if I want to,' he said tensely.

'I'll do it if you like.'

'No.' He shook his head. 'That would be cowardly.'

She looked at him as he stood there brooding, the poetry book on the desk disregarded.

'I'll think about it,' he said brusquely.

Her father was reading the *Daily Telegraph*, her mother working on her latest water colour in the room grandiosely known as 'the studio', Simon sticking stamps into his album. Jocelyn, setting her Iris Murdoch novel aside, felt the peacefulness of the household gently embrace her. She had spent the morning with her mother, window-shopping interspersed with some real shopping and coffee in one of their favourite haunts in the High Street. It had been soothing, undemanding, a perfectly restful occasion. She had treated herself to a new top, hip-length and with the high, round neckline now in fashion. She had examined it critically before buying, for Jocelyn rarely rushed into anything, and her mother's approval had played a crucial part in her decision to go for it. When they reached home her father had still been in the garden, with Simon busily lending a hand. Dennis Wiltshire had come in eventually, slowly washing his hands under the kitchen tap before going upstairs and changing into something 'more civilised,' as he inevitably put it.

'Bought the town up, have you?' he had remarked dryly over the light lunch all four ate together. Laconic, his eyes heavy-lidded but not dull, he regarded his wife and daughter with the sceptical amusement that was his defence against an unpredictable world. He had survived warfare with Monty's Desert Rats to return a much quieter man than hitherto, finding the comparative security of a banking career exactly to his taste. A slight limp was the consequence of experience never spoken of, and any attempt to draw memories of El Alamein out of him were rebuffed with an untypical shortness of temper.

'Not quite,' returned Laura Wiltshire equably, 'but Jos did get a new top.'

Dennis grunted. 'We've been busy, haven't we, young man?'

Simon nodded, his mouth full.

'Simon's always busy,' Laura had acknowledged.

Proving this hours later, Simon carefully lodged a British Honduras stamp into its correct place in his impeccably kept album. Just like his grandfather, Jocelyn reflected; maybe he'd end up as a bank manager too. Nothing of the journalist about him, so far as she could see. But what had Steve been like as a boy? She couldn't imagine him ever sticking stamps into an album. But she imagined he had always loved reading, like Simon. When they'd first started going out together, he had even been writing poetry. He'd had some poems published, in good magazines too, but it was years since he'd written any, to her knowledge. He would no more talk about it than her father about the war. Men! They were incorrigible.

Thinking about him now, she began to worry. Was he taking his tablets, two a day? They kept his heart beating regularly. Oh, she wished he hadn't volunteered for this stupid job! It may set him back again, after all the care she had taken of him. It had been a serious operation; he'd been in hospital for three weeks. Subbing, with its regular hours – even though they were worked at night – had seemed ideal. But there was always that itch in him, to be back on the road reporting! 'Subbing!' he'd say contemptuously. 'Just fiddling round with bits of paper.'

Suddenly missing him, she went to the French windows and looked out. But she saw little. Miserably she returned to the sofa and tried to read again. Her father gave her a speculative glance over his glasses. He seemed about to say something, but changed his mind. Her mother came into the room busily. 'Now, what would you lot like for supper?'

'Please, Mum, let me do it.' She sprang to her feet.

They ended up cooking a meal together, mother and daughter sharing the evening as they had shared the morning. The problem of Steve receded, temporarily.

Steve had been hoping they'd send Derek Ryan down from Manchester but it was Charlie Hopper who turned up just after six, playing the chirpy, incorrigible press photographer to perfection. 'What's this going to be then, son? Snatch job, is it?' he asked at the bar in the residents' lounge.

'That depends. He might co-operate,' replied Steve, trying not to make his distaste too obvious.

'What? Welsh professor caught with his pants down? Do me a favour.'

'You never know. Don't jump to conclusions.'

'Conclusions! That's a good one.'

'How do you mean?'

'Well. The only conclusion I'd come to is that he's for the high jump.' He swigged his pint confidently.

'We don't know that for certain.'

'Well, what are we doing here then, eh? That's the story, init?'

'Not necessarily.'

'What? Who're you kidding, Steve?'

'The relationship is the thing. Not the consequences.'

'Bloody hell. I thought I was working for the *Comet*.'

What was this oafish Cockney doing in Manchester? Oh, why hadn't they sent Derek Ryan or Harry Saunders!

'It's a good story anyway,' insisted Steve. 'Academic and film star.'

'And you think they're going to admit it, do you? What planet you living on, son?'

'The same as you.'

Charlie stared at him scornfully. 'Snatch picture, boy. Take my word for it.'

Steve went up to his room, more worried than he cared to admit. The story seemed to be disappearing before his eyes. What if Haydn Lucas didn't turn up tomorrow? Maybe Bill Merrick had been wrong about the meeting. He could be at Jill Manders's place, anywhere. He'd have to start digging deep. How long would the newsdesk give him on the story? A fear he had subdued flared up fiercely, a fist tightly grasping his stomach. *What if someone else got the story first?* He'd open the *Mirror* or the *Sketch* on Monday morning and find the kind of splash he was dreading. Hell! He'd have done better to ignore Bill's phone call and carry on subbing. It was safe, secure, a doddle compared with being out on the road.

He sat on the bed miserably, thinking of Jos. What he'd give to be with her now! And Simon. He'd even agree with his father-in-law on some minor political point, old Tory though he was. He felt lonely, fed up, worried sick, almost – but not quite – ready to give it all up for a nice, cushy job in PR.

'I'm going out,' Annette said suddenly.

'Bit late, isn't it?' said Nigel, as the *Keystone Cops* whirled around on the box. 'Where are you going?'

'To see Mam and Dad, of course,' she replied irritably. 'Where else?'

'I don't know.' He was irritable himself now, miffed by the edginess she had been showing all evening, and feeling uncomfortable too, for fear that she had picked up on something in their earlier encounter in his study. 'They'll be going to bed soon, won't they?'

'It's only just gone nine. They don't go that early.'

'OK then,' he shrugged. 'Please yourself.'

As soon as she stepped out of the house, Annette had a sudden, exhilarating sense of freedom. It took her by surprise, even shocked her. What did it mean? She decided it was to do with the tension she had been feeling all day, culminating in their exchange of words – not really an argument – over when they should tell Rob things he ought to know. Come to think of it, Nigel had been acting strangely too. First, there was the sight of him wearing his office braces with his gardening clothes that morning – a tiny point, but oddly disturbing – and then his taking himself off to his study while *Dr Who* was on. He'd always been a fan of *Dr Who* and loved watching it with Rob. Why not today? And why plump himself down in his study to read poetry? Normally he could shut himself off, wherever he was, to read whatever he liked. Oh, what did it matter! She'd feel better after being with Mam and Dad.

There was a freshness in the air that spring evening that confirmed Annette's sense of release as she walked briskly downhill. She loved the subtle scents that, for her, were the essence of the season. They mingled with the briny smell of the breeze coming off the sea to produce a heady mix that stirred her senses. Her irritation with Nigel was swept away, as by the brush of a hand, to be replaced by a deep sense of gratitude that she had been born where she was, and remained there after her marriage. She allowed herself, briefly, to imagine what life would have been like if Nigel had whisked her away to a big city, Cardiff or Birmingham. Those endless streets! She'd have felt shut in, like a beast in a cage. Merely thinking of it gave her a sense of suffocation. But, she thought with an inward smile, there'd been no danger of that with Nigel. He was perfectly content to be a small-town solicitor, and they were doing very nicely, thank you. He was a country boy at heart; even Glanaber was too big for him. She knew he envied his brother Adrian his role in the family farm down in Carmarthenshire, and she knew too (something she suspected Nigel was unaware of) that Adrian resented this envy. He took after his father; there was a mean streak in him. Nigel was more like his mother, more open and generous-hearted.

The wide road commanding vast views of Cardigan Bay narrowed down into an urban terrace of tall Victorian houses, some of them converted into flats with the relentless expansion of the university. Now she was in the town itself, passing tennis courts and a bowling green and then the town hall, with its trim beds of tame civic flowers. A couple of turnings took her to the council flats where her parents lived, a grey three-storey building blending effortlessly with its neighbours. Inside, she walked up two flights of stone steps and rang the bell of number nine. Her mother answered the door, a small figure with a triumphant expression.

'Thought you might be coming,' said Lorna Morris complacently.

'What made you think that? I didn't tell you I was.'

'Just had a feeling, that's all.' She shut the door behind her daughter. 'I've got news for you, but sit down first. It might be a bit of a shock.'

Annette ignored this, as she ignored so many of her mother's idiosyncrasies. 'Hullo, Dad.'

'Hullo, love,' returned Ted Morris, not taking his eyes off the telly. 'What brings you here this time of night then?'

'Not so unusual, is it?'

'Eh? No, course not – bit late for you, that's all.'

'I'll go away if you like.'

'Don't be so touchy, girl,' said Lorna. 'Sit down.' Her brown eyes gleamed. 'Well, aren't you gonna ask me?'

Annette sighed. 'Ask you what, Mam?' she asked patiently.

'Who I seen today.'

'Well, who have you seen, Mam?'

'Him. Steve.'

'Who?'

'Your old boyfriend.'

'Oh.'

'Sorry, gel. Thought I ought to tell you.'

Annette recovered quickly. 'No odds to me. Where was he?'

'Walking down Darkgate Street, large as life.'

'Did he see you?'

'No. He was across the road.'

'Well. That's all right then. I'll have a cup of coffee, Mam, if that's all right with you.'

'Is that all you're gonna say?' Lorna stared at her daughter, disbelieving.

'What else should I say, Mam?'

'Well, what's he doing here? Don't you wanna know?'

'Not particularly. Why should I?'

'Well, for a start…' Lorna stopped herself just in time. She had almost said the unforgivable – 'He was the father of your baby.' Instead, flustered, she came out with, 'I'll go and get your coffee then.'

Annette's face flared crimson. Discreetly, her father avoided looking at her. Steve! she thought. In Glanaber! For how long? And why? Would she bump into him? Oh, she hoped not.

'What are you watching, Dad?' she asked, for something to say, though she knew very well it was the very same programme about early Hollywood that Nigel was watching up the hill. The *Keystone Cops* had given way to Charlie Chaplin, twiddling his walking stick and splay-footing out of shot. As the scene faded and the smarmy-faced presenter came back into shot, the laughter of the studio audience sounded more strained than ever. How did they get them to laugh like that? Did they pay them, drug them, and offer incredible inducements?

'Nothing on these days,' Ted was saying. 'Don't know why I bother.'

Normally Annette would have teased him, for if there was nothing on telly why was he always watching it? Now, however, she was distracted by the thought of Steve being in town.

'Like a biscuit?' asked Lorna abruptly, returning with the coffee.

'No thanks, Mam.'

'Please yourself.' She lit a Park Drive resentfully: she'd looked forward to a good gossip that her daughter obviously wouldn't provide.

'He's doing something on that principal bloke, I 'spect,' Ted said, with a sidelong glance at Annette.

'What you talking about?' Lorna asked sharply.

'Principal of the college. Going about with that woman, in't he?'

'What woman?'

'That film star. Jill thingy. They were on about it in the Nag's Head the other night.'

'Don't know what you're on about.' She looked at her daughter. 'Do you?'

'Nigel did say something,' Annette replied carefully. 'But he doesn't like gossip.'

'Who is she then – this *film star*?' asked Lorna sarcastically

'Jill Manders. You'd know her if you saw her, Mam – she's been on telly a bit.'

'Don't look at it like your father, do I? Too busy, me.' Lorna sniffed. 'What's she been up to then?'

'I told you – she's been doing what she shouldn't with the college principal,' said Ted.

'Why din't you tell me 'bout it then? Keeping it all to yourself!'

'No skin off my nose. Don't bother me one way or the other.'

'I dunno – these clever Dicks. No better than no one else, when it comes down to it. Worse, if anything.' Lorna dragged on her fag complacently.

'Reckon Steve must be reporting it,' said Ted. 'Nothing else to bring him down here, is there?'

No, Annette thought, with a bitterness that surprised her. Nothing in the least.

After she had left, her parents settled into an edgy silence. Ted flicked the occasional glance at his wife, which she steadfastly ignored.

'Trust you,' she said eventually.

'What now?'

'Honest to God. If your pocket was as big as your mouth, we'd be millionaires.'

'Say what you bloody mean, for God's sake.'

'Nothing to bring him down here indeed! How d'you think she felt, you saying that?'

'Don't know what you're talking about,' Ted muttered.

'Yes, you do. You know very well.'

Ted glowered at the screen.

'Should have married him. And she knows it.'

'For God's sake.'

'More her sort. Too late now.'

Tinny laughter from the telly mocked them.

7

STEVE GAVE CHARLIE Hopper the slip, not fancying a night's boozing. He walked the prom restlessly in the direction of the castle ruins, the dark tower overlooking the sea silhouetted against the last of the light. He remembered sitting up there with Annette, the girl he had nearly married. The town was full of memories. He remembered another woman, too, an older woman saying, 'Who's to know then, eh?' And slipping her shoes off...

No! He would *not* go down that path. All that was long ago... he had done so much since.

On the way back to the hotel he detoured to the harbour. The tide was out and three boats were marooned on the mud bank on the far side from the quay where he stood, with his back to the sunset. A chill breeze ruffled the surface of the river. The ghost of a past he thought he had outgrown brought stirrings of nostalgia and regret. If only he'd stayed in Glanaber fourteen years ago... His eyes turned towards a single row of dwellings abutting the harbour. His breathing quickened as he took in what he saw... could that really be Back Row? Brightly painted in colours that harmonised with one another, the old fishermen's cottages had a picture-postcard appearance. Even from where he stood, he could pick out number four. Someone was sitting in the backyard, reading a paper. The backyard where the woman had once stood, slatternly and provocative, pointing out the rat shit that she hoped would be her passport to a council house. And so it had proved.

Where was she now? Where was Vi, the little girl who had

scampered away so that her mother could be alone with 'the man from the paper'? And where was the self he had been – unschooled in the ways of the world, an easy target for a woman of easy virtue?

He turned away suddenly, and hurried back to the hotel.

When he went downstairs next morning, Charlie was already tucking into his breakfast. His fair, gingerish hair, swept straight back, stood up slightly, giving him the appearance of a surprised cockatoo. Stilettoing his bacon vigorously, he gave Steve the briefest of glances.

'See they're at it again,' he said, nodding at the Sunday paper on the table.

'Who?'

'Wotsit and Thingummy. That Russian pair of jokers.'

Steve scanned the upside-down photo on the front page.

'Oh, Brezhnev and Kosygin.'

'That's what I said. Must think we were born yesterday.'

'Why, what've they been saying now?'

'Filling Gordon Walker up with a lot of claptrap. God, it's enough to make you weep.'

'Let's have a look.'

'Help yourself.'

Charlie landed another smudge of tomato sauce on to his plate from the bottle. SOVIETS PLEDGE PEACE the headline shouted above a report that the 'duo' who had succeeded Kruschev six months before had promised 'peaceful co-existence' during their 'historic' talks with British Foreign Secretary Patrick Gordon Walker.

'Peaceful co-existence, eh? Well, that's nice to know, isn't it?' Steve said cheerfully, generously sprinkling his Rice Krispies with sugar.

'Peaceful my arse. If he swallows that he'll swallow anything.'

'Why shouldn't they mean it? They don't want war, do they?'

'Don't they? Well, I'm not so sure.'

'Don't be silly. Why should they?'

'Because that's the only way they can get anywhere, isn't it? War on the West.'

'The Russians hate war,' said Steve hotly, roused now. 'Look at their losses last time. They ran into millions – far more than ours.'

'Yes, and they had millions left after. All ready to sweep through to France and then us.'

'That would mean nuclear war,' scoffed Steve.

'Would it?'

'Of course it would. The Yanks wouldn't stand for it.'

Charlie gave him a pitying look. 'You really think the Yanks would commit suicide for us? Do me a favour.'

'That's the whole basis of their foreign policy. Massive retaliation.'

'Massive bollocks,' said Charlie impassively.

'Well, if that's what you think... what are they doing in Vietnam then?'

'Boosting their arms industry. That's what Eisenhower was on about a few years back, wasn't it? Military-industrial complex, remember?'

A man hunched over Steve. Thin, blotchy hair, wrinkled skin, dusty grey suit... the bloke who'd been in hotel reception when he arrived. Where *had* he seen him before? 'Full English breakfast, sir?' he murmured breathily.

'No thanks. Just poached egg on toast – that OK?'

The man nodded. 'Coffee or tea, sir?'

'Coffee please.'

The man crept away. Steve put the paper aside. Charlie crunched into his fried bread.

'Not a bad day,' Steve said pacifically. Charlie grunted.

Steve had tried ringing the principal late last night. There'd been no reply. Their strategy now was to park themselves outside his house and await his return. Once he turned up, with or without his mistress, they'd follow up the drive and nobble him. 'Snatch picture, you wait,' Charlie said equably.

Steve felt as nervous as he'd been on his first big job in the Street. If he cocked this up, he'd be finished! He could never go back to subbing, with his tail between his legs. What he'd do, God only knows. He jammed his morning tablets into his mouth, swigged a large gulp of water.

It was a lovely spring morning, the sort of day that made the natives swear never to leave Glanaber. Walking to the promenade railings opposite the Prince of Wales Hotel, he stared at a calm sea nibbling the shore. The 'golden' sand depicted on the front of the town's tourist guides was, in reality, as gritty as ever. Why was this so when, a few miles to the north, Borth and Ynys-las had such perfect beaches? The geological mystery had always perplexed him. Maybe, some day, they'd find a way of putting this right. Maybe not. Glanaber! Fourteen years ago he'd stood like this, gazing out to sea, restless to get away. And there'd been someone beside him, a slim girl with chestnut hair... He turned about suddenly. It was time to give Jos a ring. Of course, she was still at Guildford – she had told him the previous evening she'd be staying overnight. It was no great surprise.

His mother-in-law answered. 'Hullo, Steve,' she said. 'How are you getting along?'

'OK, thanks.' Her friendly voice and Scottish accent

cheered him, as it always did. If only he could feel warmer towards her husband! 'Got your story yet? I was surprised when I heard what you were up to.'

'Well, can't get out of practice too long, you know.'

'Well, mind you don't overdo it. I'll get Jocelyn for you. Hang on.'

Always Jocelyn to her parents – never Jos. An exchange of words in the background – indecipherable. Then: 'Hullo, darling! How are you feeling?'

'Fine, thanks.'

'You sure now? Did you sleep alright?'

'Like a top. What about you?'

'Oh, so-so. Not the same though, is it?'

'No, it's not.' Filled suddenly by a warmth of feeling for his wife, he added: 'I missed you, Jos.'

'I missed you too.' The briefest of pauses. 'Well, what's on the agenda today?' She spoke lightly, but Steve sensed rather than heard the underlying anxiety in her voice.

'Getting hold of this fellow,' he replied.

'No signs of him yet then?'

'No.'

'Nor his girlfriend?'

'Afraid not.'

'Ah well. I expect they'll turn up.'

Steve was speaking from a call-box, not from his hotel bedroom where he might easily be overheard by a nosy parker on the switchboard, but he was still cautious: had been so ever since a detective had warned him against being indiscreet on the phone at any time. Accidental crossed lines and deliberate tapping were, he was assured, ever present dangers.

'You're taking your pills, are you?' asked Jos anxiously.

'Yes, don't worry.'

'I'll be glad when you're back. I'm not sure you should have taken this job on, darling.'

'I can't go on subbing all my life, Jos,' he said, more sharply than he'd intended. 'This'll do me good. Get me out of a rut.' But even as he spoke, he felt that unaccustomed failing of the nerve that had haunted him ever since he had arrived in Glanaber. He seemed to be sliding on ice, with no firm foothold anywhere.

'How's Simon?' he asked abruptly.

'He's fine. I'll get him for you. Simon!' she called. 'Daddy's on the phone.'

After the call, Steve went back to his room and slumped on the bed. The excitement of the chase had gone before it had even begun. He put it down to his illness; he felt tired to the bone.

At ten o'clock, a rap on the bedroom door. Charlie stood outside. 'You fit? Time to get moving, son.'

'Don't need two cars, do we?'

'No. Come in mine. You look knackered. Didn't have a woman in there last night, did you? Naughty boy.'

'Do you mind? No such luck, mate.'

Charlie chuckled. 'How'd we get there then?'

'Easy enough. It's only two minutes away.'

Steve felt strange, as if he were intruding on his own past. The town was at once familiar and oddly foreign, as if it had been placed in another dimension. The street they drove along from the prom had the insubstantiality of a film set; yet it was on an upper floor of the tall building they were passing that he had worked, as a raw young reporter. Who was there now? Did the office still exist?

'Quick,' Charlie was saying. 'Left or right?'

'Oh – left.'

'No bloody choice,' Charlie muttered. 'One-way street.'

That too was new! They'd be having traffic lights in Glanaber next. The broad thoroughfare into which they turned, however, seemed little altered. The late Georgian and early Victorian houses on their left, some of them pillared and porticoed, faced the world with the same assurance. Charlie swept past them, blasting the horn unnecessarily at a pedestrian who, reaching the central reservation turned and stared coolly at this interloper. Steve recognised him instantly as Goronwy Pritchard, resident bard, cadaverous and, Steve was sure, more free than ever with his gnomic pronouncements. Soon they were turning into Brynpadarn Road, abode of the social and cultural elite of Glanaber.

The house that had been occupied by successive principals stood alone, gabled and aloof, at the end of a drive lined by sombre, reflective trees. Steve was prepared for a long wait; he had slipped out early from the hotel to buy some Sunday papers to pass the time.

'You sure this is the right house?' asked Charlie in a peculiar voice, as he slowed down to park at the roadside.

'Positive. What the hell's happening?'

'Search me.'

A young, fresh-faced policeman – much shorter than the London fuzz, Steve thought irreverently – detached himself from the group at the open gates of the drive and leaned over.

'Can't park here, I'm afraid, sir.'

'Why not?' asked Charlie sharply.

'Incident.'

'What sort of incident?'

'Can't tell you that, I'm afraid.'

'Come off it, mate. We're Press. Can't you see?' Charlie waved a hand at the card stuck permanently on the windscreen. 'We've got an appointment with the principal,' he lied.

'Well,' said the cop, with the faintest of smiles, 'he won't be able to keep it, I'm afraid. The gentleman's deceased.'

'Deceased!'

'You mean he's dead?' said Steve incredulously. 'Professor Lucas is dead?'

'I'm afraid so, sir.'

'Christ almighty,' breathed Charlie.

'When did he die?' asked Steve.

'Can't tell you any more, sir.'

'Why all this kerfuffle?' demanded Charlie. 'Was he murdered or what?'

Another blue-uniformed figure, larger and older, lumbered over threateningly. 'Who are these people, Evans? Are they giving you any trouble?'

'No trouble, sir,' wheedled Charlie, changing his tone to fit the superior rank. 'Just want to know what's going on, that's all. We had an appointment with...'

'Who are you? Not from the *Dispatch*, are you?'

'*Dispatch*? What *Dispatch*?'

'The local paper,' put in Steve. He leaned over. 'We're from the *Daily Comet*, officer. We were hoping to see the principal today. Could you tell us what's happened precisely? We'd appreciate it if ...'

'A statement will be issued in due course,' said the superintendent officiously. 'Now I must ask you to move on, or I shall have no alternative but to put you under arrest. Evans! See to it.'

'Yessir!' The young cop all but saluted. 'Now then. You heard what the super said. Move on please.'

'For Chrissake,' fumed Charlie. He fiddled with the gearstick, playing for time. Big-shot super was out of earshot now. 'Just tell me, mate,' he pleaded. 'Topped himself, did he?'

The young cop gave the briefest of nods, slapped the bonnet officiously for the eyes of those watching. 'Off you go,' he said loudly.

'Thanks, pal,' said Charlie softly. 'Owe you a pint.'

He drove past the staring eyes, parked farther along the road. 'Well,' he said. 'What you gonna do about that then, eh?'

'Do a story, of course.'

'You got enough to go on?'

'Plenty. Few more quotes I need, that's all.'

'Cops won't give you much.'

'Don't need them.'

'What about the blonde?'

'What about her?'

'Don't know where she is, do you?'

'Doesn't matter. Got all I need for tomorrow. Firm it up the day after.'

Charlie smiled. 'That's my boy. I'll get busy then.'

He got out of the car, walked back and began snapping the police outside the house, to the extreme annoyance of the superintendent and the satisfaction of his minions, who stamped important looks on their faces while pretending that nothing was happening.

Tim Crossley was in charge of the newsdesk that Sunday, keen to put one over everyone and get himself promoted.

'You sure about this now? They really were having it away?'

'Positive.'

'Where d'you think she is then – Jill Manders?'

'God knows. She's got a place on the Welsh border – could be there, I suppose.'

'Hop along there then, will you? Get some quotes before you file the story. Make it juicy.'

'Hang on, Tim. She's sixty miles away – if she's there at all.'

'That's not far. For God's sake, Steve…'

'Look, mate. Sixty miles in rural Wales is like a hundred and sixty in Essex. She may not be there anyway and if I go chasing round like a blue-arse fly I won't have time to write the story up, will I? Anyway she could be in London – or Monte Carlo for that matter.'

'No need to put on that tone of voice,' said Crossley, playing the big-time news executive, not very convincingly. Steve could picture him wriggling his fat bum on his chair, a chunky mass of cut-throat ambition. 'We've got to get this bloody story in the paper.'

'Don't I know it? It's my bloody story, isn't it?'

Steve remembered Crossley's first day on the paper, a raw recruit from the *Little Noddy Review*, or some such. He wasn't going to be pushed around by him.

'Get an agency on to her,' he said. 'There's a good one in Oswestry. Try her London address too.' He spelt it out. 'I've got enough to go on for tomorrow. We can flesh it out for Tuesday.'

'Well, make your story hot and strong,' said Crossley loudly, so that everyone around him would hear. 'We'll get going this end, full blast.' He slammed the phone down.

Steve felt years younger. His old confidence had returned. He was on to a story, a cracker! Possible intros swam mistily in his brain. He'd got enough to go on already, too right he had! Haydn Lucas was dead, so he couldn't be libelled. You could say he ate babies for breakfast, and the *Comet* wouldn't have to pay out a sou. The police would be issuing a statement later, the usual sort of thing. Lucas would have been 'found dead' at his home... 'foul play' would not be suspected. All this could be translated into plain English for *Comet* readers. The question was, how much should he reveal about the affair with Jill Manders? Obviously he'd have to say something, or there wasn't a story. The unsuspicious death of a college head in a Welsh backwater wouldn't have them spluttering over their boiled eggs in Bromley. But should he name her, or merely hint at the relationship with a 'famous British film star'? He'd have to write up the story on the assumption that they wouldn't be able to nail her for an interview that day, so he'd have to rely on his own hunch of how things stood between them. Well, he was clear enough in his own mind. They'd been having it away. Of course, he couldn't go so far as to say that. It would have to be a 'close friendship'. But everyone knew what that meant.

Back in his hotel bedroom, he screwed a sheet of copy paper into his portable typewriter. Then – not before time – he remembered to take one of his tablets.

8

'WHAT DO YOU mean, we've run out?' asked Ivor Morgan.

'What I say,' his wife Shirley replied. 'We haven't got any of those locks left.'

'Jesus Christ! When was Roberts round last then?'

'I don't know – last week, I think.'

'I didn't think we were so short.'

'Bloody hell. You're supposed to be keeping an eye on that sort of thing.'

'Can't do everything, can I? And stop swearing at me.'

The shop door's sharp *ping* silenced them. Ivor, grey-overalled, erect, smiled at the customer, a woman with dark, angry eyes and an odour of neglect. 'Morning, Muriel. What can I do for you then?'

'Firelighters. The usual.'

'One box or two?'

'One'll do. What d'you think I am, made of money?'

She scrabbled in a worn brown purse for the cash. Shirley remained on the far side of the ironmongery shop, half-heartedly tidying a shelf and inwardly seething. She was a woman who had gone to seed, her once slender body now lumpy and unprepossessing, in a dress that did nothing for her except confirm every one of her thirty-eight years. As she pushed objects this way and that, in a poor attempt at purposefulness, she impatiently swept back a stray lock of hair decidedly darker than it had been in her youth. Ivor's eyes flickered with annoyance as, only too aware of her distracted presence in the background, he served Muriel Jenkins with the good humour which was an essential part of his business persona.

'Thank you very much, Muriel *fach*,' he said, taking her money and handing her change. 'Always a pleasure to see you.'

Shirley shot him a sardonic glance and unnecessarily fiddled around with a kettle, confirming its new position by banging it down hard.

'*Diolch yn fawr iawn*,' Ivor called after the retreating figure of Muriel, who disobligingly failed to pull the shop door tight.

Ivor firmly closed it, only to encounter his wife's scorn: 'Next time you lick her bum give me some warning, will you? I nearly puked over these new gadgets no one wants.'

'Only trouble with you is,' Ivor replied phlegmatically, 'you've got no mind for business.'

'I've got no mind for arse-licking. Good God, anyone'd think she's a duchess.'

'Her money's as good as any duchess's, love.'

'Yes Muriel, no Muriel, three bags full Muriel,' mimicked Shirley. 'What's happened to you, Ivor? You didn't used to be like this.'

'You didn't used to be like that, either.'

'Like what?'

'Like you are.'

'No,' she said harshly. 'I don't suppose I did.'

So she was down that self-pitying track again. It was her excuse for everything – a mother so senile that she couldn't remember who she was, or anyone else either. Well, it was hard – hard for them both, not just her – but hell! You just had to get on with things, didn't you? And she'd started letting herself go when her mother wasn't half so bad as she was now. Ivor remembered how Shirley had been when he'd married her — vivacious, full of fun — and wondered why it was that she'd altered so much. Was it his fault? If so, how? Impatiently he picked up the paper he'd bought from the nearby newsagent's before opening up the shop. He skipped the front page — Frank Cousins sounding off again about something or other — but gave the pin-up girl on page five more than a passing glance. *Iesu mawr*! Some figure on her. Feeling Shirley's eyes on him — she had her own built-in radar, that girl — he flicked the page over. 'Jesus,' he breathed. 'The bloody principal's dead,' he said, louder. 'It's all in here — about him and that film star.'

'What?'

'The bugger's dead. Christ, where'd they get all this from?'

She hurried over.

'They've got her name in here too — can they do that?' Shirley said.

'I dunno. They have, whatever.' Excitedly they read the story through, shoulder to shoulder, the paper flat on the counter.

'Wonder how he died? They don't say, do they? Heart attack, d'you think?'

'More to it than that,' said Shirley shrewdly. 'Look at this — *crime is not suspected*, it says.'

'So?'

'Well, that's what they put in when there's been funny business, isn't it? Remember that comedian who topped himself? That's what they said then — I remember.'

'You mean... you think he did that to himself?'

'I don't know, do I? But he might have.'

They looked at one another, awestruck, their little tiff forgotten.

'Funny Muriel didn't say anything,' Ivor mused.

'She hardly knows she's alive, that one. Anyway, she didn't know about it, probably. We didn't, did we?'

'Only because we were out all day. Every bugger knows probably, 'cept us.'

'Look who's written this!' cried Shirley, pointing. 'Didn't you notice?'

'No, I didn't,' said Ivor sharply. 'Why the hell should I?'

'Is he here then, do you think?'

'I don't bloody know, do I?'

Their whole demeanour had altered. Ivor had a dark, resentful look, while Shirley, stoked with mischief, had brightened considerably.

'One in the eye for Annette if he is,' she said. 'Isn't it?'

'I don't know what you mean.'

'Well, he went off to London to get away from her, didn't he? To better himself. He has too, by the look of things.'

Ivor was silent.

'He'd still be doing little bits in the *Dispatch* if he'd stayed here,' Shirley added.

'What's it matter?' Ivor growled.

'Doesn't matter to us, but it does to her, doesn't it?'

'How does it?'

'Well, she might not have lost the baby if he hadn't buggered off.'

'Jesus girl, you say some stupid things!'

'Oh, do I? No more stupid than you.' She flounced away, disgruntled.

Ivor sighed.

'How you feeling today then?' Jocelyn asked, ringing early before setting off on the school run.

'OK,' Steve replied cheerfully. He was half-dressed, having showered in tepid water in the scarcely three-star en-suite bathroom.

'Did you sleep alright?'

'Yes. Fine.'

There was a small pause, as Jocelyn wondered how much he was concealing, if anything.

'When'll you be back then?'

'Tomorrow, I hope. I've got to see this woman today.' He was repeating what he'd told her the night before, after the news agency had tracked Jill Manders down to her border cottage.

'Ah yes. The famous film star,' Jos said sarcastically. 'Well, watch she doesn't gobble you up, honey.'

'No chance of that. I don't taste very nice today.'

'Can't someone else see her? You've done the main piece, haven't you?'

'It's still my story. You know what it's like.' She should have known better than to ask, he thought impatiently. But that was Jos all over: she liked to keep his job at a distance, as if it had nothing to do with her. He doubted if she'd even buy the paper to see his page six splash, complete with the by-line that still gave him a kick – even after years in the Street of Ink.

'Well, look after yourself. And,' she added warningly, 'don't forget to take your tablets.'

'I won't, don't worry.'

They were away just after nine in separate cars – Charlie would be heading back to base in Manchester as soon as the job was done. He assured Steve he'd find the Manders place, no problem – 'I've got a map, son, could find my way anywhere, don't ask me to drive in convoy, can't be done' – and on a straight stretch of road just out of town, proved his confidence (and impatience) by zooming past Steve and bequeathing him a derisory blast of the horn. Steve let him go, trusting the silly bugger not to get lost in the hills.

What would he *really* get out of Jill Manders? She'd agreed to see him, but that meant little. She could easily be on her way back to London by now, leaving him high and dry. Well, he'd have to wait and see.

'Sit down.' She waved them to a low settee while she sat opposite, below the small lattice windows. 'Pull those papers out of the way, that'll give you more room.'

She lit a cigarette, settling back in a chair with chintzy covers and looking poised and self-aware. 'Bloody acting already,' Steve thought, his initial sense of unreality having been extinguished as quickly as the sunlight. He knew he wouldn't believe a word this woman said, but so what? If she gave him the quotes, that's all he wanted.

'It's good of you to see us,' he began. 'I was sorry to hear about Professor Lucas…'

'I saw your piece in the *Comet*,' she cut in swiftly. 'What exactly were you implying?'

'I wasn't implying anything. I was simply giving the facts.'

'Come off it. You're saying we were lovers in effect, weren't you? All that stuff about "close friendship" – any fool knows what that means.'

'You *were* close friends though, weren't you?'

'Of course we were. Very close.' As his eyes became used to the semi-darkness, Steve could make out hers better. They were cold, guarded, decidedly not the eyes of a grieving lover. 'Couldn't be much closer, in fact.' She drew on her cigarette.

'So I was right then.'

'Of course. I'm not denying it.'

'You were lovers.'

'I was going to bed with him, yes. If you call that love, so be it.'

'What do you call it then?'

'Fucking. What do you?'

'All depends,' said Steve languidly.

'Look, Mr Whoever-you-are. I've known Haydn for about a year. I've been going to bed with him for six months, off and on. He was great fun.'

'I'm sure.'

'You don't have to say anything. Just listen. The thing about Haydn is that he was a great big fraud. He wasn't a nationalist at all. He just pretended to be, to get the job.'

'What was he then?'

'Bugger all, politically. I'd say he was Labour, more than anything. Maybe Communist, I don't know.'

'Communist?'

'Christ, what's it matter? These are labels. I tell you, he wasn't interested in politics.'

'What was he interested in then?'

'His career. He was interested in that alright. He got what he wanted too, didn't he?'

'You mean the principalship?'

'Of course.'

'But he was prepared to put it all in jeopardy.'

She frowned. 'How?'

'By having this affair with you.'

'I don't understand you.'

'It's obvious. The college authorities would never condone a thing like that. They'd have had his guts for garters.'

'What a silly thing to say. Do you write in clichés as well as talk in them?'

Steve looked back at her coolly. 'Then why do you think he hanged himself?'

She turned ashen. 'He what?'

'You mean you didn't know?'

'*Hanged* – oh, Christ.'

'I'm sorry. I thought you knew.'

She made a vague movement of the hands, as if to ward off blows. Her cigarette fell to the floor. Charlie dashed forward to pick it up. 'Leave me alone,' she said faintly. 'Just fuck off.'

'I'll get you some water,' muttered Charlie.

'You mean they didn't tell you yesterday – those guys from the agency?' said Steve. 'I thought they had – when I rang up.'

She seemed not to hear him. 'He can't have,' she moaned. 'Not Haydn.' She was rocking to and fro, her face distorted.

'I'm so sorry. I really am.'

Charlie came back with a glass of water. She half-waved it away, then drank. Charlie and Steve exchanged long looks of helplessness.

'Found dead,' said Jill. 'That's what you said in the paper.'

'That's just a way…'

'I thought it was his heart. He had a dicky heart, you know that? She didn't do much for it either, the bitch. How did he do it, anyway?' she asked, her voice hardening.

'From the banisters, apparently.'

'Jesus God. How awful.' She passed a hand over her eyes. 'And she wasn't there, I suppose. No, she wouldn't be, the slut.'

After a pause, Steve said gently: 'We thought you might have been, actually.'

'What? Been what?'

'With him.'

'With him? Me? Christ.'

Charlie sat down by Steve's side. His discomfort was almost tangible.

'Weren't you living with him then?' asked Steve.

'Of course I wasn't, you dolt. I've just told you, haven't I? I just bedded him now and then.'

'But she'd moved out, hadn't she?'

'Not because of me. She's a lesbian, you fool.'

'I see,' said Steve, feeling foolish.

'She'd have moved out anyway. I helped to keep him sane.'

She drank some water, recovering.

'So that was going to be your story, was it? Hot-pants actress drives the man to suicide. Well, think on. It was her fault, not mine. Go and put that in your wretched rag.'

She put the glass down beside the ash tray on the coffee table.

'You'd better get out, both of you. I want a lie-down.'

'Can we have a picture please?' asked Charlie.

'What for? You've got plenty of me, haven't you?'

'That's why I've come here,' he wheedled. 'Just one, Miss Manders?'

'Where'd you find him?' she asked Steve. 'In the ditch?'

Steve smiled, not knowing quite how to play it.

'So what's your story going to be now? Are you going to print the truth, or what?'

'I really can't say. It depends.'

'On what, for Chrissake? Harold Wilson?'

'They may decide to drop it.'

'Drop it? *No!*' Her eyes blazed in her white, contorted face. 'You see they don't drop it, mister, or you'll answer to me. What did you say your name was – Lewis?'

'Steve Lewis.'

'Well look here, Mr Steve Lewis. I want you to go from here and write the facts. I was having an affair with Haydn Lucas. He was a lovely guy but his wife is shit. She's having it away with Brenda Coswell. You know who she is?'

Steve shook his head.

'Well, go and find out, duckie. And put her name in your sodding paper. Because if you don't, watch out. Watch bloody out.'

She turned to Charlie. 'Where d'you want it, in here or outside?'

'Both, if you don't mind. In here first, right?'

Steve went outside, keen to set down all he remembered. What a story!

'Don't forget what I said!' she cried as Charlie reversed out of the drive. 'I'll be getting your paper tomorrow!' Charlie pulled away fast. She was still screeching.

He typed out his copy, then dictated it over the phone in his room. What did it matter if someone overheard him? Now the story was in the bag, he didn't give a damn.

He exulted in it all, the punchy intro, the spicy quotes, the way he wrapped it all up. With Charlie's pictures, it would make a great exclusive. He was in business again!

He stood up, threw his arms open wide, and gave vent to a wild cry of self-congratulation, in the same league as Peter Pan's cock-crow of sheer delight!

The adrenalin kept Steve on a high all that evening. He walked along the prom, briskly and triumphantly, picturing the splash in tomorrow's *Comet*, imagining the headline he wouldn't have minded penning himself. He popped into the Black Ram, one of his old haunts, and downed a couple of pints. The landlord had changed. So had the pub. There was no one he knew there.

He rang home, told Jos he loved her, and promised to be back as soon as he could next day. Mission was accomplished. There was nothing to keep him in Glanaber any longer.

He fell asleep quickly. And woke in the early hours feeling like death.

9

THEY WERE GOSSIPING again; why were girls always gossiping? He couldn't hear what they were saying, just the general chirp and cheep of their bright, youthful voices. In the old office he might not have heard them at all, but the doors and walls here were paper-thin. You pay more these days and get less, he thought sourly, then checked himself. If he was like this before forty, what would he be like at sixty?

Nigel Allan, this Tuesday morning, had plenty to do at the firm of Richards and James, Solicitors, but was in no mood for doing it. An old tragedy and a new temptation had combined to disrupt the even tenor of his life. He thought of himself as a straightforward sort of chap, but realised he was not acting in a straightforward way at all with his wife, Annette. But how could he? He could hardly say he was attracted to another woman, could he? And it was all so stupid. He was old enough to know better. Didn't he know it!

Then there was this matter of Ocean Park. Damn place! It should never have been given planning permission. But there it was, twenty miles up the coast, and everyone with kids in Glanaber was being plagued to take them there. Big wheel, water splash, scenic railway, all the vile contraptions that went into making a so-called pleasure park. Some pleasure, when you might end up paralysed like Uncle Ned! He would sooner die than take his children there. But Annette was right, he supposed. Sooner or later he would have to tell them something.

Nigel passed a hand over his face and closed his eyes, feeling sorry for himself. Then he remembered the Principal, hanging by his neck from the banisters in Brynpadarn Road. Poor devil. What had driven him to it?

A rap on the door, which opened immediately afterwards. Glenys stood there, auburn-haired, smiling. 'We're making a coffee, Mr Allan. Would you like one?'

'Bit early, isn't it?'

'Well, we felt like one. Been reading about this terrible business with the Principal. Awful, isn't it?'

'You should be getting on with your work, not wasting your time gossiping,' said Nigel severely. 'Didn't know it was in the papers, anyway. There's nothing in the *Times*.'

'There's a big piece in the *Comet*. With photos and all. You like to see it?'

He sighed. 'If you insist.'

He left his desk and went into the main office, where Delyth, as plain as Glenys was pretty, smiled up at him. These two girls did most of the secretarial work, with a part-timer, Mrs Roach, coming in Tuesday to Thursday, ten till four.

The *Comet* lay on Delyth's desk, opened at page six. 'Let's see what the rag says then. Probably made half of it up.'

The first thing that struck him – forcibly – was the by-line, 'by Steve Lewis'. It gave him a sharp kick in the guts, seeing the name of someone he despised – the man who had made Annette pregnant, all those years ago. Of course, Lewis had offered to marry her, but thank God he hadn't! Annette had done the right thing, pulling out of the wedding they'd arranged. If she hadn't, she'd have married this miserable hack and gone to live up in London. And what might he, Nigel, have been doing now? Would he have stayed in Glanaber with Richards and James? Yes, probably: small-town life in Wales suited him very well. But there'd have been no Robert and no Joanne... strange to think his children might not have existed… but on the other hand, might the baby Annette had lost in infancy have survived? So many imponderables! He read the report quickly, hardly taking it in. 'Not much in any of that,' he said. 'All gossip.'

'Why d'you think he did it?' asked Glenys. 'Was it because of her, do you think?'

'I haven't got a clue. Could be anything. His work, possibly.'

The girls' gaze, directed at him, made him uncomfortable. Could they know anything about his feelings for Jenny Briggs? That would put him in the same category as the Principal; a man led astray by sexual desire. 'Anyway, it's nothing to do with us. Best get on with our work.' He returned to his office, shutting the door firmly.

Glenys brought in his coffee, giving him a glance that might have meant anything or nothing, and he was reminded again of the passing resemblance she bore to Annette at the same age. The same colour hair – only Annette's had been darker, chestnut rather than auburn – the same slim figure. He hadn't fallen for Annette instantly – in fact, he'd going out with a girl in Carmarthen his parents had expected him to marry… it was only after Lewis had gone up to Fleet Street that he'd really started taking notice of her. He'd been struck by the pride she had in herself, her vulnerability… she hadn't got married just to 'give the baby a name' and herself the respectability of a 'Mrs' ahead of her name. That had meant something then, in the early 1950s… of course it was all changing now, even in Glanaber. Oh yes, it had been different then…

'Great story,' rasped Kent May, the deputy editor. 'Haven't lost your touch, Steve! Christ, we've missed you for that stuff. You're wasted, subbing.'

'Glad you think so.'

'Look, I hear you're feeling a bit off. What's the trouble?'

'Oh, nothing much. Just a bit knackered, that's all. I'll be OK in a day or two.'

'Think you ought to see the local witch doctor? Just to check you out?'

'I don't think so.'

'May be an idea. Don't want you laid up again. Think about it.'

'OK, I will. Wouldn't mind a couple more days down here though – if that's OK with you.'

'Certainly! No need to rush back. Scout around a bit – you might sniff out something else, you never know…'

Steve lay back on the bed. He felt as though someone had pulled a plug to let all his energy out. What could be wrong? He was still taking his Digoxin tablets twice daily – one in the morning, one last thing at night. The old ticker couldn't be playing up again, could it? Maybe he ought to go along to the local quack…

What would he tell Jos? She'd be worried sick. Tentatively he tested a few phrases he might try out on her. None sounded convincing. He knew she'd see through them all and, with a deadening sense of anti-climax, knew too that she would use them as ammunition against him. But he would *not* leave the *Comet*. Not for her. Not for anyone.

'Call for you,' said Glenys disapprovingly, on the office intercom. 'Miss Jenny Briggs. Shall I put her through?'

'Yes, of course,' replied Nigel, instantly regretting the 'of course' and just as instantly regretting the regret. He arranged his face, although still alone in his office, so that it presented to the world a professional mask of inscrutability. It may have deceived the world, if the world had been watching, but it did not deceive himself. His true response to the call lay in his quickened heartbeat and the weird sensation (a mix of excitement and apprehension) in the pit of his stomach. It was a sensation aroused simply by the sound of the girl's name, or the appearance of her name in the local paper: and lately there had been plenty of that.

'Nigel Allan,' he said neutrally into the phone.

'Are you busy?'

'Moderately. I've got a client in five minutes.'

'Oh – I'll call back later then.'

'No, that's perfectly alright. I can give you a minute or two.'

He cleared his throat – the signal for Glenys to put her phone down.

They continued their conversation in Welsh – their first language. Their voices were immediately warmer, all formality brushed aside.

Nigel said: 'Well – how are you today then?'

'Oh, not bad. Could be better.' With her tone of voice and the slightest of pauses, she managed to convey the impression that this possible improvement lay entirely in his own hands. 'What do you think of the big news then?'

'You mean Lucas?'

'Of course.'

'Very regrettable.'

'That's a funny word to use,' she said, amused.

'Why funny?'

'Sounds as if you're addressing the magistrates.'

'That wouldn't be funny at all, *cariad*. What do *you* think of it then?'

'I think he was an idiot. But then, I always did. All that phoney stuff about import controls on people. He didn't do a thing for the language really. Suspended students who took direct action.'

'I know. Pathetic.'

'Look, let's not beat about the bush. I've got to see you, Nigel. Urgently.'

'What about?'

'The planning application. Can you come round this afternoon?'

He hesitated. 'That might be a bit awkward.'

'It wouldn't take long, Nigel. There's something worrying me. I'd like to talk it through.'

'Couldn't it wait till tomorrow?'

'It could, but I'd rather see you today. *Please.*'

The 'please' – breathily delivered – did it, as she knew it would.

'Well, I suppose I might – at a pinch. But it'd be half five, at the earliest.'

'Oh, that late? Couldn't you make it five – possibly?'

'No. Well – quarter past, maybe.'

'Lovely. Do try, Nigel. I'd be so grateful.'

'I'll do my best.'

He put the phone down, feeling foolish. Why did he let her twist him round her little finger? If he knew the answer to that, he'd know the answer to many things. But for the time being, that was an answer he would prefer to do without.

Before Steve opened his mouth, Jocelyn knew what he was going to say. She half-turned away, so that Simon could not see her expression; she didn't want to worry him. She chose her words carefully, telling Steve she'd call back later. She put the phone down and smiled brightly, falsely, not deceiving her son for a moment.

'Dad's ill again, isn't he?'

'No, not *ill*. Just tired, that's all – he's taking a little break.'

The boy looked frankly at his mother. 'You didn't want him to go there, did you, Mum?'

'No, I didn't – to be honest. But it's his work – he had to.'

Simon pondered. 'Is he going to see Nana – before he comes home?'

'Good heavens, no – she's miles away!'

'He might – he hasn't seen her for a long time.'

'Don't be silly – he went down there a few months ago. You went with him, remember?'

'That was ages ago, Mum – just after Christmas.'

'Well, it's only April now, for goodness sake!'

Guilt and anxiety combined to raise the pitch of her voice. Simon gave her a look.

She knew, just *knew*, that something bad would come of all this. He should never have gone back to that squalid little place, he should have refused the job, utterly! She had hated Glanaber on sight, the first time he had taken her there. Pinched between two hills, at the end of miles of nothingness, it seemed to be waiting to be swallowed up by the sea. The best thing that could happen to it! For something had happened to him there, she was sure, something he never talked about. They had gone there first together to visit his widowed mother, before she had moved back to south Wales to be near her old friends. The best move she'd ever made, in Jocelyn's opinion…

The fact was, she realised, that she didn't like Wales much at all. There was no logic about it – she just didn't.

He kept to his room for most of the day, getting his strength back and savouring success. By late afternoon he felt better, and decided to take a stroll. He was putting on his shoes when the phone rang.

'Reception here, sir,' said the thin, dusty voice of the man he could not quite place. 'There's a gentleman to see you. A Mr Merrick.'

'You mean he's down there now?'

'Yes, sir.'

Bill Merrick! He might have guessed.

'I'll be there in a minute. Tell him to hang on.'

He splashed cold water on his face, put on his jacket and tie.

'He's in the lounge, sir,' the receptionist said, with the ironical smile that typified his dealings with Steve.

Bill was smartly dressed, evidently a man keen to negotiate a deal in the upmarket surroundings of Glanaber's leading hotel.

'I took a chance on finding you,' he began, 'though I thought you might have left by now.' His manner, at once deferential and triumphant, was that of a card-sharper with several tricks up his sleeve.

'What can I get you?' Steve asked brusquely.

'Well, a Scotch and soda would go down nicely, thank you.'

Steve ordered the same for himself, and they sat at a table overlooking the prom.

'Good story, Stephen. Nice quotes from Jill Manders. Pretty forthcoming, wasn't she?'

Steve's obvious impatience forced Bill to come to the point.

'I think we should be looking at the tip-off fee again, shouldn't we? I mean, a story of this magnitude...'

'OK, I'll do my best. They might go up to seven-fifty.'

'Seven-fifty? Surely a thousand at the very least. You did intimate...'

'I know I did, but I'm not the editor, am I? I'll have a word with them tomorrow.'

'You haven't already?' Bill's off-the-peg look of pained surprise increased Steve's irritation.

'I'm sorry, but I've been a bit off-colour today. I'll ring them tomorrow, I promise.'

'Staying down then, are you? Looking for fresh angles?'

'No, just resting. How's Betty today, anyway?'

'Oh, much the same. The campaign gets off the ground this week, you know. *The Dispatch* is running a piece on Thursday.'

'I'm glad to hear it, Bill. I hope you raise the money.' Feeling suddenly ashamed of his dismissiveness, Steve smiled. 'Thanks for the tip-off, Bill. You were right. It's a cracking story.'

'And you were the one to do it,' said Bill quietly. 'The best thing you ever did, boy, leaving Glanaber.'

Steve, stumped for words, stared down at his glass.

10

JENNY BRIGGS WAS a slim, gangly young woman whose full breasts gave her a top-heavy look. Her large, expressive eyes were the dominant feature in an angular face which was not so much plain as unusual. They seemed to have been placed in the wrong context so that, looking at her, people often wondered what it was about her appearance that puzzled them. She realised she had an effect on people, without quite knowing why, but was shrewd enough not to waste time rationalising this but simply took advantage of it.

Young as she was, just twenty-four, she had a position in the town arising from her devotion to the cause of the Welsh language. Coming there from Caernarfon as a student, she had taken a vigorous part in the direct action campaign arising from Saunders Lewis's radio lecture of 1962, in which he had foretold the death of the ancient mother tongue of Wales unless strenuous efforts were made on its behalf. She, and others like her, had stopped the traffic on the Town Bridge by squatting in the road, turning deaf ears to the insults of the mainly English-speaking locals of that quarter of town, who had mostly never heard of Saunders Lewis and would have cared little about him if they had. She had daubed slogans on walls, painted pillar boxes green, torn up official documents written only in English, shouted insults at councillors and engaged in sundry acts of civil disobedience. This was only the beginning, she had asserted. They must achieve justice for the language, or die in the attempt. While not modifying her views in the slightest, she had lately moderated her behaviour, for she had set up a Welsh-language nursery school and could no longer afford to show complete contempt for the law. Her partner in the enterprise was Heulwen Price, a small, mouse-like woman who shared Jenny's views but lacked her flamboyance. They had the enthusiastic support of many parents, but were short of money and a suitable building. Jenny now believed she had found the latter, but it needed modifying, and this is where her friendship with Nigel Allan was proving useful.

'Well,' she said, squatting on an upturned wooden crate in what had been the front office of a failed accountant, 'what do you think?'

'Well,' he responded carefully, 'it might be suitable. Only… it's a bit large, don't you think?'

'Oh, we wouldn't need all of it. Just this room and the one across the hall.'

'I see. And that's a possibility? I mean, they'd be willing to do that?'

'Oh yes. They've got somebody interested in the upstairs. A dentist.'

'Really?' Nigel smiled faintly. 'You don't think the children might be upset by the screams of the tortured?'

'Come on now, Nigel. This isn't Sweeney Todd. I'm sure they'd be quite civilised.'

'Well, I'm glad to hear it,' remarked Nigel, surprised that she had heard of Sweeney Todd. 'In that case…'

He was distracted by the angle of her legs as she sat bestride the crate; her knees were together, but her legs were splayed out in a way that was perfectly decorous but strangely exciting. Moreover, the curl of her eyelashes was oddly alluring, and so was much else about this young woman. There was no real reason why, as Jenny and

Heulwen's solicitor, he needed to inspect the premises at all; this was more the province of an architect. But there was, between Jenny and himself, something that might be deemed an understanding. They were attracted to one another; he was married; she needed him, both as a business accomplice and as an older friend wiser in the ways of the world than herself. The understanding did not preclude the hint from Jenny that, at some time, sexual favours may be offered him. The relationship, thus finely balanced, afforded both of them pleasure of a delicate and exquisite kind. There was absolutely no reason why either of them should feel guilty, or compromised in any way whatsoever.

'So you think we should go ahead, do you?' she asked, looking up.

'I don't see why not. How's the money side looking?'

'Not bad. We're getting lots of support.'

The supporters, he knew, included her father, a Caernarfon jeweller who knew how to tap patriotically-minded businessmen.

'Well then. Carry on. Why not?'

'And you'll go on... representing us?'

'Of course. Why shouldn't I?' He laughed, briefly and awkwardly. 'It's of mutual benefit, isn't it?'

'I hope so. Indeed, I hope so.'

She stood up, and he took a step back instinctively.

'You know, Nigel, we rely on you a lot for... advice and things,' she said in a small, breathy voice.

'That's all right. I'm only too glad to give it,' he blustered, feeling foolish and gauche.

'Well... so long as you know.'

She gave him a long look, then: 'Well, I mustn't keep you

any longer,' she said briskly. 'Your wife will be expecting you, I'm sure. Thank you for coming.'

'That's quite all right. Give me a ring any time. Keep me in touch with developments.'

He stood there awkwardly for a moment, then stepped out of the building.

It was over dinner that evening that Steve solved the mystery of the man in reception he knew he had met before, but could not place. 'PC Thomas,' he said to himself wonderingly. 'That's who he is!'

It all came back to him – the theatrical way that Thomas used to give evidence in the magistrates' court, holding the Bible high in his right hand while swearing that he would tell the truth, the whole truth, and nothing but the truth. It may have impressed some, but not Steve, who had been convinced that the man would swear black was white to get a conviction. There were other memories, too – notably of the time that PC Thomas and another copper had barged into the party thrown by his old girlfriend, Annette, and her flat-mate Shirley, on the pretext that there'd been complaints of too much noise. He could see them now, sitting smugly with their helmets perched on their knees, proud upholders of the Law. Idiots! But how could he have forgotten?

He stared out of the window, seeing nothing... aware that it was not simply the passage of time that had fogged him, but the fact that the man looked so dusty and dispirited now. It had been different before – he'd been a smart-looking chap, a right know-all. What had happened to him, to bring him so low?

Was he in reception now? He seemed to appear in the hotel at odd times, performing a number of roles, sometimes receptionist, sometimes waiter: Steve could swear he'd even seen him driving an important-looking guest to the railway station. Was he a taxi driver too? Anything was possible.

The placing of this man played odd tricks with Steve's mind, sharpening his recollection of events in a formative year in his life. He had got his girlfriend 'into trouble', as they used to say in those days, proposed to her and been accepted, had gone off to his new job in London thinking they would be married in a couple of months' time – only to get a letter from her calling it all off, a letter he had kept to this day. And then, a year later – or was it two? – she had written to him again, a letter he had torn up because it held so much pain, telling him about the death of her baby... *their* baby.

Christ!

The waitress was standing by his table, a pretty brunette with a friendly smile.

'What can I get you now, sir?'

'Nothing, thank you.'

'You don't want a sweet?'

'No thanks. I'm full up.'

Another time he might have flirted with her a little – perhaps even risked a mild double entendre. But not now. His appetite had gone.

She picked up his plate. At least he'd managed the first course.

'Coffee then, is it?'

'Yes please.' He relented. 'That'd be nice.' He smiled.

She wiggled her hips as she walked away, to show he was forgiven.

'All right,' said Nigel grumpily. 'I'll tell him tonight, if you like. But I really don't see the necessity.'

He had arrived home from work a little later than usual after meeting Jenny, ready with a perfectly valid excuse that he didn't need because Annette was bothered by something else – the fact that they never took their son Robert to that dreadful funfair, Ocean Park, and that they had not told him why. Good God, did you need some *reason* other than the fact that it was a bloody awful place? Yes, according to his wife.

'We must, we really must. Please, Nigel,' she pleaded.

So here he was, at Robert's bedtime, stumping upstairs to tell their seven-year-old the truth.

Annette was reading him a story. Rob listened attentively, sitting up in bed, his small hands curled up on the white sheet. He seemed scarcely aware of his father until the story ended, when he gave him a questioning look.

'Enjoy that?' asked Nigel.

Rob nodded. Nigel sat on the bed.

'We thought we'd tell you a bit more about Ocean Park… why we don't like to take you there,' ventured Annette.

Rob's eyes darkened.

'It's not that we're being spoilsports,' said Nigel. 'Don't think that because it's not that at all. It's…'

'I know,' said Rob. 'You think it's dangerous so you don't want me to go there – you said.' He flung himself down, burying his face in the pillow.

'Yes, but listen,' said Nigel earnestly. 'It's not just that. Something happened to someone we know at one of these places – that's why. Someone in the family.' He looked despairingly at Annette. She nodded. Rob was quite still.

'I had an uncle – Uncle Ned. He was thrown off a ride – it was horrible. He was in a wheelchair the rest of his life – I can see him now… and he'd been so active till then. He played rugby – that sort of thing… I'm sorry, son.'

Annette and Nigel looked at one another. Nigel could not decide whether or not to squeeze Rob's shoulder, make some gesture.

'Where's he now?' a muffled voice asked.

'He's dead, son, I'm sorry. He died quite young.'

The boy lay quite still. Then he screwed his face around, looked at his mother.

'Is that true, Mum?'

'Of course it is. You don't think your father would lie to you, do you?'

Rob buried his face in the pillow again.

'I still want to go there,' he said. 'It's not fair.'

Nigel felt a chill deep inside, a sense that never again would he command the boy's trust. For though he had told him the truth, he felt that Rob had sensed the lie at the heart of him – his burgeoning relationship with Jenny Briggs. It was ridiculous, but there it was. He felt the boy saw right through him, to the core of his deceitful heart.

'Very well, then,' he said heavily. 'We'll talk about it some other time.'

Annette leaned over and kissed the top of the boy's head. Nigel did the same.

The boy did not stir. His parents left the room, bowed down with a sense of failure.

'I'm going round to Rachael's,' said Annette later. 'Don't mind, do you?'

'Why should I?' said Nigel heartily. 'Give her my love.'

They were both relieved to be without each other for a while, though neither would have willingly acknowledged it. Nigel felt a sense of failure, that he had dealt – he believed – so awkwardly and unsuccessfully with their son. Annette had not reproved him for it, but he was sure she was secretly blaming him for the clumsy way he had gone about telling Rob why such places as Ocean Park were out of bounds. What he did not know was that, the matter now dealt with, however unsatisfactorily, she was preoccupied with a question at once more ambiguous and more central to her well-being – that of the presence in Glanaber of Steve Lewis.

After a last glance in the hallstand mirror, and a final fluffing of her hair, she hesitated momentarily before opening the door, as if she were having doubts about the venture, then went out decisively. Seated in her trim Austin A35, she started the car in second gear (a bad habit Nigel could not cure) and drove off.

Rachael and Gethin Miles lived eight miles out of town, in a new bungalow in a village on the main road to Machynlleth. Gethin was a short, cheerful man of thirty-five, Rachael three years older ('Cradle-snatched me, she did,' Gethin insisted benignly). Childless, they pursued moderately successful careers – Gethin in public relations and publishing, Rachael in admin in Glanaber University.

'Just going out,' Gethin assured Annette, as she slipped through the door. 'Don't take offence, bach. Got a business meeting.'

'Don't believe him,' scoffed Rachael. 'He's going to the pub.'

'Did I say I wasn't? Strictly on business though.'

'Business! Lifting the elbow's the only business you'll do tonight.'

Gethin rolled his eyes in mock exasperation, and Annette smiled back.

'Talk as much as you like, girls,' was his parting shot, 'but not about me, I hope.'

'Don't flatter yourself,' his wife retorted.

Rachael, petite, olive-skinned, had the Levantine look of the grandmother she had never known, inheriting not only her appearance but mannerisms which had skipped a generation. One of these was the flicking of her middle finger against her thumb, a tic of which she was generally unaware. She was, however, conscious of the shapeliness of her body, which was at once the envy and despair of women who found the onset of middle age treating them far less kindly. One of these was Annette, whose struggles with the cellulite fortunately did not make her ill-disposed towards her closest female friend. Annette could, after all, console herself with the thought that the effects of child-bearing put any mother approaching forty at a physical disadvantage.

Alone together, the two women relaxed in the atmosphere of intimacy they had long established between themselves. They were utterly at ease with each other, enjoying the kind of close friendship in which the sharing of secrets is possible but not obligatory. The delicacy which sustains such an intimacy was evident now in the way that Rachael forbade to ask directly why Annette had rung earlier to say she would like to call around: their meetings were usually arranged a day or two in advance. They chatted in a desultory sort of way until Annette said, 'I don't suppose you've seen today's *Comet*, have you? No, of course you haven't.' She puffed nervously at the Silk Cut cigarette Rachel had given her, before stubbing it out prematurely.

'I suppose it's full of the Principal, poor devil.'

'Yes, but not just that. There's a lot about Jill Manders as well.'

'Is there now? What's it say then? Come on.'

Annette took the cutting from her handbag.

FILM STAR'S SEX FROLICS WITH 'FIREBRAND'

Great fun in bed, says Jill Manders
by Steve Lewis

Screen goddess Jill Manders spoke last night for the first time about her secret love affair with Welsh firebrand academic Haydn Lucas.

Prof. Lucas, 48, principal of Glanaber University, was found dead yesterday at his home in the west Wales seaside resort of Glanaber.

I understand that his body was found hanging from banisters. Police say that crime is not suspected. An inquest will be held.

Tory MP Toby Begg headed a campaign for his sacking after his call last year for new laws stopping English 'colonists' from settling in Welsh-speaking areas.

A shocked Jill Manders told me at her remote country cottage near Newtown in mid-Wales:

"Haydn and I were lovers, but we didn't live together. He was great fun. People had the wrong idea about him.

"He wasn't a Welsh nationalist at all. He just pretended to be, to get the job.

"I don't think he was really interested in politics. He said things just to stir people up.

"He had a bad heart but kept this to himself. He was a very courageous man.

"Did I drive him to suicide? Don't make me laugh. There were lots of problems in his life. I gave him the emotional support he needed.

"I'm devastated – absolutely devastated."

So it went on. Rachael tossed the paper aside.

'Well?' said Annette. 'What do you think?'

'The man's a fool. Why'd he have to go and kill himself? Mind, I always thought he was a bit – '

'No, not that. I mean the report in the paper.'

'Oh. Well, par for the course, I suppose. I never read the rag. You don't either, do you?'

'Sometimes. Actually I know the man who wrote that.'

'Do you now?' Rachael was intrigued. 'Old boyfriend, is he?'

'Bit more than that, Rach. He's the one. Ceri's father.'

'Ceri's…' A picture flashed into Rachael's mind, of Annette stooping, putting daffodils on a grave. A small, plain headstone bearing the initials 'C.M.' Ceri Morris. Annette had taken her there just once, to share that much of her sorrow.

'My God.' Rachael glanced at the cutting again. 'Steve Lewis.'

'Silly, isn't it? I didn't think I'd mind.'

Rachael took a deep breath. 'I think a drink is called for, don't you?'

'I suppose Nigel knows all about this, does he?' she asked, mixing the gin and tonics.

'Of course. He's known all along. I told you that, didn't I?'

'Yes. But you didn't tell me who the father was.'

'I didn't see the need. Are you sorry then?'

'For what?'

'That I told you.'

'Don't be silly. Why should I mind? Proper dark horse, aren't you?' she said lightly, handing Annette her drink. 'Cheers.'

'Cheers.'

Rachael sat where she had been before. Annette's face was partly in shadow. She looked tense and pale.

'How much did you tell Nigel?'

'Everything.'

'So he knows it was this man?'

'Of course.'

'I know what you're thinking,' Annette said, after a moment. 'I'm a tart.'

'Don't be stupid. I'm just wondering about him. This reporter. Did *he* know?'

'About what?'

'The baby.'

'Of course. Couldn't help knowing, could he? We were going to get married. It was all arranged.'

'Why'd you call it off then?'

'Why does anyone do anything?'

'That's no answer,' Rachael said, after a pause.

Annette said nothing.

'Did he know the baby died?'

'Oh yes. I wrote and told him… He wanted to come down for the funeral.'

'And did he?'

'No. I stopped him. I told him it was none of his business.'

'You didn't!'

'Well… maybe not like that. But it's what I felt.'

'Jesus, Annette.'

'Why?'

'Well… most blokes would've run a mile, wouldn't they? They wouldn't want to know.'

'Well.' Annette shrugged.

Silence shrouded the room, stifling, oppressive.

Rachael said: 'You're still in love with him, aren't you?'

'Don't be stupid.'

'Yes you are.'
'Don't be stupid.'

Steve heard that strange bird again, in the middle of the night. What was it, curlew, peewit, lapwing? Whatever it was, it seemed to hold all the earth's woes in its cry. He got out of bed, pulled back the curtain, stared through the window. An almost full moon, half hidden by clouds, cast a pale light on the sea. Words came to him, unbidden. The beginning of a poem… possibly. He thought of writing them down, but simply got back into bed. He had done with poetry.

11

Simon was in bed, it was past nine o'clock, there was nothing much on telly, and Jocelyn was doing her tatting. It was something she had taken up recently, after reading about it in a magazine: '*There's been a revival of interest lately in this ancient craft, associated more with sedate Victorian times than our own. But working women of today are finding the skill and artistry involved both relaxing and fulfilling. In essence it is a kind of 'lace' making with cotton, using a small hand shuttle…*'

She had found it frustrating at first rather than fulfilling, but having overcome her initial clumsiness she began to feel she was getting somewhere.

She was going along well when the doorbell rang. A tall, lean figure stood there – Jack Palmer, secretary of the tennis club. 'Hi, Jos,' he said smoothly. 'Hope you don't mind me calling. I was just passing…'

'Oh.' Her initial surprise was supplemented by something else, a shiver that was only part pleasure. 'How nice to see you, Jack. What can I – How can I help you?' she asked, avoiding the ambiguous 'What can I do for you?' with a sudden glint of caution.

'I'd just like a word with you, if I may. About Friday.'

'Friday?'

'The annual meeting. Don't tell me you've forgotten!' he reproved archly.

'I had actually. Steve's away on a job. You'd better come in. Would you like a coffee?'

'Love one.' He stood in the hallway, smiling, assured.

'Milk and sugar? I can't remember.'

'Milk please, no sugar. The old weight, you know. Got to watch it.' He patted his flat stomach contentedly.

'Haven't we all. Well – go and sit down. I won't be a tick.'

She flurried about in the kitchen, wondering why she'd asked him in, not seeing how she could have avoided it. There was something about Jack Palmer that discomfited her – a charm that women found seductive. There were rumours about him: there always had been. His wife seemed to cope, but there was an ambiguity about this childless couple that people found disturbing. It was part of the climate of the times, the swirl of sexuality and ill-defined promise that went with the Beatles and Rolling Stones and miniskirts and discos and the sense that nothing would ever be quite the same again.

She put the tray down carefully – coffee, sugar bowl, biscuits.

'What's this, Jocelyn, if I may ask?'

'Oh – that's my tatting.'

'Tatting? What's that when it's at home?'

She explained. 'Never heard of it,' he confessed. 'Looks damn difficult to me. Doesn't seem part of your scene really.'

'Oh? Why's that, Jack?'

'Too antiquated. You're a thoroughly modern Millie.'

'You've got the wrong name, Jack. I'm Jos.'

He smiled cosily. 'Where's Steve then?'

'Down in Wales. They sent him on a job the other day.'

'Did they now? I thought he was desk-bound these days.'

'He is usually,' she said, tight-lipped.

'Ah well. Something just up his street, I suppose. Back to base and all that. Big story, is it?'

'Sort of.' She didn't feel like going into details and felt

uncomfortable, with him sitting there. He seemed perfectly at ease, legs stretched out, an athletic forty-year-old with touches of grey mottling his sideburns.

'Is he back by Friday, do you think?'

'I haven't got a clue, Jack. They could put him on another job after this. You know what it's like.'

'Who'd work on a paper, eh? Glad I'm not in that business.' He smiled, a shade too flashily for her liking. 'Well – maybe you can come yourself. It'd be great if you could. I'd like as many there as possible. Some important things coming up.' He listed them: trouble with the council over plans for a new clubhouse, one or two members getting stroppy, treasurer keen to put up subs, usual sort of stuff. Nothing especially urgent, that Jocelyn could detect. 'Be glad if you can make it,' Jack confided. 'I'd like your support over the fixture list. I know you've got strong feelings.'

'I don't know about that. It's just that we play too many matches. It's getting ridiculous.'

'I agree with you entirely, Jos. We should thin it out. What's the point of playing St Mary's year after year? They can hardly raise a team. It's a total waste of time.'

'I know, but nobody listens. You know what the older ones are like. We've been playing St Mary's since the year dot, so we've got to go on.'

'Syd and Bella.' He grimaced. 'Don't remind me.' He sat up straight, slapped his thighs. 'So you'll come then, will you? Help to put those old buggers in their place!'

'I can't promise, but I'll do my best.'

'Good girl.'

When he had gone, she wondered about him. She had her suspicions about Jack. But then she had her suspicions about Steve. Did he have suspicions about her? There were absolutely no reasons why he should have, but it would be nice to give him cause. She thrust the thought aside, and went back to her tatting. But now it bored her and she switched on the telly, feeling suddenly dissatisfied.

Shirley Morgan had the consuming discontent that often overtakes people approaching middle life, though she herself would have been hard put to find a satisfactory explanation. On the surface she was living a comfortable life, with a son and daughter who presented no great problems, and a hard-working husband who with her help had built up a moderately successful business from nothing. Their ironmongery store in Water Street ticked over nicely with the sale of door handles, lawnmowers, paraffin, nails, hammers, glue and all the oddments of domestic life that are never missed until they become necessary. Moreover, Ivor Morgan was a popular man who came within the definition of 'pillar of society'. He belonged to the Rotary Club, contributed to charitable causes, lived what would have been regarded as 'a Christian life' while rarely attending church or chapel and, had he only known it, was very close to being raised to the magistrates' bench. He had been urged to stand for the town council, but maintained he had 'no time' for such matters. He was content enough to plod on with his family and business matters, offending no one if he could help it and building up a healthy stock of investments which he hoped might one day serve him well in his old age.

So what was bugging Shirley? She had a permanently cross look, a snappy tongue, and had worn less well than Ivor. Some might have suspected that, at thirty-seven, she was suffering the early onset of the menopause, but the truth was more subtle. She was missing in her husband the elements that had drawn her to him in the first place: the suspicion of a certain wildness in his nature curbed only with difficulty, the glitter in his eyes when he spoke of people he hated or distrusted, the sense that any moment he might throw off the restraints of civil life and reveal something untamed and barbaric. She wondered, obscurely, if the change from working with his hands to running a shop had something to do with it. He had been far freer with his cash when he had far less of it than now. He wasn't exactly *mean,* but he was certainly careful. 'You've lost your entire spark, Ivor!' she had cried out to him once, only to be answered with a frown. 'Spark? What bloody spark? I'm not an electrician.' Yet there was much to be said for him: he was kind to her and the children, steady, reliable. Everything a husband and father ought to be.

That evening, Shirley was at her mother-in-law's. She got on far better with Eileen Morgan than with her own mother, a cantankerous widow forever complaining about the ache in her legs her doctor did nothing about. 'Doesn't give a bugger, that one,' Beryl Tucker grumbled to whoever cared to listen. 'Won't put me on nothing 'cos he says it won't do me no good. Can't be bothered, more like.' Eileen had been widowed far longer than Beryl but had adjusted far better both to this and to the curse of old age. She lived alone in a small house sensibly modernised which she had no intention of leaving until 'taken out in a wooden box,' she declared.

Eileen was often irritated by Shirley's pettishness, but prepared to make allowances. She knew her son could be a trial (indeed, all men could) and that Shirley was going through what she privately thought of as 'a bad patch'. The bottom line, however, was that Shirley was as good a daughter-in-law as she could hope to get in an imperfect world, far better than any wife her younger son Lennie was ever likely to acquire. At the thought of him, her face darkened. He'd turned out a boozy, thieving waster who was likely to end up in prison, the way he was carrying on. It was not Lennie who was occupying her thoughts at the moment, however, but her elder daughter Sally, because Shirley had asked after her.

'Oh, Sal's fine. She wrote the other day. She's just got herself a new flat.'

'Has she? Does she like it?'

'Loves it. It's her own too – she's buying it with a mortgage.'

'Cor! Must be doing well for herself.'

'Well, she doesn't get a fortune. Nurses don't. But she loves the work.'

'Funny,' said Shirley pensively. 'I didn't think she'd like it in London. I thought she'd be back here in two minutes.'

'Not Sal. When she puts her mind to something she sticks to it.'

'Yeah… like that time she was in the San. She stuck it out in that place all right, didn't she?'

'Mm.' Eileen pursed her lips, none too pleased to be reminded of the time Sally had been stricken with tuberculosis. Convinced her daughter had no hope of recovery, she'd wanted her to discharge herself from the sanatorium so that she could end her days amid the comforts of home. Then the wonder drug Streptomycin had come along – to save her, and countless others.

'Wish I was living in London,' Shirley said vehemently. 'I'm sick of this place.'

'Why – what's bothering you?'

'Everything. They all know your business round here.

You can't even go in the bath without them washing your back for you.'

Eileen smiled. 'I know what you mean. But it's nice in a way. It means they care, I suppose.'

'They don't care. They're just nosy.'

'I'm sorry you feel like that,' Eileen said gently.

'Oh, don't worry. I'm just a pain in the butt. I get on Ivor's nerves.'

'No you don't.'

'Yes I do. You know I do. I snap his head off. We had a row yesterday – over nothing! I wonder he puts up with me, honest to God.'

'Ivor knows when he's well off, believe you me.'

'I dunno about that. Maybe he should've married someone else.'

'Don't be soft! Why do you say a thing like that?'

'Because it's true. He nearly did, didn't he? He was going out with that Annette.'

'Don't remind me!' Eileen cried. 'He had a lucky escape.'

'What, by marrying me?'

'Yes! Of course he did. She's good for nothing.'

'You really think so?'

'Of course. What else can I think? Look what happened to her.'

Shirley frowned. 'You mean – losing the baby? That wasn't her fault though – was it?'

'Wasn't it? I don't know so much.'

Shirley looked wonderingly at her mother-in-law. What did she mean? Eileen didn't say.

The subject was dropped.

Shirley felt better, without quite knowing why.

Steve didn't recognise her at first. She had her back to him and looked as anonymous as any of the other mid-morning customers in the Pelican Café. She was sitting two tables away, her back erect, dark auburn hair tumbling down to her shoulders.

It was her voice that did it, coming to him loud and clear and sending a shock wave through him that froze him in the act of lifting the cup to his lips. He couldn't make out the words; it was simply the timbre of her voice – as familiar as if he had heard it only yesterday – that identified her. He stared in its direction, only to meet the eyes of a man just taking his place at the table that separated him from Annette. The man, beetle-browed, surprised and suspicious, gave him a long, cold look in return, and Steve looked away hastily, staring down at his frothy coffee as he wondered what to do.

Annette! Did he *want* to see her again, after all this time? It would be easy just to slip out without being seen – she didn't have eyes in the back of her head. But that high, clear voice had a hypnotic effect. He could not move – could not think – all he could do was wait till it rose again above the murmur of voices and the hiss and splutter of the coffee machine at the counter. Ah! There it was. And now the words were quite clear – 'He *didn't*!' – and he knew exactly how she would appear as she said them. He raised his eyes to look past the man on the next table, to see Annette throw her head back as she laughed, that staccato laugh he remembered so well, along with everything else about her. How could he *not* have recognised her at once, even though her back was turned? Again he met the cold glare of the beetle-browed man but this time he did not flinch, staring at him briefly before looking beyond to the table where Annette was sitting opposite someone he could not see. Was it a man or a woman? A sudden movement by Annette enabled him to catch a glimpse of her companion – a dark-haired woman, smiling. Steve felt a relief he knew to be absurd – what was it to him who she was with? He stared down at his paper, but for all he saw of it the pages might have been blank. Should he go and speak to her? What would he say? Would she rebuff him? Why should he want to talk to her, anyway? But he did. Most certainly he did. There was a hole where his stomach ought to be and he felt like a seventeen-year-old. The moments passed and now he could hear nothing from that next table but one. He looked up. They were still there.

'Good God. If it isn't you.'

A sallow-faced man plonked himself in the chair opposite. 'I was wondering if I'd see you. You've got some things wrong in that piece of yours in the paper.'

He was babbling on as if only a day or two had passed since they'd last seen each other, not fourteen years. What the hell was his name?

'I could have told you all about him and Jill Manders weeks ago, if you'd asked. Why didn't you keep in touch with me? You said you would when you left.'

Gordon, Gareth, Gwyn? Something like that. He willed the man to go away – all he wanted was a word with Annette!

'There's a lot more going on round here than that, I can tell you. Much bigger stories. Corruption on a big scale. I can tell you things that'd make your hair curl, boy! I'd name names too. I don't care.'

Jet-black hair slicked straight back, he looked across the table at Steve, who stared past him and the beetle-browed man to where Annette and her unknown female companion were sitting. For God's sake, why didn't he belt up?

'Where can I see you? I can't talk here. How long you down for, Steve?'

Gerwyn! That was it. Gerwyn Hopkins. He used to be a clerk in the brewery, always full of tales of seamy goings-on in the town. A frustrated gossip columnist who'd have made a mint up in Fleet Street.

'Is that OK then – tomorrow night in the Coopers?'

'I don't know,' said Steve helplessly. 'I may have gone back by then.'

To his horror, the two women were on their feet. He'd left it too late! But now he didn't want to be seen – not like this. She'd simply give him a glance and ignore him – he knew it. He rested his left elbow on the table, concealing his face with his hand. He felt rather than saw them pass, a table's width away – Annette going out of his life for a second time!

'I'm sorry, Gerwyn, but I can't stay now. I've got an appointment – nice seeing you again.'

'Don't go yet, mun.'

'I've got to – I'm late already.'

'Give me a ring then, will you?'

'Yes – yes.'

'Don't forget now. Hey – you don't know my number though, do you?'

'I'll look you up in the book – I promise.'

'I'm ex-directory. Hang on a minute.'

Atrociously slowly, he took a pen from his inside pocket and fiddled around for a piece of paper. Steve needed all his strength of will not to rush straight out. She'd be gone – he'd never find her!

'Here you are, boy. Don't forget now – it'll be worth your while.' He winked, slowly and absurdly.

'Thanks.' Steve grabbed the paper and hurried out. Left

or right? He hesitated. To the left, Pier Road with its cafés and assortment of shops ran down to the Pier Theatre and the prom, to the right it continued only a short distance before abutting with Darkgate Street, Glanaber's busiest shopping street. He stepped from the kerb into the road, to give himself a better view, then stepped smartly back as a car hooted and narrowly missed him. Damn! Hell! He'd lost them. But then, way to the left – how could they have got that far so quickly? – he spotted the two women going past a toy shop. Dodging the crowds, he hurried after them.

12

So! HIDE YOUR head, Stephen Lewis. See if I care.

It was obviously him. She'd faltered a moment on her way out of the café, then pressed on. If he didn't want to see her, so be it. She didn't give a monkey's.

But outside, she began to have her doubts. What made her think he was deliberately snubbing her? Maybe he hadn't seen her at all!

Yes! Of course he had. Why else should he hide his face like that? Who was he afraid of? And what was he doing with Gerwyn Hopkins? Oh, another story no doubt. Gerwyn was full of sensations. He was a small-town wannabe, always looking to get in the news either directly or indirectly. Just the sort to latch on to a Fleet Street reporter.

'Hang on,' said Rachael. 'You got a train to catch or something?'

'Sorry,' she said breathlessly.

'What is it, Annette?'

'It's him. In there.'

'What? You mean…?'

'Come on. I don't want to see him.'

'Where was he?'

'Couple of tables away. Talking to someone. He pretended not to see me.'

'*Did* he? Are you sure?'

'Of course I'm sure. I ought to know, didn't I?'

'Why are you worrying so much?' Rachael asked, struggling to keep up with her.

'I'm not worried.'

'You certainly seem to be.'

'Well, I'm not. I just don't want to see him, that's all.'

'Why should you see him, if he's still in the Pelican? You don't seriously think he's following us, do you?'

'He'd better not.'

They were approaching the point where Pier Road met the promenade, with the Pier Theatre directly opposite. This was where they always parted company – Annette going to the left, Rachael to the right.

They stopped at the corner. Rachael stared back at the way they had come, intrigued. 'What's he look like?' she asked.

'Don't look!' Annette cried passionately. 'I told you, I don't want to see him!'

'Well, I do. I've never seen an ace reporter before.'

'Don't be stupid! He isn't an ace. He isn't anything.'

'For God's sake, Annette. Pull yourself together. You're acting like a schoolgirl. Is that him?'

'Come *on*!' Annette tugged her round the corner.

'Take your hands off. *Please.*' Rachael, laughing, freed herself. Annette strode on, along the prom. 'I didn't see anyone – honest,' called Rachael. 'Stop a minute – *Annette.*'

Annette didn't look back. Rachael stared after her. Then, with a shake of the head, she went the other way.

Annette reached her parked car. She put her shopping on the back seat, swiftly looked around, and got behind the wheel. After a quick look in the driving mirror, she pulled away. As she reached the Old College on the seafront, with its quaint architecture once dubbed 'Early Marzipan' by an Edwardian wit, she had to stop to let some cars pass the other way. Glancing to her right, she saw Steve standing on the pavement. Their eyes met. He half-raised a hand. She ignored him. She drove on.

He rang just after two. She knew it was him before she picked it up.

'How did you know my number?' she asked.

'I found it in the book. You're the only Allan there with two As.'

'Fancy that.'

'How are things?'

'Very well, thank you.'

'I saw you this morning by the college. You pretended not to see me.'

'Like you did.'

'What?'

'In the Pelican.'

'Oh.' A pause. 'I'm sorry.'

'It doesn't matter. What do you want, Steve?'

'I'd like to see you.'

'No. What's the point?'

'There's something I want to talk to you about.'

She did not answer.

'Annette?'

'You shouldn't be ringing me, Steve. I don't want you to.'

'I haven't, have I? I never have.'

'Well, don't start.'

'I won't keep you long, I promise.'

'What are you still doing down here, anyway? I thought you'd have gone back by now.'

'I'm not too well. They told me to stay down here a bit longer.'

'What's wrong then?'

'Oh, nothing much. Just a minor heart condition.'

'I thought you'd got over all that, long ago.'

'It came back. I've had an op.'

'I'm sorry to hear that, Steve.' She realised she was clutching the wire tightly with her free hand and let it go.

'Don't worry, I'll be OK.' A pause. 'Look,' he ploughed on. 'Can I see you for five minutes?'

'Why?'

'It's hard to explain. It's about Ceri.'

'*No.*'

'Please, Annette. It's important. Where can I see you?'

'You can't. It's impossible.'

'I just want to know where she's buried.'

'Why?'

'I want to put some flowers there.'

'What on earth for?'

'I just do. I'm her father, for God's sake.'

'Don't I know it.'

'Well, I've got a right.'

'You've got no rights at all. Leave me alone, Steve.'

'See me tomorrow in the cemetery. Half past ten.'

'I can't.'

'Yes you can. I'll be just inside the main entrance.'

'*No.*'

'Thanks, Annette.'

'*Steve.*'

The line went dead.

'So he thinks it'll be alright then, does he?' asked Heulwen Price, giving her flatmate a keen look.

'Yes. No problem at all,' replied Jenny Briggs, shaking the dripping lettuce over the sink.

The two young women conversed in Welsh, as they

always did. To do otherwise would be not only unnatural but shameful.

'Will he help us with the application?' Heulwen took a newly-washed radish from a bowl.

'Of course. When the time comes.'

'Useful chap, isn't he?'

Jenny gave her a glance, but said nothing. In jeans and T-shirt – her denim jacket thrown over a chair – she might have stood as a symbol of mid-Sixties young womanhood.

Heulwen nibbled the radish absently, her mind on greater things. 'What's he really like then – this Nigel?'

'He's OK. Knows his legal stuff alright.'

'I don't mean that. I mean – personally.'

'He's very pleasant. Sympathetic.'

'Oh, I'm sure. Married, I suppose?'

'You know he is. I told you.'

'Ah yes. I forgot...' She added, carelessly: 'How long have you known him then, Jen?'

'I don't know. Why do you ask?'

'Oh, nothing special... Doesn't seem your type, that's all.'

'*Iesu mawr.* What is my type, Heulwen?'

'You should know.'

Jenny clamped her hands down hard on the sink.

'What are you trying to tell me, Heul?'

'I'm not trying to tell you anything. I'm just curious, that's all.'

'About what?'

'Whether you intend shagging him or not.'

'I might if I get the chance. Satisfied?'

Heulwen smiled. 'Let me know if you do.'

'I'll send you a postcard, right?'

Nigel came home that evening, looking strong and dependable. Annette fussed over him, though not so much that he noticed. He was tired and the kids bothered him a bit with some fractious quarrelling at bedtime. He shouted at Rob and the boy stumped up to bed looking injured. Annette would normally have taken Rob's side but wanted only to mollify her husband that evening. She felt confused by Steve's phone call and guilty about not telling Nigel about it. But how could she, without making it more important than it was? And she had no intention of opening old wounds. Nigel had been marvellous about the baby she'd had by Steve, and his staunch support had gone a long way towards persuading Annette that she had really fallen for him.

He sat reading the *Telegraph* while she knitted a cardigan for her mother, half-looking at a TV quiz hosted by Hughie Green.

He rattled his paper irritably. 'Must you look at that rubbish?'

'Not if it bothers you, darling.'

'I can't stand that man. He's a complete phoney.'

'I know.'

She switched off the set. As she resumed her knitting, the room seemed oppressively quiet.

'I'm sorry,' he said suddenly. 'Look at it if you like. Don't mind me. I'm just in a bad mood, that's all.'

'You're tired, Nigel, that's your trouble. You're doing too much. When's Stella coming back, anyway?'

'Oh, not long now, I don't suppose. She's probably back by the autumn.'

'Autumn! That's months away.'

'It'll soon pass. It's hard for her too, isn't it?'

Annette's knitting took new pace, registering her

annoyance. It was all so typical. Stella was a career woman – she'd been to college. Annette had never had a career. All she'd been was a shorthand typist. Ten a penny. Not that she'd minded at the time. But now it seemed so unfair. They'd never have let *her* take time off to have a baby. Especially an illegitimate one.

'It's so unfair though, isn't it?'

'What's unfair?' he said absently.

'Giving her all that time off. To have a baby.'

He grunted.

'They wouldn't have let me.' She instantly regretted the words, would have snatched them back if she could.

'No,' he murmured.

She stared at him, appalled. Is *that* all it meant to him?

'That's stupid. Absolutely stupid,' he fumed.

Her eyes brightened.

'Do you know what Wilson's done now? I didn't think even *he* could be so stupid.'

She threw down her knitting, left the room.

'What's up with you?' he said.

He shook his head, at the impossibility of women.

Steve was there ten minutes early – he couldn't wait a moment longer. It was another brilliant May morning, sunlight driving thick shadows from tall evergreens down on to the tarmac strip leading from the cemetery entrance to the graves themselves. This was the way the shiny-black hearses came, giving death a glossy respectability mocked by the unseen corruption six feet below. He remembered Scoop Matthews standing here, hunched and claw-fingered, reverentially gathering the names of mourners for the obituaries page of the *County Dispatch*. Scoop, the last of the old school; no self-respecting hack did that sort of thing any more.

While remaining within sight of the entrance – he didn't want her saying she'd turned up but found no-one there – Steve ran his eyes over some of the epitaphs. Among the hackneyed tributes and Biblical verses, simple tales still had the power to shock. A six-year-old boy had been swept away by a mill-race; three brothers slaughtered in Earl Haig's trenches; a young woman killed by a bolting horse. The size of the Victorian tombstones made Steve ponder: what would they cost today? Anyway, they probably wouldn't be allowed; after two world wars, death itself had been cut down to size. His thoughts turned to his father; no memorial to him here. He had been cremated in Shrewsbury, his ashes scattered somewhere in the Vale of Glamorgan, his mother wouldn't say exactly where. 'I don't want you there with me,' she instructed. 'This is just between the two of us.' He had long learned to live with his mother's whims, and accepted this despite the hurt. What choice did he have? But he would like to have done some of the scattering himself, and known just where the winds had blown these grey flakes of what had once been the material image of his progenitor.

He had no doubt she would turn up, though why he was so sure of it he couldn't say. It was a conviction deep in his bones – or 'in his water', his Auntie Grace (more correctly, Great-Aunt) would have said. He was as sure of it as he was sure that he and Jos would never have any more children, and that one day he would live in Wales again. He did not try to find a link between these last two convictions, nor did he wish to do so. They were simply part of the framework of his thoughts, as irrefutable as his date of birth or the identity of his parents. Viewed rationally, there was little or no reason why Annette should indulge his whim to see her in the cemetery. From her point of view, it was a highly dangerous idea. Why should she risk being seen in his company? It would cause tongues to wag, providing fodder for the gossip mongers. And yet, and yet... she had not hung up on him, even when he'd mentioned their baby. And he'd detected something in her voice that shored up instinct with the merest sliver of logic; something not strong enough to be sympathy, still less affection, more an unspoken acknowledgement that their past intimacy and its tragic consequences had created a tie between them that, however fragile, was still real. As he waited, an excitement built up in him which he tried to subdue. He knew he was not being honest with himself. He was using their dead baby as an excuse. It would be a nice gesture to put flowers on her grave, but nothing more than that. He did not grieve for her: how could he? He had never held her, or even seen her. She was no more than an idea. But she was a way of getting to see Annette again... the only way. And he wanted that. He did not quite know why, but he wanted that.

Absorbed in his thoughts, he was not at once aware of her approach. Then he looked up. She was in a smart two-piece suit, the black polo-neck sweater clinging to her throat.

'Annette,' he said.

'I can't stay long. Come on, let's get it over with.'

She began walking briskly along the narrow path through the cemetery. He caught her up. Neither said a word. He felt foolish and guilty, as if he had been caught out in a shameful act.

'It's good of you to come like this,' he managed.

'It's not good at all. It's stupid. I don't know why you

rang me. I told you not to. Good job Nigel didn't answer the phone.'

'I thought he'd be at work.'

'He was.'

'You mustn't do this again. Do you understand? Never.'

'OK. It's just that I'm down here for a job, and I thought...'

'I know that. I saw it in the paper.'

So she'd read his story. He grasped at this lifeline. 'Hell of a thing isn't it, this business with the Principal.'

'I'm not in the least bit interested, Steve. Though it's the sort of thing the *Comet* goes for, I expect.'

'We had a tip-off about it.'

'Did you now.' She was looking straight ahead, as if not seeing anyone would mean that she herself would not be seen. But there was no one in sight. The graves were shrouded in a deep silence broken only by their words.

'I'll be going back tomorrow.'

'How's your wife? I can't remember her name, I'm afraid.'

'Jocelyn. She's fine.'

'How many kids have you got now?'

'Just the one, Simon. And you?'

'It doesn't matter, does it?' She wheeled around suddenly. 'Look, Steve, this is totally ridiculous. I'm going to show you the grave and then leave you. I don't ever want to see you again.'

'You won't, don't worry.' Then he heard himself saying, 'Why didn't you let me come to her funeral? You had no right to keep me away.'

'What?'

'She's my baby as well as yours. I wanted to be there.'

'You…'

'I'm sorry, Annette, but I mean it. I was really upset. I still am.'

'You were up in London. I was married. What the hell right did you have? Christ, I can't believe you're saying this.'

'I wanted to see her. Before she died. I know why I couldn't, but all the same…'

She was shaking her head, wretchedly.

'I really loved you, Annette.'

'Stop. *Stop.*'

She hurried on again and he followed, a step or two behind. She stopped by a gnarled tree, almost bare of leaves in spite of the season.

'There.' She pointed. 'The fourth one along. You'll see her name on it. Goodbye, Steve.'

'Thanks.'

She strode away, back the way they had come. His throat was tight. He wanted to call after her, but could not.

13

'So what are you making, exactly?' Steve asked.

'Oh, just some trimming. For the cushion covers.'

'Looks complicated.'

'It isn't really. Just needs a bit of getting used to, that's all.'

Jocelyn's head was bent low as she worked. Her face, seen in profile, again gave him that strange sense of looking at the medieval painting of a woman, chaste and unapproachable, waiting for her lover to ride up on a charger. The work she was engaged in gave emphasis to the illusion. Twisting thin threads with her long white fingers, she seemed to have slipped into the role of one impossibly removed from the twentieth century. All that was required to complete the picture was a wimple. Yet she had not been at all nun-like last night. Not in the least.

Steve wanted to show interest without appearing to humour her. Lowering his paper, he looked intently at what she was doing.

'What do you call that thing you're pushing through there?'

'A shuttle.'

'Like they have in tweed mills?'

'This one's smaller. A hand shuttle. But it's the same sort of principle.'

'Funny to see you doing that. You don't like knitting.'

'Shows how weird I am, doesn't it?'

She threw him a brief, coquettish glance. Happily he ruffled the pages of the *Sunday Times*. He was glad to be home again, doubly glad not to be doing the Sunday shift he'd been due for. 'We won't expect you till Monday,' an assistant editor had assured him. 'But can you make it earlier – say half four, before conference? The Chief wants a word with you.'

'Oh, right-o. But what's he want, do you know? Not in for a bollocking, am I?'

'I shouldn't think so. You can keep your bullet-proofs for another time.'

Ever since taking that call before setting off for home, job done, Steve had been wondering what it meant. Had Gus Chapple – The Chief to all *Comet* journalists – expected more from him? He went over the story again in his brain, every word of it, worrying it with terrier-like intensity, setting it against what he knew of the situation and what could only be surmised, remembering the way Jill Manders had looked and what she had said. The way she looked... mustn't think of that too much. He'd always fancied her – but then, what man didn't?

He ruffled the paper again then put it aside, unable to concentrate. He kept thinking of Annette, and that small tombstone in the cemetery. *C.M. Died 29 August 1952. Aged 4 Months. Rest in Peace.* Ceri Morris, commemorated only by her initials. His own daughter. She'd be twelve now. In the local county school. Going there in gymslip and school hat. Learning French and Latin. Playing hockey and netball. If she'd survived. He'd put flowers on her grave. Red and blue flowers, very colourful. As bright as she'd be now. He'd bought them in a florist in Water Street. A woman assistant in the shop, not the one serving him, had looked vaguely familiar, but he couldn't place her. There were lots of people like that in Glanaber. People he thought he recognised, but wasn't sure of. Not sure enough to greet them. Sometimes he'd nodded, sometimes they'd nodded back. That was the way of things, going back to somewhere you'd lived before. The past was all around you, confusing the present. He'd only spent a few years there, after moving up from south Wales with his parents. He'd had his first job there, on the local paper. But he couldn't wait to get away. He'd wanted to see more of life, not spend his time rotting away on a small-town rag. But there'd been complications. Annette. He'd fallen for her, and got her pregnant. With Ceri. Who was now dead. Lying in that pathetic little grave bearing the initials *C.M.* Not a mention of him, of course. Why should there be? And why did he care anyway? Most blokes wouldn't give a toss.

'Penny for them,' said Jocelyn.

'Mm?'

'You were miles away.'

'Was I?'

'Yes.'

'Oh… I was just wondering what the Chief wants to see me about.'

'Maybe he's giving you a pay rise.'

'Pigs might fly.'

'Why not? You made a good job of that story, didn't you?'

'I don't know. Maybe he thinks I cocked it up.'

'How could he? You got hold of that woman, didn't you?'

'Maybe he wanted better quotes. She wasn't very forthcoming.'

'They looked alright to me.'

He rustled his paper impatiently. How could she read the Chief's mind? How could anyone?

The nun-like look returned, and a sense of unreality overcame him. Who was she? Who was he? What were they doing together?

'See many people you knew there?' she asked, after a moment.

'Where?'

'In Glanaber, of course.'

'A few. Not many.'

'Really?'

'Yes.'

'Surprising that.'

'Why? I've been away fifteen years, Jos.'

'All the same... Lots of people stay in a small town. They do in Guildford.'

'Guildford's not all that small.'

'The same applies. Not everyone goes away like you.'

'Maybe I didn't recognise them. People change.'

He thought of the man in the hotel he'd placed with great difficulty, the woman in the florist's. But Annette had hardly changed at all.

Jos screwed him a glance. 'Didn't see any old flames then, by any chance?'

'Good God no. Why should I?'

'Why not? They must be thick on the ground.'

'Don't be silly.'

'You did meet one though, didn't you?'

Steve's heart skipped a beat. 'Who's that?'

'Jill Manders.'

'She's not an old flame,' Steve said, loud with relief.

'Isn't she?'

'Of course not.'

'You'd met her before though, hadn't you?'

'Yes, but I didn't *do* anything. Good God, what do you take me for?'

'An old lech. Come on. Let's go to bed.'

When it was over, she said: 'I was worried about you, you know.'

'What on earth for?'

'Your state of health. You weren't well.'

'I was just tired, Jos.'

'All the same... you've got to look after yourself, you know.'

'I do, don't I?'

'I don't think they should have sent you on this job. It's not fair.'

'What are you talking about?'

'You've been ill. You've got a serious heart condition. It's only a few months since you had that operation.'

'But I'm OK now. You know I am.'

'You're not OK, Steve.' She was sitting up in bed now. 'You're still taking those tablets. And you've got to look after yourself. The doctor said.'

'I do look after myself. I'm not an invalid, Jos.'

'You will be if ...'

'If what? What's bothering you?'

'Oh, I don't know. Everything.'

To his amazement, she was on the brink of tears.

'Darling.' He put his arm around her. 'What is it?'

'I hated you being away. So did Simon. I don't want to go through all that again.'

'All what?'

'You know. The stuff you were doing before.'

'Reporting, you mean? It's my job, Jos. I can't stay subbing for ever.'

'Oh, Jesus.'

She got out of bed and hurried to the bathroom. He switched on the light in her absence. When she came back, he hardly looked at her.

'So we're going down again, are we?' he said, as she put on her clothes.

'I don't feel like sleeping yet.'

He followed her downstairs in his dressing gown. He would not let the subject go.

'I don't understand why you're so worried, Jos.'

'Just leave it, Steve. I'm tired.'

'Who's been getting at you – your parents?'

'What?'

'I know they don't like my job. They never have.'

'Just leave them out of this, will you?'

'Who is it then?'

'Nobody! I can think for myself, can't I?'

'You don't seriously think I can go on subbing the rest of my life, do you? I hate the bloody job. It's boring. I want to be out there, getting my hands dirty, not shoving silly bits of paper around.'

'How old do you think you are, Steve?'

'What?'

'You're thirty-seven. You're not a kid. You're too old to be a reporter.'

'Too old?'

'It's time you settled down. Do you think you can go on for ever?'

'Why not?'

'Because it's not like that – you know it. Younger people come along. You'll get pushed into the background. It happened to Bruce Farnham, remember?'

'Bruce was past it. I'm not. I can hold my own with any bugger. Why do you think they sent me on that story, for God's sake?'

'I don't know. Because you found out about it, I suppose. It was your story, wasn't it? And you're a good reporter; I'm not saying you're not.' ('Oh, thank you,' he interposed sarcastically). 'But you can't go on for ever. You've got to look to the future, that's all I'm saying.'

'Well, what's the alternative? I'm not going into PR, if that's what you're thinking. I don't want to be a paid liar, thank you very much.'

'Did I mention PR? There are other things, you know.'

'Such as?'

'Well.' She made a large, helpless gesture. 'Desk jobs. Editing.'

'Editing what – the *Wattle-and-Daub Weekly*?' he sneered.

'There are worse things.'

It was hard to believe they had been making love half an hour ago.

Ivor was totting up the shop accounts, but found it difficult because Shirley kept disturbing him. It was just the way she was these days, always going on about things that didn't matter. Tonight it was the way their eldest, Conrad, wouldn't get down to his homework properly. She was afraid he was falling behind at school. He'd never get to college if he carried on like that.

'What're you so worried about?' Ivor asked. 'He's only twelve, for God's sake.'

'Yes, and next year he'll be thirteen. And then fourteen. And then fifteen.'

'Jesus wept. You'll have him drawing his pension soon.'

'Don't laugh, Ivor. It's not funny.'

'I'm not laughing. But you're making a mountain out of a molehill. Why should he go to college, anyway? You didn't go. I didn't go.'

'And much good it did us, too. Do you want him to end up like us, slumming away in a shop?'

'He could do a lot worse. He might want to take over anyway, for all we know.'

'Oh, no. I'm not having that!'

'Why not? It's a good little business.'

Shirley made a dismissive sound.

'What's that mean?'

'Don't you want him to better himself? He's got a good head on him, that boy.'

'I don't say he hasn't. But we aren't exactly stupid either, are we?'

'Speak for yourself.'

Ivor sighed. 'I don't know what's wrong with you these days, Shirl. All you do is bloody moan.'

'You aren't exactly a barrel of laughs, either.'

'I'm not as bad as you.'

'No? You should listen to yourself sometimes.'

Ivor, sitting at a table strewn with account books and documents, made a convulsive movement of the shoulders, as if shrugging off a burden. Silently he resumed his calculations.

Shirley glanced at him, her features softening.

'Fancy a cuppa?'

'Aye, orright.'

She went to make it. He put down his ballpoint, rubbed

his face briskly with both hands. When she returned, he was sitting on the sofa.

'Time you took a break. You'll be wearing yourself out with all that.'

'Got to be done, girl.'

'You should get somebody else to do all that paperwork.'

'Who, for instance?'

'Get a clerk in.'

'No thank you. I'd rather do it myself.'

'Headstrong, that's what you are.' She sat by him.

'Headstrong, is it?' The word pleased him. 'Aye, suppose I am in a way. That's why I married you.'

'Not sorry then, are you?'

'About what?'

'Not marrying Annette.'

'Annette! Why bring her up?'

'You could have married her, if you wanted.'

'No, thank you. Not after that reporter got his hands on her.'

'I saw him the other day.'

'You did? You didn't tell me.'

'I'm telling you now, aren't I?'

'Where was he?'

'On the prom. Walked right past me he did, nose in the air.'

'Maybe he didn't see you.'

'He saw me all right. Just didn't want to know.'

Ivor sipped his tea reflectively. 'Funny time that, wasn't it?'

'How?'

'Well... everything. Got Annette in the family way, and then dumped her.'

'*She* dumped *him*, Ivor.'

'Did she? Can't remember now.'

'He was a little shit,' said Shirley vehemently.

'Hey, steady on.'

'Well he was. He was having it away with that tart from Back Row, wasn't he?'

'Oh aye. I remember that all right. Got beaten up for it too, if I remember right.'

'Serve him right.'

Ivor smiled. 'Don't like him, do you?'

'I bloody hate him.'

'*Hate* him. That's pretty strong.'

'It's how I feel.'

Ivor glanced at her wonderingly, but said nothing.

A single image had come to dominate Nigel Allan's thoughts. It was that of a slim, gangly young woman sitting on a crate with her legs splayed out. The mental snapshot would pop up unbidden at the most inconvenient times – when he was listening to a client, or trying to make sense of an official document. It would even intrude into intimate moments with his wife, a fact that slightly shocked him. He was, after all, fighting the feeling he had for Jenny Briggs, a feeling he now had to acknowledge. If he wasn't honest with himself, how could he be honest with others?

The image disturbed him because of the suggestiveness of her posture. It was impossible for her not to have known the effect it would have over him. The more he thought of it, the more deliberately provocative it seemed. Was she offering herself to him? When he allowed himself to dwell on the possibility, he felt both excitement and trepidation. This was a challenge he could do without. He was a married man:

a *happily* married man, he emphasised in the dialogue with himself he was forever conducting these days. Annette was a beautiful woman with whom he had no quarrel. He had two lovely children. His home life was comfortable. Moreover, he was a successful solicitor with a reputation to maintain. How could he possibly contemplate an *affair?* The word itself was so foreign to his nature that he saw it in italics, and even with a final 'e', *affaire* being so thoroughly French and risqué as to place the whole business quite outside the pale. Metaphorically he straightened his shoulders and squared up to temptation. He was Nigel Allan, product of a chapel upbringing in Carmarthenshire. How could he possibly be lured into a sexual liaison with a young unmarried woman? *Get thee behind me, Satan,* he thought grimly.

All the same, the image continued to taunt him. It came to him while dressing, while eating, while playing with the kids. Miserably, he had to confess to himself that he was fighting a battle of critical importance. And it was one he had to fight entirely alone. This was the worst thing of all: that Annette was excluded from the struggle. Its very nature meant he could not call on her support. The only answer, he felt, was to immerse himself in his work. And it was work he enjoyed. The sheer *orderliness* of the law answered a deep need in him. Like the family farm on which he had grown up, it was based on eternal verities: not the verities of nature, but those of justice. And justice, founded as it was on truth and fairness, supported by the accumulated wisdom of precedent, itself resembled a force of nature. He delighted in the very language of the law, the circumlocutions and archaisms that reflected the huge length of time in which present laws and customs had been in the making. He absolutely resisted the trend towards simplification of legal language, which he thought both dangerous and unnecessary. What if the apparatus of the law did seem remote from everyday matters? So it should be. Its very remoteness was a guarantee of its purity and efficacy. So he continued to use the Latinisms 'inst' and 'ult' in the letters he dictated to Glenys and Delyth, which they dutifully typed out and despatched to solicitors and barristers and court officers and the firm's clients. Their very formality and stuffiness offered protection, not only against any erosion of professional standards, but against the temptation implicit in his feelings for Jenny Briggs.

For relaxation away from the pressures of professional and filial duty, he went occasionally to the Constitutional Club, where he enjoyed a quiet drink and, occasionally, a game of snooker. The club was rarely crowded, priding itself on being a select institution with a highly restricted membership. Although it had no political affiliation, its members leaned towards a kind of latter-day Gladstonian Liberalism, a position taken by the county's MP, Cyril Davies, whose opponents were apt to say was so used to sitting on the fence that he had a permanent crease in his backside.

'Evening, Nigel.' Standing at the bar with a Scotch and water was Hubert Hughes, of Hughes and Peregrine, Estate Agents, a man of florid complexion and military manner. He liked to be called 'Colonel', a rank acquired in the Home Guard, but few were still willing to accord him this dubious dignity.

Nigel ordered a pint of Roberts' Special Mild and engaged in small talk with Hubert, who seemed even more disgruntled than usual.

'Seems they're having him cremated then,' said Hubert at last, apropos of nothing.

'Who?'

'Lucas.'

'Oh, are they?'

'Shrewsbury, next Thursday. Lovell's released the body. Opened the inquest yesterday. Just a formality. No doubt about cause of death. Blighter topped himself.'

'So it appears.'

Hubert gave vent to a throaty dismissal, a cross between a grunt and a cough.

'Never thought he had much fibre. Pandering to the Nats over that barmy scheme to keep out the English. Ridiculous.'

'It's a wonder they gave him the job of Principal, when you think of it.'

'Not a wonder at all. Typical of the way things are going. They'll be having bilingual lectures next. Instant translation.'

'There's still a long way to go before that, I imagine,' said Nigel, smiling.

'Don't be so sure. We had someone in the other day asking us to put all our literature in Welsh as well as English, if you please.'

'Did you now? Who was that then?'

'Girl called Jenny Briggs. Runs a Welsh nursery school with her pal.' He speared Nigel with a penetrative stare. 'Do some work for them, don't you?'

'A little, yes. Nothing much,' said Nigel, self-deprecatingly.

'Right little madam, she is. I gave her a piece of her mind, I can tell you.'

'I'm sure you did, Colonel.' Nigel could have kicked himself. Why was he sucking up to this idiot?

'It's going to get worse, you know. These youngsters are hot-heads.'

'Oh, I don't know. I expect they'll see sense one day.'

'Sense! They haven't got an ounce of sense. They'll be the ruin of us, mark my words.'

Nigel moved away as soon as he decently could. He mustn't start imagining things. There was no reason why Hubert should suspect him of lusting after Jenny. All the same he felt uncomfortable, realising this was a hint of how he would be feeling if his association with her developed. He couldn't afford that kind of thing. It would make him a laughing-stock. And what might it do to his marriage? Guiltily, he decided to go home straight after finishing his pint. He wasn't in the mood for drinking.

The club's copy of the *County Dispatch* was on the bench beside him. Desultorily he scanned the pages, glancing up when someone sat at the next table. 'Hullo, Arthur,' he said.

'Good evening, Mr Allan.'

Inwardly, Nigel sighed. Why did the man insist on calling him 'Mister'?

'Keeping well?'

'Quite well, thank you.'

Nigel took a deeper swig of his pint. He had nothing against Arthur Thomas, but did not relish his company. He had a defeated air and there was something odd about him. Yet it had not always been so. He had once been PC Thomas, a young constable with a forthright manner and commanding presence. Now, retired from the police force, he had a menial job at the Prince of Wales Hotel on the seafront. The gossips ascribed his decline to his wife's flighty ways, but Nigel wasn't so sure. He had seen enough of the world to know that many factors can bear on a man's self-esteem.

'Bad business about the Principal,' murmured Arthur. 'It's his wife I feel sorry for. She's done nothing to deserve this.'

'No, I don't suppose she has.'

'Thoroughly decent woman, Mrs Lucas.'

The man's lugubrious voice irritated Nigel. He could do without this.

'Of course, the Press made a meal of it.'

'Quite.'

'He was staying with us, you know.'

'Who was?'

'That reporter fellow. He booked into the Prince.'

'Did he now.' Nigel feigned indifference.

'I met him before, you know. Years ago. When he was on the local rag.'

'Really.'

'Didn't like him much. Too big for his boots. Hasn't improved either, far as I can see.'

Nigel put the paper down.

'Didn't see him, did you? When he was down here?'

'Good heavens, no. Why on earth should I?'

'Just wondered, Mr Allan. Just wondered, that's all. You know what these people are like. Real scavengers, they are. Poking their noses in everywhere. Digging. Yes, digging...' His voice drifted into silence.

Nigel gave him a hard look. Unhurriedly, he finished his pint and left.

Arthur Thomas cleared his throat. He glanced up at Hubert. Arthur's right eye flickered in the suspicion of a wink. Hubert's mouth twitched in what could have passed for a smile.

14

THE SUMMONS TO Gus Chapple's office at 4.30 meant that Steve was off to work before Jocelyn came home next day. He wasn't sorry. Last night's words still hung in the air, small invisible clouds of dissension. Reluctantly, he had to admit the force of her argument. He *was* getting too long in the tooth for reporting. There *were* new people coming along. He *would* have to think about his future. And, he thought gloomily, that was exactly why he had been summoned to the Chief's office.

He felt like company, reassurance, the lift and confidence a couple of pints could give you. But he didn't want to see his old mates from the *Comet* newsroom, especially if there were rumours about him going around. He preferred to find out his fate from the Chief himself, without any preliminaries.

He rang Ray Bounty, an old buddy from his days at the *Star*, the first paper he'd worked for after coming up to Fleet Street from Wales. Now writing a lively diary for a posh Sunday, he could be relied on for some juicy gossip.

'Saw your piece on Jill Manders,' drawled Ray. 'Did you stuff her, while you were about it?'

'No. Didn't have time.'

'You're slipping. Spent too much time subbing, by the look of it. Takes all the guts out of you.'

'You're not kidding. Feel like a lunchtime pint somewhere?'

'Might manage a quick one. Usual place?'

Ray was large, solemn, and dismissive of a pinstriped clientele braying over pints of Watneys Red Barrel and

Double Diamond. 'Jesus. The types you get here these days. I think I'll go back to the *Biggleswade Courier*.'

'That's where I may be before long, mate.'

'Why so?'

'Gus wants to see me.'

'Oh-ho. Been shagging his missus, eh? Naughty boy.'

'Not likely. Wouldn't touch her with a barge pole.'

'Getting fussy, are we? Shit. Look at that.'

A miniskirted blonde was straddling a bar stool, showing as much as she dared within very broad limits.

'If they make 'em any shorter, they'll be showing their belly buttons.'

'Not complaining, are you?'

'Yes. Strongly. Means I'm on permanent heat.'

'I'll put some bromide in your soup.'

'Bromide? That wouldn't stop me. Got it upfront too, hasn't she? Most unTwiggy-like.' Ray took a long, cooling draught of London Pride. 'Anyway, what're you bothered about? If gorgeous Gussie doesn't want you, you can always go somewhere else.'

'Oh aye. Just like that.'

'Why not? Not getting cold feet in your old age, are you?'

Steve grimaced. 'That's just it. Old age.'

Ray smiled. 'Hit the nail, did I?'

'Don't laugh. It's not funny.'

'Hey, not serious, are you? Think yourself past it?'

'According to Jos I am.'

'No kidding!'

'Too bloody true. She wants me to settle for a nice little number in PR. Think of anything?'

'Bloody hell. You in PR?'

'Or maybe the *Biggleswade Clarion*, or whatever you call it.'

'This is serious. What's brought this on then?'

'I've seen it coming a long time. She can't stand the Street. Thinks it's beneath me. Beneath her, more like.'

'Jesus, mate.'

Steve flushed, feeling suddenly guilty at slagging his wife off.

'She's worried about my health. That's part of it.'

'Mm... You're all right though, aren't you?' Ray asked anxiously. 'I know you've had some problems, but...'

'Yes, I'm fine. Christ, Ray, I'm only thirty-seven. I'm not ready for pipe and slippers yet.'

'I should think not, squire.'

They sank into gloomy silence.

'That piece was all right, wasn't it?' Steve burst out.

'On Jill Manders? Yes. Fine. Nothing wrong with it, son.'

Somehow he sounded too enthusiastic to be convincing.

Jocelyn was having a bad day at school. She hated quarrelling with Steve, and had hoped they might make it up before she left for work. But the fact that he'd slept late, or apparently so – she was sure he'd been shamming – and his refusal to say any more than a few words when he did stir himself, meant that she'd been burdened all day by last night's bickering. His mood wasn't helped by the fact that the kids had chosen this day of all days to play her up something rotten. They were good kids as a rule with only two or three real nuisances, but today even some of the better-behaved little monsters had joined in the mischief. Chief nuisance was Sophie Ledbury, a ginger-haired pest who could be a right little madam. She'd picked a classroom quarrel with Caroline French that had all but ended with them scratching each other's eyes out. She'd dearly wished to wallop both of them, as she herself had been walloped in junior school by Miss Bridges, a towering representative of the no-nonsense brigade, but free-and-easy walloping had gone out of fashion, and in her cooler moments Jocelyn thoroughly approved of this. Sorting out Sophie and Caroline, however, as well as umpteen other difficulties, had left her drained and irritable, a condition not at all conducive to calming her anxieties over the future. But when at last she had time to think, she felt glad that she'd raised matters that had been bothering her for ages. She *was* worried about Steve's state of health, and had dreaded his going back on the reporting treadmill that she was sure had led to the recurrence of the heart problems of his childhood. She was worried too about Simon, whose asthma was not helped in the least by their living in London. But most of all she was concerned about the middle to long term prospects for herself and Steve. It was obvious that he couldn't go on being a Fleet Street reporter for ever – nobody ever did – and his refusal to look this fact in the face was a constant worry. Sooner or later he'd be pushed into some desk job he'd despise – deputy this or assistant that – or dumped altogether. In less than three years he'd be forty. Too late then to plan his future, for it would be decided for him.

'Hughie brought a Spitfire to school today,' Simon said in the car, going home.

'A what?'

'A Spitfire. You know. The Battle of Britain – *duh-duh-duh!*' Through the windscreen, he machine-gunned an imaginary enemy.

'What are you doing? Stop it!'

'I'm only playing, Mum.'

'Well, don't. You know I can't stand war games.'

'Grandad was in the war though, wasn't he?'

'Yes, and he was badly injured, too, so I don't want you going the same way, thank you very much.'

'Did his mum stop him playing war games, Mum?'

'I don't know – how should I know? I wasn't born then.'

'I just wondered, that's all.'

Jocelyn gave him a sideways glance, uneasily. There'd been something new in his voice lately – an assertiveness that hadn't been there before. He was growing up. Come October, he'd be ten.

'Mum,' he said, more pliantly, 'can I make models, like Hughie?'

'It depends,' replied Jocelyn, after a moment.

'I'd like to make model planes – like he does.'

'Not Spitfires, I hope.'

'Why not, Mum?'

She gripped the wheel more tightly. 'You know why – I told you.'

'But if they're only *models*,' he said more slowly, 'they don't matter, do they? I mean – they're not killing anyone.'

'They're still war machines. Models of war machines.'

'But...'

'You can make models of something else – airliners or something.'

Simon muttered.

'What was that?' she asked sharply.

'Nothing.'

What she had heard, barely distinct enough to be heard, were the words, '*Not so much fun.*'

Marjorie Smith's office door was always open, and so was the door to the inner sanctum beyond it. Gus Chapple, editor of the *Daily Comet*, knew better than to allow himself to be closeted, alone and unobserved, with sexy women, scheming politicians and corrupt businessmen who might afterwards accuse him of saying and doing things of which he was completely innocent. Blackmail comes in many guises. Marjorie, his secretary, provided the eyes and ears of propriety, forever alert to what was happening in the boss's stronghold. He trusted her implicitly and was right to do so, for she could be both tactful and ruthless in dealing with the endless problems that confronted the editor of a national paper. She was diplomat, confidante, friend and protector.

She was briskly typing on her electric machine when Steve looked in just before 4.30.

'He's not back yet. Take a seat.' She smiled. Marjorie got on well with all but the more self-important hacks.

Her office, ante-room to the more important one beyond, combined tidiness with informality. Her desk, scrupulously uncluttered, always had a vase of cut flowers, and the wall behind was decorated with postcards from various holiday destinations. It gave the place a summery look, as if fun and gaiety were always lurking at the edge of business. Marjorie, smart but not obsessively so, had blonde hair elegantly styled, a retroussé nose, and a chin slightly more prominent than that required by conventional notions of beauty. Her age could have been anything between thirty-five and fifty. Little about her personal life was known to anyone on the paper, except perhaps the Chief, Gus Chapple. She did not encourage speculation.

The phone rang, and she was still dealing with the call when the Chief arrived. He had a broad butcher's face, a steady pink that deepened to fiery red in moments of excitement or irritation. He had lately taken to cigars and was smoking one now as he bustled in.

'Hullo, Steve. Sorry to keep you. Come along in.' Inside his office, he waved Steve to a chair and sat on another opposite, instead of behind his desk. Steve was weirdly reminded of a time when an earlier boss had done exactly the same: Gwyn Meredith, editor of the *County Dispatch* in Glanaber, who'd been trying to persuade him to stay on the paper instead of going up to Fleet Street. Coming so soon after his few days back in Glanaber, it gave Steve a strange sense of déjà-vu. 'Been at a CBI bash. Waste of bloody time. Should've known better. Never mind.' He made a strange motion of the shoulders, as if wriggling free of an impediment.

'How are you feeling now? Haven't been too well, I gather.'

'I'm OK thanks, Chief.'

'Did you see a quack down in Wales, when you were there?'

'No, there was no need. Just rested for a day or two.'

'I think you should see one here, soon as possible. Just to be on the safe side.' He was speaking quickly, not looking at Steve.

'I'm due for a check-up soon.'

'Good.' Chapple looked thoughtfully at his cigar, holding it vertically and then tapping away the ash. 'Funny business, that professor topping himself. Why'd he do it, do you think?'

'The woman, I suppose. Jill Manders.'

'H'm. Not what she said though, is it? Talked about his private problems. Correct me if I'm wrong.'

'Yes. She did.'

Steve felt a sense of foreboding. He knew all about the Chief's fishing technique, playing with a catch before he snapped it up. It was the first time he'd been a victim of it.

Gus Chapple looked sharply at Steve. 'Who's Brenda Coswell?'

'Brenda who?'

'Coswell. The name should be familiar to you.'

An image clicked into position in Steve's mind. Jill Manders, eyes blazing with quiet fury, saying, 'His wife is shit. She's having it away with Brenda Coswell.'

'Friend of Haydn Lucas's, wasn't she?'

'Not quite. Friend of his wife's apparently.'

'So it appears.'

'Why didn't she figure in your story, then?'

'Was she relevant?'

'She might have been, if you'd bothered to take up the lead Jill Manders gave you.'

How the hell did *he* know about it?

'It was all very vague,' Steve said. 'And it was off the main point. He had an affair with Jill and then topped himself. That was the story, surely.'

'But it's not the truth, is it?'

'The truth?'

'The truth is many-sided. But we don't have to deal with it, do we? We're in the business of stories. The quick fix. Sexy film star shags prof who then tops himself. Very neat, very exact. But not the truth. Not by a long chalk.'

Pensively he puffed smoke towards the ceiling.

'Oh, you did all right, Steve. But I happen to know Jill Manders. She rang me and told me what she'd told you. Said I should kick your arse. I told her to get stuffed.' He smiled. 'If you'd missed your deadline by chasing some mythical

lesbian affair I'd have had your guts for garters, no worries.'
He stubbed out the cigar. 'You don't have to do the subbing
shift tonight, by the way. You're off subbing entirely.'

'Oh?'

'Don't look so surprised. You're wasted on the subs' desk.
You must know that yourself. Subs are ten a penny, good
writers are like gold.'

Steve was reminded of the old newspaper adage: *Facts are
sacred, comment is free.*

The Chief, back at his desk, fiddled with a bilious green
paperweight shaped like a frog. He tapped his desk with it
thoughtfully.

'How was it back in Wales then – OK?'

'Yes – fine.'

'Fancy going there again?'

'Another story?' Steve asked, surprised.

'More than that.' He gave Steve one of his direct, man-
to-man looks. 'We're starting something big, Steve. A colour
mag. Part of the paper – like these Sunday supplements, only
they're full of arty-farty shit. This'll be down-to-earth. Off-
beat stories. Something to get your teeth into. I want you to
cover Wales for us. Interested?'

'Christ.'

The Chief grinned. 'Gob-smacked, are you? Thought you
would be. They all will. Can't wait to see their faces.' He
looked exultant.

15

I T WAS JUST after two o'clock and that time of the month. Annette's periods weren't as heavy as they'd been when she was younger but they still troubled her, giving her a gritty, messy feeling. She took a couple of Anadin for her headache and wondered what to do with herself. She'd be meeting Rob from school in an hour and had thought of sorting out some old clothes to take to one of the charity shops that were springing up, but wasn't in the mood. Ever since the encounter with Steve, she had felt unsettled and at odds with herself. It had been so weird seeing him again, especially as he hadn't changed all that much. But what had she expected? He had looked older, naturally, and had filled out a bit, but so had she. It was in the nature of things. What was so weird was the fact that they hadn't seemed like strangers to each other. It was as if they'd been apart for only a few weeks, not fifteen years. And he still aroused the same mix of sensations in her, attraction balanced by irritation and resentment. That phone call he'd made to her at home, what a bloody cheek! And the way he'd got round her, persuading her to go to the cemetery with him. Why had she done it?

But she knew exactly why. Because she still felt guilty at keeping him away from Ceri's funeral.

But how thoughtless of him – to bring it all back like this! As if she hadn't relived her baby's death, time and again through the years. The horror of it – waking up to see her lying lifeless in her cot. She'd clutched her tight, willing the warmth of her own body to penetrate the child's. Ah, the hopelessness of it! The self-recrimination, the refusal to accept that it was *not her fault,* as everyone kept telling her. The nights of wakefulness, of going over everything that had happened. The way she had put her down to sleep the night before – that especially. 'You did nothing wrong, Annette,' her doctor had assured her. 'You're not to blame in the least – remember that. We had a post-mortem – death was due to natural causes. It was an act of nature. *It's not your fault.'* The words had tolled in her head, bereft of comfort. And in the background, unheard, the poisonous words she knew some would be saying. '*Serves her right. It's a judgement on her.'* She saw it in their eyes, even if she didn't hear it from their lips. *God's judgement on an unmarried mother.* In the small west Wales town of Glanaber, the Victorian age had lingered long. And in some respects, it was lingering still.

An hour to kill before meeting Rob. She decided to go and see her mother.

Lorna Morris was putting up new curtains in the living-room. 'Just in time to help me, girl. Come along, make yourself useful.' A peremptory manner came easily to her. It helped to snap Annette out of her dejection. 'Got these at the sale in Daniel's. You should take a look yourself.' She stood precariously on a chair, in spite of Annette's protestations. 'I'm all right, girl, leave me be. I've always done it this way, you know very well. Damn! Pass me another hook, these plastic things keep breaking.'

At last the job was done, and they had time for a cuppa. 'Spring-cleaning, that's what they were always doing this time of year. Remember your Gran going at it hammer and tongs? Turned the place upside down, wore herself to a frazzle. Took years off her life, I'm sure, but there was no telling her. Catch me doing all that, but there's no need now, is there? 'Course, we don't have coal fires, that's what made all the dirt. Filthy, they were. That Rayburn we had up in Pen-bryn was bad enough, got on my nerves it did. Got it made now, I keep telling your father when he grumbles. Yes, he'll be home soon, getting under my feet as usual. Probably stop him altogether soon, they're getting rid of a lot of part-timers. How's Nigel anyway? Pity we don't see more of him, anyone'd think we got the plague.'

It embarrassed Annette, the increasing distance between her husband and her parents. They had seemed to get on so well at first, but now she wondered if he had always looked down on them. She had never put it to him in these terms, and she knew that if she did he would vigorously deny it, but how else could one explain the fact that he avoided them whenever possible? When she visited them in their little council flat, either alone or with the children, he usually made some excuse for not going along as well. He was too busy, or too tired, or found some other reason. Yet there'd been a time when he'd appeared to enjoy having Sunday tea with his in-laws, with fish paste sandwiches and home-made cakes and, as a special treat, trifle with hundreds and thousands on top and a tin of 'evap'. He had talked about what was going on in the world with her Dad, who although no great shakes on current affairs had held his own with his son-in-law. Their politics differed – Dad was Labour and Nigel Liberal, and at election times that had led to some pretty rousing arguments. Now, looking back, Annette felt that Nigel had simply been patronising her father. And there'd been a great deal left unsaid, for Annette knew that, at heart, Ted Morris felt himself to be socially as well as intellectually inferior to Nigel. Not a mention was made of Ted's criminal record: he'd done time in Swansea prison for stealing mail as a postman. But the past, though never spoken about, could not be ignored, and

Annette knew how it had confirmed her father's low opinion of himself, making it impossible for him to see himself as her husband's equal.

'He's all right,' she said, answering her mother's question. 'Working too hard though, as usual. It'll be a bit easier when Stella gets back to work. That shouldn't be long now.'

'H'm! And who's going to look after her baby for her?'

'I don't know, Mam. I suppose she's worked that out.'

'Don't hold with these working mothers. Their place is at home with their babies. What's the good of having children if you don't look after them yourself?'

Annette let this pass. 'Dad working today? I thought he had Mondays off.'

'They're short-staffed so asked him in. Don't know why he bothered. They'll be getting rid of him soon, by the look of things. That's all the thanks you get.'

'It's awful, that. What'll he do, do you think?'

'Have to look for something else, won't he? Can't live on air. He's only fifty-eight – too young for the pension.'

Annette felt uncomfortable, as she always did when she thought about her parents' finances. Her father's part-time work as a messenger at Glanaber University brought in only a pittance, and they'd be seriously struggling without top-up payments from the Assistance Board. She hated them going along cap-in-hand like that – they were entitled to the money, but it was somehow demeaning. 'We'll help out, Mam, you know that,' she'd offered – even pleaded – more than once, only to be met with a snapped 'Don't be daft, girl, what do you take me for?'

Reading her daughter's thoughts, Lorna said: 'Don't worry – we'll manage. I can always do some cleaning again, if push comes to shove.'

'No, Mam – you mustn't!'

'Not too proud, 'Nette – you know me.'

'I know that, but…' Annette shook her head violently.

Lorna gave her an ironical look. 'Anyway, they've got enough on their minds at the college, what with all that scandal in the papers. Don't know what gets into their heads, messing around like that.'

'I couldn't be bothered to read it,' lied Annette.

'Didn't you? It was all over the *Comet*.'

'So it seems.'

'Had his name in big letters – Steve Lewis. Right across the page.'

Lorna met Annette's silence with a sidelong glance.

'Didn't see him when he was down here then, did you?'

''Course not. Why should I?'

'Just wondered, that's all.' She stirred her tea, unnecessarily. 'Nice flowers you put for Ceri the other day,' she said casually. 'Where'd you get them, Hardwick's?'

Annette flushed.

'No,' she said, after a moment. 'Charlie Griffiths's.'

'Ah.'

Annette's reaction told her mother all she wanted to know. It was not she who had put the flowers there.

'Cover Wales?' repeated Jocelyn blankly.

'Yes. He thinks I'm the man to do it.'

'I'm sure he does. But do you want to?'

'Haven't got much choice, have I?'

'You mean – he's just pitching you down there without so much as a by-your-leave?'

'He *is* the boss, Jos.'

'I thought he liked you!'

'He does. He wouldn't be giving me the job otherwise, would he?'

'You mean you think he's doing you a *favour* – sending you down to Wales?'

'Why not? Christ, it's not Siberia, is it?'

'It might as well be. Oh, Steve, you can't let him do this to you.'

'What choice have I got? Anyway, I thought you wanted me to get another job.'

'Not this! You'll still be reporting, won't you?'

'No – that's the point. I'll be doing off-beat stuff. Tudor Powell will still be doing the hard news from Cardiff.'

'And you're happy with that? You've always been one for hard news, haven't you?'

'Well, maybe it's time for a change. I can't go on for ever, can I? You told me so yourself.'

Jocelyn, confused, stared at nothing. Steve pounced.

'It's something different, Jos – it really is. No one's got wind of it yet – it's so hush-hush not many even know at the *Comet*. It's a feather in my cap really – I'm in at the start of something new. They'll all be doing it one day – the *Express*, the *Mail*, the *Mirror*. It's a great idea – a magazine in with the paper, only not so precious as the Sunday colour supplements.'

'You wouldn't have said that a year ago,' Jocelyn almost whispered.

'Well,' returned Steve, thrown slightly, 'a lot's happened since then.'

His increasing ill-health... fatigue, shortness of breath... the operation to stretch the heart valve affected by his boyhood rheumatic fever... the worry of it all... his temporary transfer to the subs' desk... Jocelyn saw it all again in quick-motion.

'Where would we live then?' she asked.

Steve felt a surge of triumph, hardly able to believe victory was so easily won.

'I don't know. Where would you like to live?'

'Not up to me, is it? You're the one who's made up your mind.'

'I'll go on my own if you like,' Steve offered. 'See how things work out.'

'Oh yes,' she said sarcastically.

'What's that supposed to mean?'

'I thought we were married.'

'We are, aren't we?'

'Well then.'

He sat beside her on the settee. He considered taking her hand, decided not to.

'There's Simon to consider,' she said.

'I know... Now's the time to move, if we're going to. Before he gets to high school.'

'He'll have to learn Welsh, I suppose.'

'Depends where we live. He won't have to, everywhere.' He was guessing; he simply didn't know.

'He won't like it a bit, moving to Wales.'

'I know that, but...'

'He'll hate it. Really hate it. Leaving his friends.'

Obvious phrases sprang to mind – *Is that the criterion? It happens every day. We can't stay just for him. It'll do him good – broaden his horizons. He'll have to like it or lump it.*

They all stayed unspoken.

Jocelyn sighed. 'If you want this job, we'll go. I don't get much choice, do I?'

'Yes you do.'

'No I don't. You know I don't. It's your work and that's it.'

'You make me sound like a monster.'

'He's the monster. Gus Chapple.'

He's not really, Steve wanted to say.

A shout came from upstairs. They looked at each other, startled.

'Another nightmare,' said Jocelyn. 'He's had a lot of them lately. I'll take a look, see he's all right.'

Nigel was the attentive husband and father that evening, helping Joanne with her maths homework and playing Subbuteo with Robert. Nigel was a dab hand at flipping the small table-top footballers, but he let Robert win a couple of games before Annette called time and sent the boy up to bed. She tried to forget her irritation with her mother and was in a mood to count her blessings.

They watched telly together, foregoing fighting the flab by enjoying the Black Magic chocolates they'd been given by friends they'd invited around.

'I'm thinking of going to that meeting in the Castle Hall tomorrow,' he said at bedtime. 'Care to come?'

'What meeting's that?'

'The Welsh Language Campaign. Out for equal status for Welsh and all that.'

'No use me going there, is there? I wouldn't understand a word they're saying.'

'Mind if I go on my own then?'

Propped up by pillows, Annette looked up from the book she was reading. 'Why should I? Don't get involved in any riots though.'

'Not likely to, am I? I've got a reputation to keep up.'

He slipped into bed beside her. Something in his tone of voice, a studied carelessness that reminded her of the amateur theatricals she had always hated, made her suspicious.

'Are you sure it's not too political for you? I mean, you've always avoided that sort of thing, haven't you? Bad for business and all that.'

'No, it's not political at all. It's the language pure and simple. I've never avoided that, have I?'

Annette made no comment. Nigel felt uneasy. He should have done more for the language – and the children – by sending them to the Welsh medium junior school, but Annette had opposed this. He feared the little Welsh they'd picked up from him at home would in time be buried too deep to be any use to them. They would be monoglot English unless – irony of ironies – they became bilingual in another way in secondary school: bilingual English and French, perhaps, or English and German. He imagined Jenny Briggs's scorn, if they became close enough for her to deride him like this. Her large grey eyes looked at him gravely out of nowhere, and in a vain attempt to escape them he slid down between the sheets.

Simon was lying on his back, his arms thrown up in an attitude of surrender. He was breathing through his mouth, something he shouldn't do, but at least he was asleep. He looked small, frail, vulnerable.

'You poor little devil,' murmured Jocelyn. 'What's to become of you?'

She glanced around the room. Already it looked posthumous. It was as if she were already in an unknown future, looking back to past delights that would be forever out of reach. Everything was precious: the photos of Simon's idol Jimmy Greaves stuck on the bedroom wall with Blu-Tac, the stories of Narnia on the white-painted bookshelf, the singles stacked beside his record player, the very counterpane... all had become as much part of the buried past as the beads and statuettes forlornly keeping company with the remains of Tutankhamun. She stepped softly to the window and peered through the curtains. The street lamps bathed Gladstone Road in their ghostly orange light. Then, peculiarly, a scene as spectral as the artificial light presented itself to her imagination. She saw, as if painted on a veil, two headlands hemming in a huddled town with a stretch of sea between. With a gasp, she let the curtain fall back and went downstairs.

Steve was still sitting where she had left him.

'Is he OK?' he asked.

'Yes. Fast asleep.'

'Good.' He smiled.

It was as if a great time had elapsed since she had last seen him. She could not believe he looked no older.

'Sorry to spring all this on you,' he said.

'It was sprung on you, wasn't it?'

'It was a bit.'

'I don't know how he can do this to you.'

He shrugged. 'It's the way of the world.'

'It's no way to treat you. Perfectly heartless.'

'Come on, Jos,' he said consolingly. 'It's not as bad as all that. He thinks he's doing me a favour – getting me back to the old country.'

'Yes. The one you left umpteen years ago,' she said bitterly.

He gave her a curious look. 'I was ambitious. I wanted to see the world. I haven't done so badly, have I?'

'Who said you had?'

He had a sudden urge to confess: *I saw my first love in*

Glanaber. Her name's Annette – we made a baby together. We were going to get married but she broke it off. She had the kid but it died. She wrote to tell me but stopped me going to the funeral. What do you think of that, Jos? I know I should have told you but I didn't. And now, you know what? I still care for her – Annette. I saw her the other day. We went to the cemetery together. She showed me the kid's grave – my kid's. I put some flowers there.

The moment passed.

'So,' she said. 'Where do you think we'll be living then – Cardiff?'

'God, no. I don't want to go there. That's not the real Wales.'

'No? Where's the real Wales then, Steve?'

He shrugged. 'Somewhere central, I suppose. I need to get around, north and south.'

She saw the two headlands again. The huddled town, with the sea between.

'Don't tell me,' she said. 'Glanaber.'

'What makes you say that?'

'It's obvious. I can read you like a book.'

'You don't like the place though, do you?'

'You know I don't. But you've made your mind up, haven't you?'

'Well… there's a lot to be said for it. It's a university town. There's plenty going on there. The schools should be good.'

'Well then. End of story.'

The finality of the phrase chilled him.

16

'BLOODY WELSH SPEAKERS! Who do they think they are?'

Ivor Morgan scowled down at the paper he was reading.

'Why? What've they done now?' his wife asked indifferently.

'They're having a protest meeting in the Castle Hall. I'd shoot the bloody lot of them.'

Shirley gave him an odd look. 'You speak Welsh yourself, don't you?'

'Yes, but not like they do. They do it just for show.'

Sitting on a stool in the shop, he rustled the paper angrily. 'Look what they're after – equal status for Welsh. You know what that means, don't you? Rate demands in Welsh. Summonses to the court. Every blessed form in Welsh. Think what that'll cost, mun! The rates are sky-high as it is. They'll go through the roof!'

Shirley shrugged. 'Don't suppose anyone will take notice of them.'

'Won't they! Won't they just! Look who's behind them. All that college crowd for a start. And the BBC in Cardiff. They're full of Welsh nationalists – always have been.'

'Somebody's been at the emulsion,' frowned Shirley. 'I'm sure there was more than this here yesterday. Who's been in here, remember?'

'How do I know? I don't remember everyone who comes in the shop.'

'Oh, that's all it means to you, does it? You don't care if the paint gets nicked.'

'Of course I care!' He flung the paper down on the counter. 'Let's have a look.'

He went to the neatly-stacked rows of paint in the far corner.

'Here – look,' said Shirley. 'I'm sure this was full to the end. I can't remember anyone buying paint yesterday, can you?'

'I never sold any, whatever. You may be right. Bugger it.'

'We should have a better system. Make it more secure.'

'How do you do that? Nail the bloody things to the wall?'

'Don't shout at me, Ivor. I'm only trying to help.'

'I know you are. But it makes me mad! All this thieving in town. It's getting worse. Will Donogue's boy was in court the other day for nicking tools from Jim Stanley – did you see that? A respectable family, too. I blame the schools myself.'

'What have the schools got to do with it?'

'They're too soft. When I was in board school you got a good thrashing just for looking at a teacher.'

'Oh, that was all right, was it?'

'It taught you what's what. Kids do what they like these days.'

'If someone had thrashed Conrad you'd have been down the school like a shot.'

'That's different.'

'Oh, is it. Different because he's your boy, I suppose.'

'If he'd done something wrong I'd have hit him myself.'

'Not with me around, you wouldn't.'

Ivor shifted uncomfortably. 'Any idea who might've took it? How'd he manage it anyway? You can't put two pint pots in your pocket.'

'Might have been a woman. With a shopping bag.'

'Could have been, aye. Who was in here then?'

'Mrs Rees the Manse.'

'What? She wouldn't do it.'

'Why not? They're always moaning about money, aren't they?'

'Don't be silly, girl.'

'Well – might have been one of your Welsh speakers then.'

The Castle Hall stood on the crest of a mound within sight and sound of the sea. Slightly shabby but still respectable, it resembled one of the seaside landladies who had clearly seen better days but still had pride in herself. It provided a platform for modest theatrical productions, poetry readings and public meetings such as that called by the Welsh Language Campaign.

It was an unseasonably chilly evening, a brisk north-easterly wind harassing the sea into a fretful worrying of the foreshore. Nigel Allan stood, hands in pockets, gloomily staring out at the bay from his house high in Constitution Road. He felt torn in two. One part of him longed to go to the meeting, another part desperately tried to hold him back. What made the decision so difficult was that his emotions were so deeply involved. He was in love with Jenny Briggs, and his whole idea of himself was threatened.

The defining moment had been a casual meeting the day before. She had just posted a letter and, turning, had seen him walking down Darkgate Street towards her. Her whole body had stilled, as if she had suddenly been deprived of movement. The look she gave him, grave, intense, almost took his power of speech away.

'Ill met by moonlight,' he managed, stupidly.

'What?'

'Shakespeare. Only it's not moonlight, is it? And you're not Titania.'

'No, I'm not.' But instead of being annoyed, as he thought she had every right to be, she had smiled, and the curve of her lips was so perfect that he seemed to be seeing it for the first time.

Standing there, they let people pass them on either side like the flowing waters of a river.

'Busy day?' she said.

'Busy enough. But I've finished now. What about you?'

'Oh, the usual. I'd like to talk to you again soon. About our plans. We want to press on with them.'

'Naturally. Well, any time.' They were conversing in Welsh again now, as usual.

'Are you coming to the meeting tomorrow night?'

'Of course,' he replied, though he hadn't been absolutely sure until then.

'Well, we can talk about it afterwards then. Come back for a coffee with me, will you?'

'If you like.'

'Do *you* like, that's the point.'

'Yes, I do. Very much.'

Now, staring at – but not seeing – the vast panorama of the troubled bay visible through his big front window, Nigel almost wished that this moment had never been, for it put him at the edge of a precipice. If he went to the meeting, he would be sure to go home with Jenny Briggs. If he went home with Jenny Briggs, God knows what might happen. Again he had that inward vision of her squatting on an upturned wooden crate, knees modestly touching but her legs splayed out, and he knew that come what may, he could not stay in that evening.

'Haven't you gone yet?' Annette asked cheerfully. 'You'll be late if you're not careful.'

'Doesn't matter if I am. These things never start on time anyway.' He kissed her, then the children, the Judas kiss of all betrayers.

'I won't be coming straight home. I'll probably nip into the club for a pint.'

'You'll need it then. Are you going to speak at this thingy then?'

'Not likely. I'll be keeping a low profile.'

'Watching brief, is it? May mean some business for you!'

There was a moment when, stepping outside, he might still not have gone. The breeze was exhilarating, its freshness and freedom the very essence of spring. Even as he breathed deep of it he knew that if he did what he had never done before, there was nothing in nature astringent enough to purge him of the guilt that would follow. He hesitated, then plunged on.

'Friends! We are met here for a reason. A very important reason. The best reason of all. To express ourselves as Welsh men and women. To fight for the language we love. The language that is threatened as it has never been threatened before. And with it our whole way of life – our culture – I might almost say – yes, I *will* say – our very reason for living!'

The speaker, tall, thin, fortyish, had flaxen hair neatly parted to the left, with boyish waves that made him look younger than his years. His smart lightweight suit contrasted with the deliberate drabness of the denimed students in the audience.

This was Trefor Martin-Rees, librarian and aesthete, a man dedicated to advancing Welsh culture. With quiet passion, he argued the case in endless committee meetings for more reading matter of every kind in Welsh – romances, Westerns, do-it-yourself manuals, magazines, comics – argued it usually in the face of indifference or mockery. His most radical idea of all – a television channel broadcasting entirely in Welsh – was regarded as so fantastic that his sanity was called into question. Still he persisted, a quiet visionary whose day had not yet come.

'Equal status,' he declared now, from the platform. 'That is our demand. The right to use Welsh in every facet of our everyday lives. Why should rate demands and council minutes be in English only, here in Glanaber, where Welsh is the first language of a large part of the population? Is that fair? Is that right? Is that just?'

'No!' came the expected cry from the floor. He beamed.

'Then there are tax demands – why don't they make them bilingual? And TV licences? And summonses to the courts – why should they all be in English?'

'Why should they be in any bloody language?' called out a voice from the back of the hall.

Martin-Rees swayed back, like a boxer caught by a sucker punch. He stared helplessly down, trying to locate the source of this outrage.

'Who wants summonses, for God's sake – and tax demands? What's it matter what bloody language they're in?'

Stunned silence gave way to an angry murmur as bodies swivelled around to face the heckler. Gerwyn Hopkins, the man who had buttonholed Steve in the Pelican Café, stood his ground defiantly.

'The trouble with you lot is, half of you are students. You

don't pay the bloody rates, so you don't care what they are. Have you ever thought what it would cost to have all this stuff printed in two languages? It's crazy!'

'*Not half so crazy as you!*'

'*Siddown!*'

'*Chuck him out!*'

Hopkins, face deathly pale below his jet-black hair, made a sweeping gesture of denunciation.

'I'd have you locked up, the lot of you. I'd...'

Hands clawed out, trying to pull him down. He thrust them away angrily. People were on their feet shouting. On the platform, Martin-Rees's microphone was seized by the chairman of the meeting, Jac ap Glyn, broadcaster and don.

'*Gyfeillion* – friends – please, let's have some order. Let Mr Hopkins have his say. He's never short of words – he's always writing letters to the press. Now, sir, make your point so that we can continue our meeting!'

'I've had my say – I'm going!' Hopkins stormed out, to a following wind of ironic cheers. Jac ap Glyn sat back with a satisfied look, his reputation as sage and wit confirmed. Nigel Allan, embarrassed by his proximity to Hopkins, tried to look as if he wasn't there. It was then that his eye caught that of Jenny Briggs, who had risen to her feet several rows in front of him. He had not seen her till then; had half convinced himself that she had stayed away after all. He had at once been both relieved and disappointed. If she was absent, he could go home to Annette with a clear conscience, relieved of that awesome temptation... a coffee with Jenny, alone in her flat, a coffee that might be a prelude... to what? She smiled across the hall at him, jauntily waved a hand before sitting down as a flustered Trefor Martin-Rees resumed his speech, not quite where he had left off. And suddenly Nigel ached for her, an ache that possessed his entire body and soul. Deaf to the words of Martin-Rees, blind to the people about him, he twisted his hands together as he imagined the incomparable delights of her body. Those splayed-out legs rising to the bush in her crotch, that flat stomach with the navel he would stroke oh so delicately, those full-nippled breasts he would kiss and kiss again... mouth dry, heart pumping, he almost swooned in his imagined ecstasy. There was no wish now to be relieved of this Eden, only a longing for it to come about. How many more words must he hear, how long would this meeting last? Trefor Martin-Rees sat down, another speaker took his place, and Nigel listened as best he could – applauding in the right places, while hearing nothing.

'Great meeting!' exclaimed the man next to him afterwards. 'Just what the doctor ordered. That'll set the cat among the pigeons.' Nigel, getting to his feet, looked across towards Jenny, but could not see her. Surely she couldn't have gone out already? People tried to push past him – '*Esgusodwch fi* – Excuse me.' He couldn't stand there for ever. He began moving along the row himself. On no account must he miss her.

The wind had strengthened, whisking scraps of paper along the road, flattening trouser legs against shins. The west tower of the castle was a black hulk against ragged clouds that held the last light of this fretful day. The white manes of sea horses skimmed the leaden sea. Nigel stood on the far pavement, nervously clutching his coat collar, trying to look invisible. Acutely conscious of his status in the town, he was torn between lingering there for no apparent reason and simply going home. Suddenly he was ashamed of his feelings for Jenny. What was she to him? More importantly – what was he to her?

And suddenly she appeared, leaving the hall with a young man whom she was staring at intently. That first, split-second picture stamped itself indelibly on Nigel's memory. Her pale face, tilted, contrasted sharply with his lean, swarthy features. He was speaking animatedly, gesturing to emphasise points, the very picture of strength and purpose. Nigel stood stock-still, transfixed. They swept past, a few yards from him. He might have been invisible.

'You're home early,' said Annette. 'What was it like then?'

'Oh – very good.'

'That all?'

'How do you mean?'

'Well... did they threaten revolution or something?'

'Not quite.'

'Didn't go for a drink in the club then?'

'No. Couldn't be bothered.'

She looked at him narrowly. There was something out of kilter about him. She couldn't quite put her finger on it. It gave her an odd sense of danger, as if a dark angel had touched her with its wing.

17

'BUT I DON'T understand,' said Laura Wiltshire, frowning. 'I thought you hated Glanaber.'

She was drinking mid-morning coffee with her daughter in their favourite café in Guildford High Street. It had mock-Tudor beams in keeping with the town's cherishing of a colourful past which the civic authorities were trying hard to reconcile with plans for discreet modernisation.

'I never said I hated it,' replied Jocelyn. 'I just haven't been too keen on it, that's all.'

'You could have kidded me. You let Steve go there on his own, when his mother was still living there. You told me you felt stifled by it.'

'I can change my mind, can't I? Anyway I've got no choice. I've got to go there. It's Steve's work.'

Laura gave her a keen look. 'That's something I don't understand. It's all come about so quickly. One minute he's subediting, the next he's sent to the back of beyond. Is he being demoted, or what?'

Jocelyn flushed. 'Of course not! I told you why, Mum. They're starting a new magazine.' She lowered her voice. 'Only you mustn't *tell* people about it.'

Laura smiled ironically. 'I don't see anyone to tell who'd be interested, don't worry. Come on, have a biscuit.'

'No, thank you.'

'I've upset you now, haven't I?'

'You never upset me.'

'Fibber.' Laura thought of making a flippant remark about

a childish upset that had long lost its sting, but changed her mind. This was too serious a matter. She put her hand up to her hair, brushing it quickly three or four times unconsciously – a family trait inherited from her father, and his father before him – which revealed to Jocelyn, more than anything else could have done, that her mother really was under stress.

'It'll be all right,' she said gently. 'Don't worry, Mum.'

'Easy enough to say, Jos. But what about Simon in all this?'

'What about him?'

'Well, what are the schools like in that part of Wales? Have you thought about that? He's doing so well now.'

'He's only nine, Mum. He'll adjust. We're not going to darkest Africa, you know.'

Instantly she could have swallowed the words back, aware that progressive people did not speak of 'darkest Africa' or even allow such thoughts into their heads.

'I wish you were in a way.'

'What on earth do you mean?'

'There are good schools for white children in the colonies.'

'Mother! Please!'

'That's a wicked thing to say, I know.'

'I don't know how you can say it.'

'I'm an old Tory, you know that. So's your father. We're worried about you.'

'Why? Do you really want me to leave Steve? Is that what you're saying?'

'No, of course not. But we're concerned about your future. *His* future too. I thought we were agreed, he's too good for this sort of life. It's time he got out of it.' Laura saw she had struck home. 'Look. Your father was talking to someone the other day. There's a job coming up in head office… a good job in PR. Steve's got an excellent chance of getting it, if he wants it. Dad's got contacts.'

'A job in London?'

'Yes! And not just London.' Eyes gleaming, Laura seized the moment, almost – but not quite – giving way to the temptation of grabbing her daughter's hand across the table. 'He'd travel the world, Jos. It's a brand-new job, I tell you. The sky's the limit.'

Jocelyn shook her head unhappily. 'He wouldn't want it, Mum.'

'How do you know? Try him! PR's the thing today, Jos. He doesn't want to go hacking away on the *Comet* for ever, does he?'

But that's just what he did want. Jocelyn knew it.

'Going back to Glanaber? You're not serious?'

Edna Lewis's thin body tautened as she listened to her son explaining why. She sat bolt upright in the chair she kept beside the phone near the front door; Steve had never been able to convince her that the proper place for a phone was the living-room, not the domestic Siberia of the hall.

'But what does Jocelyn think of this. Is she going with you?'

Edna, her violet eyes perplexed, ran her free left hand down the length of the telephone cord and then back again. Confused images came and went in her brain, not all of them pleasant.

'I find this hard to take in, son. It's all so sudden.'

'But you're glad for me, aren't you? You're glad I've got the job?'

'I suppose I am, if you want it. But I still don't understand.

You wanted to go to Fleet Street – and now you're going back where you started.'

'Yes, but...' Patiently he explained. It all made sense to him because he wanted it to make sense. But as he went through it all again – as he had gone through it with Jocelyn – he knew that he was not being completely honest, that there was far more to it than he was prepared to admit.

'Just a minute, *bach*,' said Edna sharply, as she grasped the essence of what was happening. 'You say you'll be covering the whole of Wales for this new what-d'you-call.'

'Right.'

'Well, you could live in Cardiff, couldn't you? You'd be just down the road from me then.'

'That wouldn't work, Mam.'

'Why not?'

'Well, that's where all the newsmen are for the nationals. I don't want to be mixed up with that lot.'

'What difference does it make?'

'A lot. Anyway it's too far away.'

'Far away – *Cardiff*?'

'Yes. From the rest of Wales. It takes all day to get to Bangor – you know it does.'

'Why would you want to go to Bangor?'

'If there's a feature there I'd go. Look, Mam, I keep telling you – this is something new. I'd be looking for off-beat stuff. I can't get that by sitting in a pub in Cardiff – I've got to be in the middle of things.'

'Glanaber – the middle of things?' said Edna faintly.

'Geographically it is. It's plum in the middle – you know that.'

Edna took a deep breath. 'All I know, son, is that you're going against all you've ever told me. You broke my heart when you went to London when you did – and your father's heart too. No, no, listen now – don't interrupt. Stay where you are, son – don't risk it. You know what I mean by that. Don't risk it.'

There was a long silence.

'I can't, Mam. There's no future for me here. I've got to go.'

'And have you told Jocelyn? About Annette – and the baby?'

'No. Not yet.'

'Time you did then, isn't it?'

Tell her. How could he? He had always kept it a secret. There was no need for her to know. It was part of another life – a life he had lived before meeting Jocelyn. He thought he had put it all behind him – the little town at the edge of the world, with its sea forever fretting and its petty feuds and endless gossip. He had shaken its dust from his feet when he went up to the Street to live the life of an adventurer. And what adventures he'd had! The 'Steve Lewis' by-line had meant something. But now? He felt unsure of himself. His life had irrevocably altered.

The change was evident in the way that people spoke to him and looked at him. He was still on the subs' desk, but merely filling out time till the launch of the Saturday mag. He was no longer given the front page splash to sub. That was now entrusted to Tim Marks, who'd lately come up to the Street from the Midlands. He was still in his twenties, bright, energetic, and full of promise. He was Smythe's blue-eyed boy and Scottie thought highly of him too. The three of them were often in a huddle as deadlines approached and the tempo got faster. Steve was ignored. When he went for a pint in the office pub in the unofficial evening break, his old mates among the hacks had less to say to him than before. Subtly he was being edged out. He was yesterday's man.

It was obvious that, from the Chief down, the verdict – unspoken to his face but most certainly bandied about behind his back – was that he had fallen down on the Jill Manders story. He was tired of agonising over it. Should he have spiced it up more? Perhaps. But it was too late now. What was done was done.

They had to cope, however, with a very unhappy son. 'Do we have to go, Mum?' Simon asked plaintively. 'I want to stay with my friends. I don't *want* to move schools.'

'I know that, darling, but… people *do* have to move home, you know, because of their Daddies' work.'

'But you don't like it there – you've told me!'

'Well, that was very wrong of me. You'll love it there – I know you will. It's by the sea – think of all the fun you'll have.'

'No I won't – it's full of *Taffies*!'

'*Taffies*? What do you think your father is, for goodness sake?'

But Simon had fled the room.

It was all over. But then, it had never really started. There'd never been anything between him and Jenny Briggs, not really. Only a few words and glances that might mean anything – or nothing. Now, after seeing her march off from the meeting without even a glance in his direction, Nigel knew for certain that she didn't give a toss about him. He felt an enormous sense of relief. He could get on with his life without even thinking about her.

Except that… she would still be consulting him about her

plans for the nursery school. Except that... he still felt that ache in his guts for her.

Well, they would have to meet strictly on business terms. He was quite determined about that.

18

MEURIG OWEN PULLED down his lower lip as he stared into the bathroom mirror. The nagging toothache that had kept him awake half the night meant a visit to the dentist could no longer be postponed, and he had a visceral dislike of dentists stemming from his schooldays. In the middle 1940s, school dentists had been a feared species. Even now, he could easily call up memories of that ghastly rubber bib tied around his neck before the horrid mask was clamped stiflingly around his nose and mouth, to be followed by weird, gas-induced hallucinations. And then the horror of returning to consciousness, his mouth blood-filled and the dentist's voice hollow and remote, the spitting of mucus and blood into the receptacle at the side of the leathery chair, the plug of cotton wool shoved over the raw cavity that he would feel gingerly with his tongue for days afterwards. Ugh! Going to the dentist now – twenty years on from that time – was nowhere near the nightmare it had been then, but the memories were still vivid enough to persuade him to postpone the inevitable for as long as possible.

Blast it! He'd have to fix up to see someone pretty damn quick, then ask Emyr John for time off – an ordeal almost as bad as the toothache. There was the get-together that night, too – he couldn't miss that. The Castle Hall meeting had been all very well, but they had to get on with the serious stuff. The English who still ruled Wales – and the Welsh quisling MPs who still connived in the fraudulent game of 'democracy' acted out in Parliament – wouldn't be broken by the likes of Trefor Martin-Rees and Jac ap Glyn. Trefor and Jac were worthy enough – that was the word for them, worthy – but too soft by far. Something harder was needed – another Owain Glyndŵr! He clenched his fists instinctively as he called up the name and doused his face in cold water. For a few precious moments he managed to forget his toothache. Then it returned with full force, causing him to drop the towel to the floor. Bugger!

Clad only in underpants, he hurried back to his living-room-cum-bedroom and pulled on the green slacks he was wearing to work that day. He'd much prefer denims, but that useless prat Emyr John insisted on something 'decent'. Jacket and tie always, even on Saturdays. Meurig had once been bold enough to turn up for work in open-neck shirt and sweater, only to encounter the full wrath of an outraged Emyr. 'We have to maintain standards,' the silly sod had cried. 'Go home and change at once!' He'd had half a mind not to go back, then common sense had prevailed. He couldn't afford to lose his job. More's the pity.

Now, his toothache raging, Meurig grabbed a red tie and did it up with a flourish. Always a Windsor knot, which his father had painstakingly taught him – 'bigger it is see, son, makes more of an impression.' Nothing to do with respect for the royals – not likely. Dad had as little time for them as he had himself.

Meurig never ate much breakfast and didn't feel like any today with that toothache, but he knew he'd be hungry if he didn't have at least a bite so managed half a round of toast with his coffee. Hell, but it was hard chewing only on the one side! It slowed him down and he'd be late, especially as he had to ring the dentist on his way. What was his name now? He'd been to him once before, for a filling. Carlton, that was it. Derek Carlton. Would he be there now, before nine? Well, somebody might – one of those two girls he employed. Anyway, the first thing was to find a call box working. They were often vandalised these days, even in Glanaber.

After a last glance in the stained mirror above the mantelpiece – Christ, his face was swelling out like a balloon – he pulled on his jacket and left.

It had been a bizarre episode, but it was over now. She would never see him again. She could carry on as if it had never happened. Annette determined to struggle out of the state of confusion in which Steve's visit had left her. She even averted her eyes from copies of the *Daily Comet* in newsagents. She busied herself about the house, doing the rigorous 'tidying-up' she generally ignored. *Spring-cleaning, just like Gran,* she thought ironically. But, gripped by restlessness and dissatisfaction, she began to think in larger terms about her future. Was she simply to be a wife and mother for ever? Joanne was ten, Robert seven. Why couldn't she manage a part-time job? Surprised by the adventurousness of the idea, she paused in the act of shaking a pillow. She might be able to… *might.* But it would all depend on the children being willing to stay on at midday for school dinners. Joanne did so now and then, but Rob insisted on coming home. 'I hate school dinners!' he had protested, when she had suggested it. 'But you've never tried them.' 'I've seen them – they're yucky.' Which had resulted in Joanne calling him a big baby. Of course, she could try again. He might be persuaded now, but she wasn't very hopeful. Joanne was a different matter. The novelty of having a working mother might well appeal to her. And by helping out like this she'd be proving how grown-up she was, compared with her little brother. But, Annette wondered, just what work would she find? She couldn't go back to her old job at Richards and James, Solicitors – it didn't exist any more. Delyth and Glenys were coping very well with the secretarial work she and Rita used to do in the old days. It was where she had met Nigel, when he had been a young solicitor and she a secretary. Imagine working for Nigel now! Imagine *wanting* to work for him. So what was there? Her only qualifications were in shorthand and typing – she had never been to county school, where people came out stuffed with O levels as they were now. So she'd still have to be a secretary of some sort, she supposed. Part-time secretary, too, for she'd have to meet the kids from school – she wouldn't let anyone do *that* for her, even if she managed to find someone willing.

Going downstairs, she wondered what had happened to Rita. They'd been quite close once, sharing confidences with each other – though Rita had always been far more conventional than herself. Poor Rita! She'd been truly shocked when she'd broken off her engagement to Steve. 'But what about the baby?' she'd cried. 'You can't have a baby if you're not married!' As if. But for a pregnant woman wilfully to refuse to marry the father – that was something quite beyond her understanding. Her relief when, after Ceri's death, Nigel had married Annette was profound. 'You won't find many men who'd do that,' she had observed piously. And Annette had been annoyed with her – truly annoyed. Of course you wouldn't! she thought. But Nigel wasn't doing it out of pity for her, was he? If there'd been any suggestion of that, she'd have told him where to go! She hadn't been forced to marry *him,* either – no way. Her latent crossness with Rita, flaring up briefly, suddenly amused her. All that water under bridges! She'd like to see Rita again but heaven knows where she was – somewhere in south Wales by now with a husband and kids, no doubt. The common lot.

The recollection of Nigel's sheer decency, however, made her pause outside his study. Should she dare to tidy it, just a little? It was sacrosanct. She only went in there to vacuum-clean the carpet, and that didn't take long. He was a tidy individual. Therefore the room didn't need tidying. Case proved. But something – a feeling she could scarcely analyse, still less explain – tempted her to delve uncharacteristically into her husband's privacy. She opened the door, and stepped in. Everything was in order. The uncluttered desk, the row of legal books above it, the old cabinet he had bought at a sale for the 'genuine antique' look of it... what had she expected to find? She was about to go out again when her eye caught a book that somehow seemed out of place. Thrust between two thick legal tomes, it had a slim spine and bright green cover... the Welsh poetry collection she had spotted him reading the other day. She took it off the shelf, feeling unaccountably guilty. Why shouldn't she look at it? She flicked through the pages, spotting the word *cariad* – at least she understood that much. *Cariad*... darling... love poems, obviously. What was he doing reading love poems? He wasn't what you'd call a romantic. One poem had a thin pencil mark running down the side... Nigel's own marking? It had to be – this was a new copy, not second-hand. Why had he done it? What made this poem so special? Oh, how she wished she spoke Welsh, at that moment! She put the book back, and then paused. She took it out again, found the page, and carefully copied the poem on to a blank sheet of paper.

She finished it, took a deep breath, and tip-toed out like an intruder.

'See the dentist? In working hours? How bad is this toothache then?' Emyr John, proprietor of Holloway Books, glared suspiciously at Meurig.

'Very bad.'

'Too bad to put up with? Have you tried sucking a clove? That's very good, I believe.'

'I've tried that, Mr John,' Meurig lied. 'It's done no good at all. It's giving me gyp – I can't go the whole day like this.'

'Well, I suppose you'd better get it taken out. If you can find someone to see you, that is. I doubt if you will though, at such short notice. You can always try Dan Eddistone, I suppose. He's not very busy these days, I gather.'

Dan Eddistone! He'd rather go to Purnell the butchers – that'd be a lot less painful, he reckoned.

'I'd rather try Carlton, if you don't mind. I've been there before.'

'Well, please yourself. Go and ring him from a call-box. Can't have you using the phone here – I'm expecting an important call.'

'Thank you, Mr John. *Diolch yn fawr.*'

'Be as quick as you can, mind. This is all very inconvenient.'

If only he knew he'd already booked an appointment on his way in to work! thought Meurig as he hurried pointlessly along Pier Road. Well, serve the lonely skinflint right. Emyr John never let anyone but himself use the shop phone for personal calls. Meurig lingered a minute or two outside the phone booth at the top of Darkgate Street – he was tempted to cross the road for a quick coffee in the Pelican Café, but didn't want to push his luck – then ambled back to the bookshop. How long could he put up with working for this miserable old devil? He'd been there two years now, since leaving Coleg Harlech – two years too long. If only he'd completed the course at the so-called 'College of the Second Chance' for mature students, he might be in university by now – but it was no use going down that road again. What was done was done. He had to look to the future. And the future, for him, lay in what happened to Wales.

Back in the bookshop, Emyr John said with a lethal smile: 'I've got a little job for you today. I'm sure you'll enjoy it.' He looked at Meurig gloatingly. 'I've had a lot of requests for books about royalty lately. They're lying all over the place. I want them all put in proper order.'

'Would that be Welsh royalty or English, Mr John?'

'Both. But naturally, the English will predominate. We haven't had our own royals for centuries – except for the Princes of Wales, of course.'

'The English princes.'

'The only princes, Meurig.'

'I don't recognise them myself, Mr John.'

'What you recognise or don't recognise isn't my concern,' said Emyr sharply. 'All I'm concerned about is what my customers want. And there's a big demand for royal books, as well you know. The public can't get enough of them. There'll be a bigger demand too, in the next few years, with Prince Charles coming up to his twenty-first birthday.'

'Why, what difference will that make?'

'Well, he's Prince of Wales, isn't he? There'll probably be a big investiture ceremony, like there was in 1911 for his great-uncle in Caernarfon.'

'You were there then were you, Mr John?'

'Not quite, young man. I was a mere babe-in-arms.'

Meurig could not quite conceal his smile. One up for the rebels.

'This is far too difficult,' said Rachael Miles, studying the slip of paper Annette had handed her. 'I'm still a Welsh learner, you know. Gethin can do it better than me.'

'No! I don't want to involve him. All I want is the gist of it. You can manage that, can't you?'

'I can try.'

They were having mid-afternoon coffee in Glanaber's newly-built Arts Centre, part of the university complex where Rachael had a job in admin.

'It's a love poem, obviously. Who's it by?'

Annette told her.

'That explains it. It's got lots of modernisms. Not the sort of thing they teach you in Welsh classes. Why do you want to know this, anyway?'

'I came across it,' Annette replied evasively. 'It seemed sort of – interesting.'

Rachael gave her a look. 'Come off it! I'm not buying that. You're not in the least interested in Welsh poets, and you know it.'

'Nigel is. It's in a book he's reading. He's marked it off specially.'

'Has he now? I wonder why?'

'So do I.'

Rachael flicked her right middle finger against her thumb, a sure sign that her interest was aroused.

'And you copied all this out for me? Why didn't you bring the book?'

'Well, I didn't know how long you'd take. I thought you might want to take the poem away with you.'

'And he might miss the book, you mean? You didn't want him to know?'

Annette nodded.

'You cunning little devil. Who is she?'

'Who?'

'The woman he's having an affair with.'

Annette frowned. 'Affair? I never mentioned an affair, did I?'

'You don't have to. It's written all over you.'

'Just translate the poem, Rachael. I don't want an inquest.'

Flicking moodily through *The Tatler* in Derek Carlton's waiting room, Meurig wondered why dentists put such monstrous garbage in their waiting rooms. Those old copies of *The Pig Breeder* and *Yachting World* were bad enough, but this! He glanced distastefully at the glossy photographs of silk-toppered gents at the races with their ladies, and wondered how on earth the Bertie Wooster world of privilege had endured so far into the twentieth century. The English were welcome to these buffoons, but why should the Welsh be saddled with them too? Oh yes, Harold Wilson was in No. 10 and a Labour government still nominally in control, but he – Meurig Owen – was under no illusion about where the true power still lay. In the hands of the Establishment, that dead weight of inherited wealth and tradition only thinly masked by the political pantomime that passed for democracy in these benighted islands. '*The Hon Antony Hetherington-May and his bride, Lady Penelope Mainwaring, after their wedding at Bride's Norton,*' declared the caption under the picture of a chinless wonder and his horse-faced bride. And how many miners and steelworkers in Wales had died to provide the wealth for such lifestyles as theirs?

Meurig threw the magazine down, ashamed to be caught reading it by the man sitting opposite, whom he had scarcely noticed before. Now, however, his eyes caught those of the stranger, veered away then returned. He was a youngish man, late thirties possibly, with a neat moustache and an ironical expression to which Meurig responded with a rush of recognition. He had never seen him before, but it was not the man's identity he recognised but something far more fundamental. Unnoticed by the elderly woman who was the only other occupant of the waiting room, the two men exchanged a long look. Meurig's guts twisted in the old convulsion, half pain, half ecstasy.

19

'NIGEL!'
Briefcase in hand, he pretended not to hear her. He quickened his pace, giving the merest of glances to left and right before crossing the road. He felt a tightness in his chest, as if he had been running. He was aware of the shallowness of his breathing, the thumping of his heart.

Suddenly she was alongside him, tugging his sleeve. 'Nigel! Didn't you hear me?'

He stopped, filled with exultation at the sight of her, desperately trying to disguise it.

'No, I'm afraid I didn't,' he said stiffly. 'Where were you?'

'Just behind you. You *must* have heard me. What's wrong, *cariad*? You look funny.'

'I don't feel it. Look, Jenny, I'm in a bit of a rush now. I've got to…'

'There *is* something wrong. Have I upset you? What is it? Tell me.'

Frowning, grey eyes troubled, she looked genuinely confused. How could she be doing this, after cutting him dead outside the Castle Hall? And what had she been up to afterwards?

'What happened the other night then?'

'What do you mean?'

'We were supposed to be having coffee together.'

'Oh!' Her hands flew to her mouth. There was no mistaking this – she wasn't pretending. 'I'm sorry – I clean forgot. Oh, Nigel.'

'Forgot!'

'What can I say – the meeting. So much bullshit – that awful man… I just wanted to go home. Where were you then?'

'Outside, waiting for you. You passed within three feet of me,' he exaggerated.

'I didn't! Oh, *cariad*, what can I say? I didn't see you, honestly. Why didn't you say something?'

'You were otherwise engaged.' He was putting on an act, playing the cold fish – the phrase *his lip curled* actually sprang to mind, while inside him was pure joy at the sight and sound of her, the very *nearness* of her.

'You mean – oh Nigel, you've got the wrong idea, that was only Meurig.'

'Only?'

'You don't know?' She sensed his true frame of mind, and relief swept away her confusion. 'Look, Nigel, I've got to explain – come back and have a coffee now.'

'I can't…'

'Yes you can. It'll only take a minute. Come on.'

She put her arm through his and marched him back the way he had come. He caught one or two people staring. He knew he shouldn't be doing this, but in five minutes' time – less – she was unlocking her front door, and he was following her in.

'Why are you telling me this?' Steve asked angrily.

'I thought you ought to know. I'm sorry – I shouldn't have mentioned it.'

'You know what I think of PR – we've been through all this a dozen times.'

'I told you, I'm sorry. Forget it.'

'How's your mother know this, anyway?'

'I told you – Dad told her.'

'Sounds like a lot of baloney to me. I doubt if the job exists.'

'So you think he's telling fibs?'

'I didn't say that. He's probably just mistaken.'

She swept out of the room. His anger drained out of him. It struck him that she'd been keeping this to herself for days. It had cost her an effort to mention it.

He knew exactly how she'd be looking. Face set, eyes avoiding him, she was flinging newly-washed clothes into a basket.

'I'd do it if I could, Jos. But I can't. It would kill me.'

It wasn't worth a reply. He knew it. She knew it.

'Maybe it's best if I *did* go on my own to Glanaber,' he ventured.

'That's just what you'd like, isn't it?'

'Why do you say that?'

'Because it's obvious. There's nothing you'd like better than to have me out of the way.'

'That's stupid. Absolutely stupid.'

'Is it?'

'Yes, it is. Why should I want that?'

'You tell me.'

She had her back to him now. He had a sense of unreality. They had never spoken like this before. He felt they were on the brink of something irrevocable.

'Why are you talking like this?'

She didn't answer.

One wrong word, and who knew what might happen? A strange mixture of emotions possessed him, trepidation mingled with excitement. A stray wisp of hair on the back of her head caught his attention. There was something pathetic about it. The whole shape of her seemed vulnerable. A sound came from upstairs – Simon busying himself with something. A fleeting vision of Annette, walking away from him in the cemetery. He stepped forward, put his arms around her from behind.

'I want you with me,' he said. 'If you don't go, I don't.'

She stood perfectly still. He kissed the top of her head.

'Do you really mean that?'

'Yes.'

She turned, her eyes full of tears.

'I've got to be certain.'

'I am, love. Don't worry.'

They kissed. He held her. But Steve felt a sense of betrayal – of whom, or what, he could not be sure.

As soon as he stepped through the door, Nigel realised he had done the wrong thing. This was simply a place where he should not be. The strangeness of it – the look of the stairs, the deep blue carpet covering them, the very smell of the stairwell – cried out a warning to his soul. And the presence of Jenny, her nearness, had a tumultuous effect on him. Her pale face seemed luminous in the half light, her grey eyes preternaturally large. The sheer physicality of her overwhelmed him and he stood, dazed. 'Well?' she said, smiling. 'Go on up. It won't bite you.'

He was only half-aware of the framed photographs of old Glanaber on the left-hand wall of the stairwell, the softness of the carpet, the sudden clarity of his footsteps when the carpet gave way to lino near the top. On the narrow landing, he stood aside as she opened the door.

His instant impression was of spaciousness and oddity.

The room was strangely shaped with ceilings sloping unexpectedly, and there seemed, at first, scarcely any furniture. Directly opposite, flush against the wall, was an old wooden table, a piece of driftwood on it holding half a dozen oranges. There were patchwork rugs that brought back memories of his great-aunt Emily's house in Carmarthen, and a Victorian sampler confirmed his sense of being transported back in time. A low settee, its red plush faded, held a cushion in either corner. To his right, by the tall sash window, was a high-backed armchair, its narrow struts close together. Along the opposite wall was a narrow divan bed covered by an Indian bedspread. Do sit down, she said, pointing to the bed. As he sat, he could see the sky through the window, sky and seagulls.

'Don't really want tea or coffee, do you? I've got a really nice Italian white. Care to try it?'

'Love to.'

Her eyes were luminous, and the angularity of her features was softened by something indefinable. She seemed possessed of a secret that gave a zest to this encounter. As she gave him his glass, he noticed the thinness of her wrists, which in his keyed-up state added to his sense of recklessness.

'Not too much sitting space here, I'm afraid,' she said carelessly, squatting beside him at an angle so that she half-faced him. 'I want to get more furniture – when I can afford it.'

'The nursery school should help.'

'Don't know about that. Depends how many send their kids along. I've had a lot of promises, but promises aren't worth much, are they?'

'They're worth something. Show the way the wind's blowing. Like the meeting the other night.'

She screwed her face up. 'Don't remind me, *bach*. Walking past you like that. It's a wonder you're still speaking to me.'

'Don't be silly.' But he suddenly had the feeling that she *had* noticed him standing there, and simply pretended she hadn't. She was talking lazily now, eyes half-hooded, and her lips looked fuller, as if engorged with blood.

'Do you smoke?' He shook his head. 'Don't mind if I have one, do you?'

'Of course not.' *It's your place*, he thought, but didn't say it.

She lit up. He wished she hadn't. Smoking didn't suit women, in his book. They looked clumsy at it, as if putting on an act.

'I think you've got the wrong idea about Meurig, you know.' She wafted smoke away, ineffectually. 'He's not my boyfriend. He couldn't be.'

'Got someone else, has he?'

'That's not what I meant. Though he could do, I suppose. But if he had, I wouldn't know about it – if you get my meaning.'

She gave him a tantalising, half-mocking look. He felt out of his depth, much younger and more naïve than this scarcely known woman.

'It's no concern of mine, anyway,' he said, trying to make light of a situation rapidly getting out of control.

'Yes it is. Of course it is. But what I mean is... he wouldn't be interested in someone like me. I'm the wrong gender.'

'Oh. I see.' He took a deep breath, feeling a fool.

'You didn't know?'

'Of course not. How could I? I don't know the man.'

'I thought you'd guess... just looking at him. All that stubble. Like a fucking gaucho bandit.'

202

He laughed, a spontaneous reaction born of surprise not humour. He had never heard the word from a woman before, outside the rougher pubs in Carmarthen. And he had seen it written only on notes passed around the courtroom, to be read by magistrates with pursed lips and expressions of affronted dignity.

'Shocked you now, haven't I?' she said, amused.

'No, not really.'

'Yes I have. I can tell. I don't suppose your wife says things like that, does she?'

'Not often, no.'

'I can imagine. What's her name, Nigel?'

'Annette.'

'*Annette*. French, is she?'

'Good God, no. What makes you think that?'

'Sounds French to me. Never know any Annettes in my life. Parents *crachach*, are they?'

Not as crachach as yours, he thought.

'He's a postman, actually – or was. They live in a council flat in town.'

'And they call their daughter Annette?'

'Yes. Why not?'

'Well, it's no odds to me, I suppose,' she said, swiftly changing stance. 'Or to you. So long as she's nice to you. Is she?'

'Yes, she's very nice.'

'Well, that's good, *cariad*.'

He felt hot and flustered by conflicting emotions, his resentment of her intrusive remarks serving only to make his longing for her more turbulent and uncontrollable.

'What do you think of this wine then?'

'It's good. Where'd you get it?'

'That delicatessen in Eastgate – Benjamin's. I love it there – it *smells* good. All those different cheeses. I expect Annette goes there a lot, does she?'

'I've no idea. I leave all the shopping to her.'

'Typical man.' She wrinkled her nose. 'Aren't you hot, in that stuffy old suit? Take your jacket off, at least. You look as if you're not staying.'

'I can't stay long, anyway,' he heard himself saying, ridiculously.

'Well, you're not dashing away, anyway. Unless you've got a pressing engagement, that is. I don't see you very often.'

Clumsily he took off his jacket, feeling absurd, unworthy of the situation. Reading those love poems, trying to write one himself, he had often pictured himself alone with her – in command, masterful. Now he felt like a schoolboy, not knowing what the rules were. Not knowing what he wanted. *I shouldn't have come in here…*

'That's better,' she said approvingly. 'Look a bit more relaxed now. Isn't this weather gorgeous? Anyone would think it was summer.'

'Lovely.'

'What did *you* think of the meeting then? You haven't told me.'

'Well… quite good, really. Some things said that need saying.'

'Crap.'

'What?'

'Waste of time. All talk.'

'What's wrong with talk? So long as it's the right sort.'

'Jesus! We've done enough talking in Wales, Nigel. It's time for some action now.' She moved position quickly, skirt riding up over her knees.

He looked away, stomach churning.

'Depends what sort of action you mean,' he said ponderously – then wanted to snatch the words back, knowing how stuffy they sounded.

'The only sort that matters. Direct action.'

'Oh!' He half-laughed, as if she had not meant it. 'That can be dangerous, Jenny.'

'So what? If we don't take risks we won't get anywhere.' She looked at him keenly. 'You know the sort of thing I've been doing. Don't disapprove, do you?'

'Doesn't matter if I do or not, does it? You'll still go on doing it.'

'You *do* disapprove. I can tell.'

'Well... I don't like the thought of you getting into trouble. It won't help, will it?'

'In what way?'

'Your plans... your career.'

'Career! *Uffern.*'

'You're serious about it, aren't you? This project of yours?'

'Serious enough. But it doesn't matter a stuff compared to...'

'What?'

'The things that *really* matter. You know what I mean.'

He had an overpowering desire to do something. To stop this useless talking. To...

'For fuck's sake.' She stubbed out her cigarette. 'You need to lighten up, Nigel.'

'Do I?'

'Yes. You do. What's she done to you, that woman? You act like...'

'What?'

'Like you haven't got any balls. Jesus! What are we doing here, Nigel?'

'I don't know,' he said stickily. 'I honestly don't know.'

'No, you don't, do you? That's your trouble. Come here.'

'I am here.'

'Come *here*.' She jabbed her finger down, an inch from her bared knee.

He moved nearer.

'That's better. Learning fast, aren't you, Nigel? Now then. Let's get this silly thing off, shall we?' She undid his tie.

He lunged into a kiss, as clumsy as it was desperate.

'Steady on, boy.' She freed herself. 'You can do better than that.'

20

THEY SETTLED FOR a terraced house in Dinas Road, the substantial work of a local builder who gave good value for money between the wars. Jocelyn had her doubts: it had been neglected, the paintwork as faded and flaky as an old gigolo, the window frames so rotten in places that they scarcely seemed able to keep in the glass. 'It's the salt in the air,' Steve said confidently. 'This'll need painting quite often, I imagine.' He was bouncy, full of confidence, 'a new man' thought Jocelyn with surprise and some resentment. If Glanaber could do this for him, why couldn't she have done it herself? With amazement, she observed his panache in beating down the asking price of the property, his sheer *expansiveness* of manner. He seemed to have grown physically, while she felt vulnerable, exposed, scarcely able to comprehend that she was now part of a town she had always regarded as alien territory. She walked the streets edgily, suspicious of everyone. Yet the shop assistants were friendly enough, often speaking – to her surprise – with Brummie accents. These were far from the beetle-browed Celts she had imagined gabbling an incomprehensible tongue and wishing her back where she'd come from. She was surprised too by something innocent and charming: the fact that, practically everywhere she went, she was in sight of hills. Some near, some far, they made a pleasant backdrop that lifted her spirits.

About the sea she was more ambiguous: this too was ever-present, their very house commanding huge views of Cardigan Bay. They were beautiful, sometimes menacing, but something in her feared the sea. It spelt power, the kind of irresistible power that might snatch her up and dash her against something harsh and unyielding. She subdued the fear, scarcely admitting it to herself, and could still take pleasure in the seascapes and sunsets. The latter were often spectacular, a mix of colours of infinite complexity and subtlety. 'Glanaber's famous for its sunsets,' Steve would say proudly. 'Turner came here to paint them, you know.' His pride in the town was immeasurable: it seemed to be a pearl of his own making. It came to her as a revelation: she would never have imagined him capable of such feeling for a place he had always dismissed as a backwater. Why had it suddenly burgeoned in his imagination? What change inside him could account for it? The subject was all the more disturbing for being so unapproachable: it was something she dare not discuss.

Unknown to herself, she was being observed. Any stranger 'from away' who settled in the town was an object of interest, and as the wife of 'Steve Lewis of the *Comet*' she was of more interest than most. The way she spoke, the way she walked, the clothes she put on – all these were keenly assessed. She was English through and through, that was obvious – but then, there were plenty of English in this university town – people from 'all over', in fact. It wasn't this that provided the meaty gossip the matrons of the town got their teeth into over morning coffee, but the question of how much she knew of his past and why she had agreed to live there. Surely she must know about him and Annette Allan and the baby! If she didn't, what did that say about her relationship with her husband? If she did, how could she bear to look Annette in the eye when they met – as they inevitably must? 'What's it matter?' an exasperated Ivor Morgan asked his wife Shirley in the ironmongery shop in Water Street. 'That was all over when she married him, wasn't it? What's it to her if he'd shagged half the women in Glanaber?' 'Typical man, you are,' Shirley retorted. 'You don't understand anything, do you?' And Ivor, scowling, would retreat into his 'office' – a cubbyhole at the back of the shop which was more escape-hatch than anything – leaving Shirley to serve the customers sourly.

Ivor couldn't understand Shirley, and truth to tell she couldn't understand herself. This rage within her was focused entirely on Steve, but why? It wasn't that she'd ever really fancied him, in those long-ago days when they'd all been young people together. He'd been Annette's boyfriend, and she'd been welcome to him. His name had been mud in Glanaber, what with his going to that prostitute in Back Row – *ych y fi*! And all the time he'd been making Annette pregnant! No wonder he'd gone up to London – he'd have been run out of town otherwise. And now he had the cheek to come back here as if nothing had happened! Shirley brooded over the way he'd cut her dead in the street the other day – she was sure it had been deliberate – but this wasn't the reason she hated him – no! It was something more than that, something deep inside her, too deep to be dug out simply by thinking about it. It was something to do with Annette, who'd become so hoity-toity since going up in the world by marrying that solicitor (wanted everyone to forget she'd been born in a council house, didn't she?) – and something to do with Ivor, who'd been going out with Annette before she'd dumped him like he was dirt.

Now, mulling over the past in her discontent with the present, a suspicion long subdued suddenly crystallized in her mind – so terrible in its implications that she tried in vain to beat it back.

What if Ivor had been the father of that dead baby – not Steve?

'Brilliant,' murmured Bill Merrick appreciatively. 'Absolutely brilliant.' He slapped the *Daily Comet*'s new magazine with his fingertips to emphasise his approval. 'You've got it all here. Great quotes from Betty. Spot-on.'

'Glad you like it,' said Steve Lewis indulgently. A sharp observer might have detected a glint of amusement in his eyes, proof of his sense of superiority over the older man.

'Like it? I...' For a moment Steve thought he was going to say 'couldn't do better myself' but he continued, 'I think it's marvellous. So does Betty. She's phoning everyone to tell them to buy the *Comet*.'

'Good.' Steve looked beyond Bill to the view from the window: the bay flecked by foam whipped up by a brisk September breeze, the roofs of the tall houses on the prom where, in another life, he had visited the flat shared by Annette and her best friend Shirley.

'How are you settling in then, OK?' Bill asked. He was paying a social call on Steve: something that would have been unimaginable during Steve's previous incarnation in Glanaber.

'Yes. Fine.'

'You know, I had the shock of my life when I heard you were coming back to live here. I couldn't believe it. You of all people.'

'Well, that's it then, isn't it? Strange what life throws at you.'

'You mean you didn't want to do it?' said Bill shrewdly.

'Not at all. I was only too happy. It's a great job.'

'Oh, undoubtedly,' Bill agreed hastily, anxious to please.

'It's made a mark already, this magazine. I was reading in the *Press Gazette* the other day...' He leapt to his feet as Jocelyn entered the room with Simon. Steve swiftly made the introductions. Bill was all charm to Jocelyn and jocular with Simon, who looked uncomfortable under the weight of this attention.

'Hasn't he given you a coffee yet?' Jocelyn said. 'Just typical. Or would you prefer tea, Mr Merrick?'

'Oh, please – call me Bill. Coffee's fine, thank you.' He flashed another smile at Simon, the slightly off-key joviality of a childless man faced by a nine-year-old. Steve detected a change in him since the spring. Bill Merrick's face seemed thinner, slightly discoloured, and the self-approval that had always sustained him appeared to have drained away. Was Betty's illness the cause, or were other factors involved?

'How's Betty today?' asked Steve, as his wife went to the kitchen, with Simon in tow.

'Not too bad at all, considering. This write-up's bucked her up, I can tell you. We never dreamed... You know, we might be able to get her to America sooner than we thought. The money's coming in fast. This should help a lot,' he added, flicking the magazine again.

'I'm glad to hear it.' But of course, Steve thought, that wasn't the purpose of the feature: it hadn't been an advertising stunt. But it had made a good human interest piece: Welsh townspeople rallying round to send local woman for treatment in America. It was one of the first of his features for the magazine that was now an intrinsic part of the *Comet*'s Saturday edition. His bosses in London had liked it, believing it would strike a chord with its compassionate readers everywhere. He had several other stories lined up: Wales was full of meaty material, so long neglected by London news editors who saw 'the Principality' only in cliché terms of gusty male voice choirs, sheep farmers with dubious habits and coal miners singing their way home from the pit when they weren't actually on strike. It was neglected too by the *Comet*'s 'hard news' man in Wales Tudor Powell, who from his base in Cardiff cast a disdainful eye on the rural fastnesses. Tudor was great at exposing the Machiavellian dealings of trade union bosses and employers in the industrial belt in the south, but disinclined to root out stories less easily come by. He was one of a coterie of Fleet Street correspondents in Cardiff who found it simpler to pool stories than set up rival camps involving all the stresses of fierce competition. On the grapevine, Steve had heard of Tudor's scornful reaction to his appointment: 'Bloody has-been put out to grass.' The words of a jealous man: Tudor had never hacked it in Fleet Street, but had simply climbed the ladder from weekly paper to evening to news agency to Wales's correspondent for the *Comet*. His opinion did not trouble Steve, who had the solid reassurance of Fleet Street success behind him. He accepted that he had suffered demotion of a kind, but this was outweighed by the compensation of living in Glanaber. It was a return journey which, he now realized, had been an inevitable part of the life script written for him by an unseen hand. He viewed the town now not as wasteland of ambition but as opportunity. He could carve out a new career more suited to the reality of what he had become: a reporter not far short of forty with health problems, already seen by young Turks in the Street as a back number. Whatever the limitations of the job, it was a whole lot better than PR. And there was Annette... He had seen her three or four times in the street (less often than he had hoped for, or perhaps feared) since coming back to Glanaber. He had greeted her, but never stopped to talk, and she had returned his greeting, politely but coolly. He had no idea what she thought of him. He remembered her words in the cemetery – 'I don't want to see you again' – but refused to take them literally. How close did he want to get to her again? Even to pose the question brought the whiff of danger. And with danger came excitement: he was not dead yet.

21

THE CONSPIRATORS MET, like many conspirators before them, in a house that was outwardly the acme of respectability. Tall, detached, gabled, it stood within a pebble's throw of the cliff railway that climbed the rocky headland that was the northernmost of the two sentinels guarding the town of Glanaber. First to ring the bell of the ground-floor flat was a dishevelled figure in tatty jeans and grubby T-shirt whose trainer-clad toes tapped the step impatiently as he awaited an answer. He gazed blindly out over Cardigan Bay, seeing only his inner voices.

'Nice and early,' said the man who opened the door. 'Come on in.'

Robyn Ifans grunted, pushing past without ceremony. He not so much ignored courtesies as trampled them to death. His host seemed more amused than offended.

'No coat? May be cold later. They've forecast rain.'

Robyn shrugged, mumbling something undistinguishable. Although young, his pale hair was thinning. His face had a raddled look, his eyes were at once wild and puzzled, as if he forever faced a question for which there was no answer.

The two men walked to a room at the end of the narrow hallway, Selwyn Cook leading the way. As he followed, Robyn's expression was one of cynicism, even mockery, a tell-tale look that disappeared immediately his host turned to face him.

'What would you like, tea or coffee?'

'Nothing stronger, have you?'

'*Jiw-jiw*, never thought of that. We don't generally drink at home. I should have realised.'

Selwyn's rabbity face registered a self-deprecation that was lost on Robyn. 'Got any coke then?' Robyn asked.

'Coke?'

'Coca-Cola.'

Selwyn spread his arms helplessly. 'Sorry, don't have any of that either. Pretty hopeless, aren't I? I'll remember next time.'

'Don't worry. I shan't bother.'

It was unclear whether he meant he wouldn't bother to drink anything, or not bother to come again.

'Who's coming then?' Robyn asked, flinging himself on to a sofa that had seen better days.

'Not sure altogether. Richard, I expect. Meurig said he would. Jenny possibly. Not sure about Maggi and Clive.'

Robyn harrumphed. 'Clive needn't bother. He's a waste of time.'

'You mustn't be so intolerant,' Selwyn reproached, with a smile. 'Clive's alright. He'll contribute.'

'Contribute? He's as broke as I am.'

'I don't mean money. I meant ideas.'

'Shit!' The fag he was rolling came apart. He tried again. 'Where's Sarah?' he asked, in a more emollient voice.

'Putting Sophie to bed.'

'Won't disturb her, will we? The baby?'

'Not if you don't bring your rock band. She's a good sleeper.'

Robyn grinned. 'Wouldn't bring that lot here. They'd frighten the horses.'

The room was cluttered in a comfortable way, with records and books piled on an old table jammed into a corner and newspapers and magazines strewn around the worn furniture. The *Daily Worker* and *Tribune* were clearly required reading, and a shelf of books in an alcove revealed works by Tawney, G. D. H. Cole and the gospel according to St Marx. Selwyn was in sports jacket, open-neck shirt and grey flannel trousers, his age mid-thirties, his squat body tending to lumpiness around the middle. He seemed not entirely at ease with Robyn, his anxiety to please showing itself in his haste to hand him an ashtray when the younger man inquiringly held up the dead match after lighting a cigarette.

'Heard the news today?' Selwyn said. 'The Yanks have bombed Hanoi again. Disgusting, isn't it?'

'What do you expect? They don't give a shit about anyone.'

'*We* ought to though. Wilson should give 'em a piece of his mind. But he's just an American lackey.'

'Not our war though, is it? We've got things nearer home to think about.'

'That's true but...'

Soft footfalls in the corridor, and Sarah Cook entered. She addressed her husband, her voice low, arresting. 'Had a devil of a job with her tonight. Wouldn't settle at all.'

'She's teething, isn't she?' said Selwyn.

'Don't I know it. Where's all the rest then?'

'On their way, I hope.'

'Late. Thought so. Be sure how you time the revolution. If it's too early in the day, you'll miss it.'

Robyn smiled, trying to catch her eye. She conveyed a sense of darkness – sexy, tremulous darkness. Dark hair, falling loose on her shoulders. Dark eyes, lit by an inner glow. Gipsyish skin, smooth as trouble. 'Where's your drink then?'

she asked Robyn, not smiling, but not indifferent either. 'Hasn't he given you one? *Arglwydd.*'

'I've offered him a cup of tea, but…'

'Tea? The boy doesn't want *tea*. Get the beer out, *diawl*.'

'Oh – have we got some then?'

'*Iesu mawr*. What world you living in, Sel? Honest to God.'

Grimacing at Robyn, she went through to the kitchen. Selwyn smiled weakly at Robyn, with a feeble half-shrug of the shoulders. A clanking in the kitchen, and Sarah returned triumphantly holding a flagon of the local ale in either hand. She swung the bottles up on to the sideboard. 'There! That'll do for starters. There's more out there, and gin and tonic in the cupboard.'

'*Jiw*, Sarah, thanks,' Selwyn said admiringly. 'Do you know, I clean forgot.'

'You'd forget your head if it wasn't screwed on. Now, can you manage without me, do you think?'

'Not going out, are you?'

'I told you, I'm going to see Nesta. Sophie should be alright. If she isn't, give me a ring. You might even manage to settle her yourself.'

She was gone in a moment, leaving behind a drabness quickly filled by the arrival of the fellow-conspirators. First Meurig Owen, in denim jacket and jeans. Then Richard Ellis, sallow, studious, eyes blanked out by shades, with an air of menace that might or might not be threadbare. Jenny Briggs and Maggi Rees arrived together, animatedly talking, bearing bottles of wine that Selwyn fussed over unable to find a corkscrew until the girls took charge. 'Thought you might be teetotal,' Selwyn joshed Maggi. 'Piss off,' she genially replied, demolishing any assumptions of what might be expected of the daughter of Dr Idwal Rees, principal of the Theological College.

'Anyone else coming, anyone know?' Selwyn asked expansively.

'Paul might be,' replied Maggi.

Robyn frowned. 'Who asked him?'

'I did.' She stared back at him defiantly. 'Any objections?'

'Too late now, isn't it?'

'So you *do* object?'

'I think we should all have a say in it,' said Robyn coolly. 'If it's going to *mean* anything.'

'What's wrong with Paul then?'

'He's English.'

'That's racial prejudice.'

'It's common sense. In the last resort he's the enemy.'

'Jesus! I never thought...'

'That's your trouble. You don't think.'

'Now now, let's not quarrel before we've even begun,' said Selwyn placatingly. 'This is a very informal meeting, isn't it? We've just come together to discuss things.'

'Are we serious or aren't we?' Robyn demanded.

'Of course we're serious, but...'

'Robyn's right,' Meurig chipped in. 'If we don't mean to do business, let's forget it. There's been too much messing round in Wales. All talk and no action.'

'There may be too much action one day,' observed Richard Ellis laconically, 'for some of us.' His quiet words changed the atmosphere of the room in an instant. In the silence that followed them, the body language of everyone there told a story. Robyn Ifans looked startled. Meurig Owen sat up straight, alert. Maggi Rees glanced nervously at Jenny. Selwyn Cook took a battered briar pipe from his jacket pocket and slowly filled it with tobacco.

'What do you mean by that, *brawd*?' asked Robyn, his voice thinner, more metallic, than usual.

'What I say.'

'You mean violence?'

'Quite.'

A frisson ran through the room like an electric charge. Maggi gasped. Meurig's eyes lit up eagerly. Jenny's expression did not alter. Selwyn looked thoughtfully at Richard, as though sizing him up. Robyn's fists clenched.

'What evidence do you have for that?' asked Selwyn. He too had subtly altered, his eyes becoming narrower, his voice more level and serious.

'Can't go into that now. Just telling you, that's all.'

'You've got to tell us *something*,' said Robyn. 'You can't leave us up in the air like that.'

'Can't I?' Richard raised his glass. '*Iechyd da.*'

Jenny said: 'Robyn's right. We've got to know if you're serious or not.'

'Oh, I'm serious alright, Jenny.'

'Well then. Give.'

Richard sipped his wine imperturbably, stretching the silence to breaking point. 'Obviously, I can't say too much. But I was over in Belfast the other day. I met some interesting people.'

'*Belfast*,' Robyn murmured.

Richard flicked him a glance. 'They're aware of what's happening here. The protests. The new mood since Saunders's lecture.'

'And?' said Meurig.

'They're proposing stronger links. If we're interested.'

'Links with who?' Jenny asked.

'Who do you think, Jenny?' said Richard.

She did not answer.

Robyn said: 'The IRA. Yes?'

'You said that, not me.'

Maggi stared down at her lap. Robyn gave Richard a long, inscrutable look. Meurig raised his clenched fists above his head, a gesture of triumph.

Selwyn said quietly: 'We've had violence already. The bomb at Tryweryn.'

'Chicken-feed,' Richard said.

The doorbell rang.

'Discussion suspended,' he added thinly.

22

'ALRIGHT,' SAID NIGEL Allan. 'We'll go there. Today.'

His children, Robert and Joanne, looked at him disbelievingly, then at each other.

'Do you mean it, Dad?' Rob asked, wide-eyed.

'Of course. Have I ever said things I don't mean?'

'Oh, Dad – *thanks*,' the boy breathed. As the news sank in, sheer joy transformed him into a dervish of delight. 'We're going to Ocean Park!' he yelled, racing around the room. 'We're going to Ocean Park! Mum…' as she came in with a vase of flowers newly picked from the garden – 'we're going to Ocean Park! Dad says so,' he added defiantly, as the news seemed not to register.

Annette, sweeping past him, coolly put the vase on a bookcase near the window and fussed over the flowers, rearranging them slightly. Rob, nonplussed, stared at her while Joanne glanced uneasily at her father, who, having announced his decision over the pages of the Saturday edition of the *Western Mail*, now retreated behind the paper again.

'Tell her, Dad,' Rob pleaded. 'We're going there, aren't we?'

The pages trembled slightly. 'Yes – if your mother agrees.'

'There you are! It's alright, Mum, isn't it?'

Annette edged a petal back into exactly the same position that it had been in a few seconds before. 'Your father can take you if you like – but I'm not coming.'

'Oh, Mum,' cried Rob, dismayed. 'You've *got* to.'

'I can't, darling – I've got things to do. Your father knows that.'

'That's not fair! We always all go together.'

'Yes, but only when we all know what's happening. This is the first I've heard of it. And you know what I think of that place – and what your father thinks too. It seems he's changed his mind without telling me.'

Nigel looked at her. 'I just thought it time – to put all that behind us,' he said sullenly.

'What, your uncle in a wheelchair? Doesn't mean anything now, does it? The funfair's suddenly a safe place for kids?'

'It is, Mum, it is. Everybody goes there – nothing bad happens!' protested Rob wildly.

'Well, you three go – I'm not stopping you. I hope you have a jolly nice time.'

She went upstairs, head whirling, and sat on the double bed she shared with Nigel, the husband whose behaviour had suddenly gone haywire. This was the latest example of a thoughtlessness that was totally out of character. The steady, even boring, lawyer had developed a disturbing contrariness in his opinions and uncertainty in his habits. He was 'delayed at the office' or had 'last-minute appointments' and his moods were unpredictable. He was snappy with the kids – and with her – though making up quickly, or trying to, and there was something in his eyes – a coolness, even cynicism – that chilled her. And now this! What was wrong with the man? Was it the onset of the male menopause the papers were full of these days? Or was it something more menacing – in which the male menopause might indeed play a part? The love poem in Welsh he had marked out – the poem her friend Rachael had translated for her – tormented her anew. Was she reading too much into it? Taken alone, it was nothing. But in association with other things, it assumed great significance. Was Nigel *really* having an affair? If so, who with – and why?

Looking out of the window, seeing only her lurid imaginings, Annette plunged deep into confusion and misery. Having her former lover back in town was bad enough. This was ten times worse.

A tap on the door. 'Mum?'

'Come in, darling.'

She smiled at her daughter, standing just inside the door, eyes troubled, face unusually pale beneath the freckles.

'I just want to say – I'm not going.'

'Why not?'

'I don't want to.'

'Come here, pet.'

The short distance between door and bed seemed to Annette to encompass not only space but time. In traversing it, she felt Joanne move from one stage of life to another. She put her arm around her lightly.

'Now,' she said, keeping her voice as light as her touch, 'what's all this?'

'You know what. It's Dad.'

'What about him?'

'He's not the same any more.'

This isn't happening, Annette thought. *It doesn't happen to people like us.* 'I expect it's his work,' she said. 'He's been under a lot of pressure lately.'

Lies. Why was she doing this? To protect him – or herself?

'I don't like him… going against you.'

'It happens sometimes. Parents don't always agree, you know.'

'It's not just that.'

Annette gave her a squeeze. 'We're OK, darling. There's nothing to worry about.'

Annette felt her daughter's misery like a stone against her side. She kissed the top of her head.

'Why don't you have a nice day out with them? You'll enjoy yourself – I know you will.'

'I'm not going, Mum. I'm staying with you.'

I ought to make an effort. I should force myself to go to Ocean Park. I've always thought that outright ban on the place ridiculous. It's a good thing to get out of the way, surely?

But she knew this wasn't the point. It was the way he'd swept it aside – without even consulting her! *That* was the point.

Nigel loomed in the doorway. 'Are you coming then, Joanne?'

She shook her head.

He gave his wife a look. 'Persuaded her, have you?'

'It's nothing to do with me. I'm not stopping her.'

'Not much.'

'*Please,* Nigel,' Annette said wearily.

Nigel fiddled with his lapel, as if assailed by sudden doubt. 'It would be nice – if we all went together.'

'I can't. I've got things to do.'

'H'm.' He braced himself. 'Well – I'll see you later.'

If he gives us a kiss, Annette thought, *it won't be so bad.*

He simply turned and went.

Heulwen Price looked across at her friend with narrowed eyes. *You've changed,* she thought. *You're not the person you were.* Jenny Briggs, unaware of this scrutiny, chomped an apple as she read a magazine. She was sitting on the divan, while Heulwen, her face half in shadow, occupied the high-backed armchair by the tall sash window on the opposite side of the room. The two young women could not have been further apart, given the dimensions of this upstairs flat, and an astute observer might have seen some significance in this, noting also that Jenny was far more at ease than Heulwen, whose edginess contrasted with her friend's composure.

Jenny turned a page. The movement, slight as it was, seemed to ignite a spark in Heulwen.

'Are you seeing him tonight then?' she asked spikily.

'Who?' murmured Jenny, still reading.

'What's-'is-face – Nigel.'

Jenny looked up. 'No. As a matter of fact I'm not.'

'Nah,' Heulwen said sarcastically. 'Too awkward I suppose. It being Saturday and all that.'

'Meaning what?' asked Jenny coolly.

'Well, family day, isn't it? Spending it with the wife and kids, I suppose. Got to find some time for them, hasn't he?'

Jenny gave her a long look. 'What's up with you then? Not jealous, are you?'

'*Jealous*? You've got to be joking.'

'It sounds precious like it.'

'You can shag the arse off who you like. It doesn't bother me.'

'For fuck's sake, Heul. What is it to you?'

'Nothing. I told you. Only – does Meurig know about it?'

'*Meurig*?' Her expression changed rapidly – first to wonderment, then amusement. 'Christ. So that's it, is it?'

'Said something funny, have I?'

'Yes. You have. Jesus. *Meurig*,' she spluttered.

'Glad I make you laugh.' Furious, Heulwen sprang to her feet. 'Watch you don't choke on that apple, that's all.'

'Don't go – please!' She too sprang up.

'I've got better things to do than – '

'He's queer, Heul – don't you see?' Jenny interrupted.

'What?'

'He's a homo, girl – didn't you know?'

'Never! Don't be stupid!'

'I thought you knew. It's written all over him. Oh, Heulwen. I'm sorry.'

'Geroff.' She shrugged off her friend's sympathetic touch. 'You're a bitch, you know that? You've changed. Utterly and completely.'

The door slammed. Jenny stared at it, dazed.

'Christ,' she said. 'Jesus bloody Christ.'

23

THE LETTER ARRIVED by first post on Monday. Steve gave the envelope a cursory glance before putting it aside for Jocelyn. He never opened her letters, nor she his: it was an unwritten rule of their marriage that they respected each other's privacy. He was going up to Dolgellau to interview a shepherd with an interesting background: one-time Congregational minister who'd discovered he was much more successful at tending woolly sheep than a human flock. There'd been something about him in one of the weeklies Steve scanned for stories to follow up. He'd been struck by a picture of the man, whose craggy features resembled those of R. S. Thomas, the poet-priest whose work Steve admired. A phone call had confirmed that the shepherd would be quotable enough for the piece to stand up. It may need some creative embroidering here and there, but nothing to get worked up about. As he checked the oil and water levels in his car, Steve whistled softly and contentedly. Things were working out far better than he had imagined.

He had thought Jocelyn would be back before he left – she was running Simon to school in her car – then remembered that she had told him she would be doing a bit of shopping on the way home. He left a note on the table: *Jos – Had to leave. See you later. Love, Steve.* He added a line, *Letter for you*, then wondered why he had done so. It was plain enough to see, lying on top of all the others.

Later, he would see it as a kind of omen.

'Haven't you finished sorting them out yet? *Arglwydd*! I gave you this job last Friday. You should have finished it by now, easy.' Emyr John, moon face pink with surprise, looked despairingly at his assistant.

Meurig Owen summoned up an expression of injured innocence. 'I didn't want to rush it, Mr John. I wanted to make a good job of it.'

'Yes, well... that's all very well but...' Emyr chuntered uncertainly, never quite sure where he stood with this young man. 'I've got other things for you to do. Get it finished in the next half hour, if you please.'

'*Iawn.*' Meurig, suppressing a smile, turned back to the task he was deliberately spinning out. The titles of the books spread on the upper floor of Holloway Books looked as dispiriting as ever: *A Pageant of Princes... Born to be Kings.* Jesus! If he had his way, he'd throw the lot into the sea. What kind of a people were the Welsh, to put up with this humiliation for centuries? To be ruled by the English was bad enough, but to have the eldest sons of their beastly royal house bearing the title Prince of Wales was truly dreadful. What made it ten times worse was the fact that some of this garbage was even written by Welshmen. Quislings every one, thought Meurig scornfully, picking up a couple of copies at random and putting them on a shelf. Well, the quicker he got on with it the better. His mood lightened with the discovery of unexpected gems – tales of the native Welsh princes who had governed the so-called 'Principality' before the Anglo-Norman usurpers took control, and a stirring biography of Llewelyn, last of the royal house of Gwynedd, whose murder in 1282 had inflicted the misery of conquest on the entire nation. Preoccupied with the challenge of giving such works maximum prominence without incurring Emyr's wrath,

Meurig failed at first to notice the arrival in that section of the shop of a man roughly the same age as himself, trendily clad in a black leather bomber jacket. The creaking of a floorboard made Meurig turn his head. The man glanced at him and smiled. Meurig's heart lurched. It was the stranger who had sat opposite him in the dentist's.

'Tooth better now?' the man asked.

'Yes, thanks,' Meurig replied. 'And yours?'

'Right as rain – now it's out.'

'Like that, is it?'

''Fraid so. What's this lot then?'

Load of shit, Meurig wanted to reply. 'Some histories of Wales,' he said instead, with an intonation which the man might or might not spot as ironic.

'Princes of Wales... extraordinary.'

'Why so?'

'Didn't think so much could be said about them. Pretty ropey lot on the whole, weren't they?'

'That's a nice way of putting it.'

'Too nice. Lot of bastards, I'd say. Correct?'

'Don't let Mr John hear you say that. He wants to make some money out of them.'

'By selling these books?'

'Of course.'

'Well, good luck to him.'

Meurig put another book on the shelf. He could not have named the title or the author. All he was conscious of was the presence of the stranger. He felt stifled, even suffocated, yet at the same time exhilarated. What stirred Meurig to the depths was what he could only have expressed as the *darkness* of him – his hair, his moustache, and something indefinable. He stood beside Meurig, unmoving, as if waiting for a response from the younger man. At last Meurig gave him a glance. The man's eyes, he observed with surprise, were not dark at all but blue – an odd, glittering blue, like something chemical and dangerous. The man smiled. 'My name's Brett,' he said. 'What's yours?'

'Meurig.'

'Care to meet later – for a drink?'

'OK.'

'See you in The Ship then. Know where that is?'

Meurig nodded.

'Eight o'clock.'

Meurig tried to say 'Right' but the word stuck in his throat. The stranger strolled comfortably away. Meurig's heartbeat slowly subsided.

24

Dear Mrs Lewis

I don't know you and you don't know me. But you aught to know that your husband was the father of a baby girl who died in infancy. The mother is Annette Allan whose married to a toffee-nosed lawyer in Glanaber. Ask him about it.

Yours truly,
A WELL WISHER

AFTERWARDS, JOCELYN COULDN'T remember how many times she read this before moving. The words had a deep-freeze effect, fixing her in immobility. A voice inside her said, *nothing will be the same again, nothing*. The words repeated themselves with the rhythm of a train, the second *nothing* being preceded by two bumps as if the train were crossing points. When at last she moved she went to the bathroom and retched.

It was a pale day, the washy light giving everything the appearance of a watercolour. Her footsteps too were muted as she walked from car to school gate to await Simon coming out. She talked easily to the other mothers and marvelled at the way she sounded so normal. Simon talked about the project they were doing on the history of the castle and she made all the right noises in return. *Annette Allan* she kept thinking. *Baby girl. Your husband.*

He arrived home just after six, full of life and bonhomie. The shepherd had been a gift, so eloquent that his words wouldn't need much embroidering after all. He'd revealed a mischievous sense of humour, too. The tales he'd come out with about his former life as a chapel minister! 'Randy isn't the word for some of those chapel women, boy. The more respectable they look, the better they like it.'

'Why'd you give it up then?' Steve had asked. 'Sounds the perfect life to me.'

'Couldn't stand the pace. Sheep are much more restful.'

Steve quoted some of this back to Jocelyn, who let him babble away, swollen with success. It was only when Simon was in bed that she said quietly, 'Who's Annette Allan, Steve?'

By then he was lounging around, half-looking at a TV sit-com. He seemed, at first, not to hear her. Canned laughter burst from the set, metallic, meretricious.

'Annette Allan,' she repeated. 'Who is she?'

'Why do you want to know?'

'Because I've had this.' She handed him the envelope.

'H'm,' he said, taking it. His face was impassive.

'I think I know who wrote this,' he said, after reading the letter.

'Never mind who wrote it. Is it true?'

'Yes. I'm afraid it is.'

'I see.'

She put her tatting aside and left the room.

He stayed where he was, tapping the edge of the letter against the arm of his chair. The sit-com came to an end.

He went upstairs. She was sitting on the edge of the bed, staring out of the window. He closed the bedroom door.

He stood awkwardly by the chest of drawers, fiddling with the trinkets on top.

'I meant to tell you,' he said. 'I'm sorry I didn't.'

'So am I.'

'It was a long time ago. Before I met you.'

'What's she like?'

He shrugged. 'Tallish. Gingery hair. What's it matter?'

'What's it *matter*?' She turned and looked at him. 'Jesus, Steve. What kind of a world are you living in?'

He flushed. 'The real world, I hope. This is all in the past. It doesn't mean a thing now.'

'Yes it does. Of course it does. I'm not stupid.'

Steve said hotly: 'It's just mischief-making, that letter. I tell you, I know who wrote it. She could never spell properly. "Ought" with an "a", for God's sake!'

'I don't care who wrote it. It could be written by King Kong for all I care! But you'd have said nothing about this – would you? You wouldn't have uttered a word.'

'I didn't want to hurt you.'

'Hurt me! Don't make me laugh.'

He made to move but she said quickly, 'Sit down. We've got to sort this thing out.'

'There's nothing...'

'Shut up.'

He sat on the opposite side of the bed to her.

'It's why you came back here, isn't it? To be near her. And the baby.'

'The baby's dead,' he said bitterly.

'Yes. But *she* isn't. God. What a fool I've been.'

'No. I'm the fool. Not telling you.'

'Was she married when...?'

'God, no. We were *going* to get married.'

She let this sink in. 'So you got me on the rebound?'

'Not really.'

'No,' she said drily. 'I suppose there were others. In between.'

They sat in silence. It had to happen, he told himself.

Sooner or later, it was bound to come out. It was a disaster. It could mean the end of their marriage. But, for all that, he felt a strange lightness of spirit. He felt as though a burden had been lifted from him.

The silence continued. In the next room Simon slept on, oblivious to the drama. It seemed strange that something did not permeate the walls to awaken him, a blast from a psychic laser gun, anything. Something in the wallpaper caught his eye for the first time, a mismatch in the design caused by the way one roll had been wrongly aligned with another by whoever had decorated the room. It would have to come down anyway: he much preferred bare walls, and so did Jos.

'Have you been seeing her – behind my back?' Jos asked, her voice pitched higher than usual, sounding uncannily like Annette's.

'Good God no – what makes you think that?'

'I wouldn't put it past you – you've had your affairs, haven't you?'

'You know I have.'

'Just one or two. That's what you said. Par for the course. Part of the job, weren't they?'

'Don't let's go over all that again,' he said wearily. 'It's all over.'

'Is it now? How nice.'

Steve's back was beginning to ache. He wanted to move but could not.

'Who do you think wrote this letter then?'

'Shirley.'

'Who's she when she's at home?'

'Local girl. Married to an ironmonger.'

'Know her pretty well, don't you?' said Jocelyn sarcastically. 'Spotting a tiny spelling error?'

234

'That's just a coincidence. I remember reading a note she wrote, years ago. She was sharing a flat with Annette. We were all together – a kind of gang.'

'Fancied you, did she?'

'Christ, no.'

'So why does she bother to…'

'Search me,' Steve said angrily. 'I don't bloody know. Anyway, can't we just drop it? It's all in the past. I'm married to you, aren't I?'

She said nothing. He flung himself off the bed, went downstairs to the kitchen.

He was drinking coffee in the living-room when she came down to join him.

She picked up the letter and tore it up slowly. 'There,' she said. 'Satisfied?'

A coldness, as from the grave, overwhelmed him. He knew his life had irrevocably changed.

25

'So you're sure of it now,' said Rachael Miles.

'Yes. Positive,' Annette replied.

'What makes you so certain?'

'The way he's changed. He won't look me in the eye any more. And the lies he tells.'

'About what?'

'Working late. He never used to. It's once or twice a week now. Mysterious appointments.'

Rachael tapped ash from cigarette. She looked coolly across the room at her friend, whose troubled eyes stared unseeingly out of the window.

'H'm… I'm almost sorry I translated that poem for you now.'

'Why?'

'It's only fired your suspicions.'

'You think I'm talking rubbish?'

'I don't know. All I know is – if Nigel *is* having an affair, it won't last long.'

'That's a comfort, I must say!'

Annette, agitated, scrabbled in her handbag.

'Here, have one of these,' Rachael offered.

'No, I can't smoke those. They make me ill.' She lit a Benson and Hedges nervously.

'You may be quite wrong you know. Have you tackled him about it?'

Annette shook her head. 'I wouldn't demean myself.'

'*Demean* yourself,' said Rachael softly. 'That's a funny word to use… Are you sure there isn't another reason?'

'What?'

'You could easily find out if you wanted to. You could have a word with those girls in his office for a start. They probably know him much better than you do.'

'Oh, thank you.'

'They'd certainly know what he gets up to in the office. If he's having secret calls or assignations or whatever.'

'They'd cover up for him.'

'No they wouldn't. You know they wouldn't.'

'I'm not sure I want to know,' Annette said, breaking the silence. 'If he wants to be like that...'

'The same as you are with Steve Lewis,' said Rachael slowly. 'That it?'

Annette stared, disbelieving. 'You bitch.'

Rachael smiled, not with humour. 'I'm sorry, darling.'

'I can't believe you said that.'

'Perhaps I didn't. It may be all in your mind – like everything else.'

'I wish it was. Do you really think...?'

'I don't think anything. I'm just wondering.'

'I haven't spoken two words to him.'

'Have you seen him?'

'Only in the street. Christ, Rachael, what do you think I am? I didn't ask him to come back here. I wish he hadn't. It's the last thing I wanted.'

'I'm sure it was, darling.'

'So why did you say that? You think I'm a slut, do you?' Weirdly, she recalled saying exactly the same words to her mother as a teenager.

'No, of course I don't. You're not a slut. You're a perfectly decent married woman. But you're in an impossible position. And it's not your fault. Not in the least. It's *his* fault – Steve's. He should never have come back here.'

'All very well saying that,' Annette said, tight-lipped.

'I know that. It's easy to say. The point is, how do we make sense of it all?'

What amazed Nigel Allan, in the early days of his affair with Jenny Briggs, is that he felt little sense of remorse. In his pre-Jenny years, an epoch that now seemed impossibly distant, he had imagined that if he ever *did* stray, he would be ravaged by remorse. But after making love to her that very first time, he had gone home feeling free, light-headed, absolved from the necessity of being anything but happy, ridiculously happy. He actually found himself framing the words in his mind, '*I feel happy*', convinced that what had passed for happiness before was but a pale shadow of what he was feeling now. He felt no alienation from Annette and the children, only a sense of gratitude for the part they were playing in the present scheme of things. He felt capable of doing anything, however wild and impractical, because whatever he did would be a celebration of the revolution in his life. It was this sense of liberation from all that had gone before that had enabled him to throw off his inhibitions about funfairs. Ocean Park! What was Ocean Park? Something to be experienced with his children – or with one of them anyway – not a symbol of lethal risk and ugly exploitation.

Yet he knew the effect he was having on others. He saw the puzzlement on Rob's face, the pinched look around Joanne's eyes, and suffered Annette's slow withdrawal from the easy intimacy they had established over eleven years of marriage. In bed, she turned her back on him, and he stared up at the ceiling, defiantly thinking of Jenny. He simply did not care. Nothing could touch him.

At work, things were fine. The firm was attracting more clients than ever, and soon Stella would be back to shoulder some of the burden. But those odious girls, Glenys and Delyth – the way they looked at him – it was intolerable! What right did they have to judge him? It was absolutely none of their business. Yet in all sorts of ways they contrived to convey their disapproval of his relationship with Jenny Briggs. It was in their tone of voice, their coldly formal manner, their meaningful glances at one another. '*We know what's going on,*' all this told him, '*and we don't like it one little bit.*' On the odd occasions that Annette dropped into the office, they were all over her – they just couldn't do enough to please her! It was amazing that she did not latch on… or did she? She certainly knew *something* was going on: that was obvious. But she said not a word. She spoke only through her actions and demeanour. Annette was nothing if not subtle.

26

JOCELYN TRIED TO pretend it didn't matter. If he'd had sex with a girl long before he'd met her, so what? It was only natural, wasn't it? And it should mean far less to her than the more recent affairs she suspected him of having, the ones that seemed to go with the job in the hurly-burly of Fleet Street. Yet, strangely, that far-distant romance *did* seem more important. Miles more important. Because there'd been a baby. Because he'd never hinted at it. And, most of all, because he'd had the nerve – the brass-necked nerve – to bring her *here,* of all places – where it had happened! How dare he? The very thought of it made her feel hot – with anger, certainly, but with other things too. Hot with shame. Yes, shame! Shame for him, and for herself. That he thought so little of her as to do that. As if it meant nothing! And it would never have come out, were it not for that ill-typed letter with the stupid spelling mistake – 'aught' for 'ought'. She didn't care who had written it, though she was mystified as to that person's motives. What she *did* care about was the mother of the baby. Who was she, this Annette? What was she like? Why had she dumped Steve after he'd gone to live in London? For he had told her all this, all the basic facts relating to the baby. She knew Annette was married to a solicitor – but what did this woman mean to Steve now? She must mean something, for why else had he chosen to come back here, of all places? When he knew that she, Jocelyn, hated Glanaber? Oh, he'd been so devious about it, so cunning, so scheming! Never once had he given a hint of his reasons! All the chances he'd had to put her in the picture, and not a word had he spoken, not a look had he given her, never once had he revealed a fraction of the truth of the matter. Oh, it was unfair, so desperately unfair, after she'd given her all for his sake, sacrificed everything for his career and his happiness. She wanted to cry, to spit, to swear, to catch the next train back to London.

And suddenly, out of nowhere, a figure from her own past came to mind – Jack Palmer, secretary of the tennis club they'd belonged to in Putney. She saw him plainly – tall, relaxed, ambiguously smiling – just as he'd been the time he'd called on her unexpectedly when Steve was away. He fancied her – he really fancied her – she knew it. And did she fancy him? Of course she did. Just a little. Any woman would – he was an attractive man. Pity she *hadn't* gone to that tennis club meeting on her own. Steve need never have known. It might have led to something. Who knows? A little adventure – possibly… Impatiently, she cast these idle speculations aside. What on earth was she thinking of? *She'd* never be tempted, she was quite certain of that. Not seriously, anyway. And she'd adapted very well to life in Glanaber, far better than she'd ever imagined. Until now! Until this stupid, squalid glimpse into the past. Now, everything was up in the air. She felt betrayed, lied to, used, miserable. All because of a dead child and an old love affair.

Put like this, it seemed absurd. Why was she taking on so? Why let the past ruin the present? Because – for her – the past *was* the present. It was newly discovered. A body blow. Something that whipped the ground from under her feet.

So she was cold to Steve, abrupt with Simon, no more in tune with anything. In bed she was an ice block, turning her back on a husband she felt she no longer knew. And she felt a strange urge, growing stronger every day, to meet the woman through whom he had fathered a baby... a daughter who, if she had lived, would today be half-sister to Simon.

Jos, in her misery, felt she had mysteriously become part of an extended family, in some ways a *junior* part, because Steve had known Annette, in every sense of the word, long before he had known her. She felt humiliated, inadequate. She *must* regain her dignity. But the only way of doing this was to get to know this other woman, Annette. Only then could she look herself in the face again.

'For God's sake!' exploded Ivor. 'Can't you do anything right, woman?'

'Don't call me woman,' said Shirley sullenly.

'Why not? That's what you are, init?'

'It doesn't sound right. It makes me sound like... a thing.'

'Well, what d'you expect? You've got these things the wrong way round again. I told you, put the paintbrushes *here*.'

'Oh, bugger off! Do it your bloody self.'

'I've got to, haven't I? If you keep making a cock-up of it.'

Ivor snorted and huffed a bit more, then subsided. After a while he shot his wife an uneasy glance. To his surprise, he caught Shirley brushing away a tear. 'What's up then?' he murmured.

'Bugger all.'

'Didn't mean to shout at you,' he fidgeted. 'It's just that...'

'Oh, for Christ's sake.' She waved it away.

'What then?'

'Him coming back here,' she managed eventually.

'Who?'

'You know who.'

He connected with an abruptness that brought a spark to his eye and an expression of wonder.

'The reporter, you mean? Lewis? But...'

'Don't! It's nothing. Forget it.'

He lapsed into thoughts not entirely pleasant.

'What's he got to do with us?' he asked.

'He's brought it all back, hasn't he? The way...'

'What?' A tinge of suspicion smeared his voice.

'Everything. The way it was then.' Out it came after an inward struggle. 'That baby. It wasn't yours, was it?'

'What?' He stared at her, astonished. 'What the fuck are you saying now?'

'Well? You were going with her, weren't you? Before...'

'Bloody hell! You think I...?'

'Can't help wondering, can I? She's such a loose bitch.'

'How long you been thinking this, Shirley?' He grabbed her by the shoulders. 'You stupid bloody bitch.'

The door pinged open. Shirley fled. Ivor, dazed, pulled himself together. The customer ambled into the shop. A stranger.

When he'd gone, Ivor locked the door and turned round the sign to say 'Closed'. Five minutes early. He stared down at his shoes, and then slowly walked to the back of the shop and upstairs to the living quarters.

The phone went on ringing so long that she wondered if she'd dialled the wrong number. What kind of an office was this? A voice inside her said *Put it down, put it down* and she almost gave way, but she knew that if she did she would never try again. It would have to be today, with Steve out on a job and her mood just right for it. She'd worked herself up to this, her gut churning and that inner voice forever insisting that it was all ridiculous, totally ridiculous. She knew nothing about this woman, nothing at all. But she had to see her. She simply had to see her.

'Richards and James, good morning,' said a woman's voice, a little husky, brisk and businesslike.

'Oh.' Jocelyn, taken by surprise momentarily after the long wait, quickly recovered. 'I wonder if I might speak to Mr Allan, please?'

She'd taken the precaution of putting a handkerchief over the mouthpiece to disguise her voice, although nobody knew it at the solicitor's.

'I'm afraid he's with a client,' said Glenys. 'Who is it calling, please?'

'Oh, don't worry – I'll call later.'

She slammed the phone down, heart thumping.

Well, she knew now that Annette's husband was at work.

Annette! She felt she almost knew her already.

They had something in common, didn't they? Steve.

Very common, said that inner voice sardonically.

27

I T WAS A grouchy sort of morning, light rain spattering the window. Annette looked out, her spirits low. She would *have* to find a job to get her out of the house. She would put an advert in the paper — it already existed in her head. *Experienced shorthand-typist seeks part-time work.* It would go in under a box number. Nobody would know it was her.

The trouble with Nigel was oppressing her. She *knew* he was having an affair, knew she would have to confront him with it. But once she did this, things would never be the same again. A line would be crossed that could never be recrossed, however long they lived. It meant she did not trust him. It meant that the very idea of a perfect marriage — or at least, an only slightly imperfect one — was dead and buried. It meant that, in her mind's eye, she had an adulterous husband, and the children a father who had betrayed their mother. It meant, in short, the end of everything that was good and wholesome.

So Annette held back, in defiance of reason. She held back even though, by so doing, she felt a fool.

Suddenly she had a sense of being observed. A woman sat in the driving seat of a car parked opposite. Their eyes met for an instant. Then the woman looked away. She seemed about to drive off, but changed her mind. She got out of the car and locked the door. Then, after a swift glance to left and right, she crossed the road.

She's coming here, thought Annette disbelievingly. And,

all at once, she knew exactly who she was. Nigel's lover – come here to confront her! How dare she? What on earth did she want to say?

The doorbell rang – a brief, peremptory summons. Annette gave herself a quick, appraising glance in the mirror, then marched to the hall. She could see the woman's outline through the frosted glass. She opened the door.

'Mrs Allan?'

'Yes?'

'I'm sorry to bother you, but – could I have a word with you for a minute?'

'What about?'

'It's something personal – could I…?'

'I don't know. Who are you?'

'I'm Jocelyn Lewis – Steve's husband.'

'Steve,' Annette repeated blankly. Then it sank in. 'Good God.'

'Please, Mrs Allan.'

Annette held the door open. She came in.

'You'd better come and sit down.'

They went into the front room.

'What's this all about?' Annette asked.

'I had a letter in the post. Telling me about your baby. I didn't know a thing about it.'

'My baby? You mean Ceri?'

'Yes. I'm sorry to intrude but – Steve should've told me. Before we came here. He didn't say a thing about it. I feel stupid.'

'Why? It's nothing to do with you, is it?'

'It's everything to do with me! Can't you see?'

'No. I'm sorry, I can't. Look, if you think Steve still *means* something… you can't mean that, do you?'

'No, I don't.'

'Then what?'

'I had this letter. That proves it, doesn't it? Everyone knows about it, don't they? In a small town like this...'

'So what? Ceri *died,* for God's sake. What are you afraid of? I don't understand.'

'No, I don't suppose you do. I don't understand myself either. To be honest.' She pressed her fingers to her eyes. 'I'm sorry.'

Annette looked at her helplessly. 'For pity's sake,' she said brokenly. She went to the kitchen, put the kettle on.

'I suppose you'd like a coffee?' she said in the doorway.

Jocelyn nodded, half-turning. 'Please.'

'This letter,' Annette said. 'Who wrote it?'

'I don't know.'

'You don't *know.* Then...'

'Steve knew. He saw a mistake in it.'

'A mistake! You mean he recognized the writing?'

'No. It was typed. It was just something trivial – an "a" instead of an "o." I know it sounds stupid. But he knew it was her – this other woman. Someone you both knew – years ago.'

'I'm sorry.' Annette was laughing. 'This all sounds so ridiculous. You come here...'

'I know. It *is* ridiculous. I know I've got a nerve – I shouldn't have done it.'

'No – no – I'm not saying that. But – I thought you were someone else.'

'Who?'

Annette's laughter was out of control. She passed the

back of her hand across her mouth, stood up, fought the mounting hysteria. 'I... I...'

'Mrs Allan!' Jocelyn cried, alarmed.

Annette flapped a hand at her, to show this was *not* something that she wanted to be called, not 'Mrs Allan', that was too... She sank on to a pouffe, weak with laughter, consumed by it.

The laughter gave way to heavy breathing, great gulps of air, then – absurdly – hiccoughs.

Jos stood over her helplessly. She touched the top of her head.

'That's alright,' Annette breathed. 'That's al- *hiccough* – right.' She took her hand, held it. Remained so, eyes shut. Then she looked up at Jocelyn. Looked steadily at her.

'So,' she said in a normal voice. 'What am I going to do about you then – eh?'

'*Do* about me?'

'Yes.' Annette stood up, brushed herself down with her hand. 'What have you really come to tell me? You're leaving your husband – is that it?'

'No. Of course not.'

'Then why come here – mm? Why poke around – mm? In a past that doesn't concern you. Dragging all this up.' She flapped her hands against her sides.

'I'm sorry. I've said I'm sorry.'

'So that makes it alright, does it? Can you imagine what it was like? They call it a *cot death* now – we'd never heard of such things. All I saw was Ceri, lying there. Ugh!' She put her hands to her head.

'I *can* imagine it. Of course I can. It must've been awful. That's why I can't understand – why he didn't tell me.'

'Steve? He's a man, girl – that's why. He doesn't give a damn.'

'But he does – that's why he didn't. Don't you see? That's why he couldn't tell me.'

'So?'

'It came as a shock. I didn't know you existed. You were going to be married, weren't you? Then you called it off.'

Annette made a gesture. 'What's it matter. What the hell does it matter?'

'It doesn't. It doesn't matter a damn.'

Annette looked at her. 'Sit down – what did you say your name was?'

'Jocelyn.'

'Jocelyn,' repeated Annette, trying the name out for size. 'Does he call you that?'

'No. Jos.'

'Mm. Right. Well, let's calm down a bit. Do you want another coffee?'

'No. I haven't drunk this yet.'

'Neither have I. What a pair, eh?' She took a deep mouthful.

'Who did you think I was?'

'What?'

'You said you thought I was someone else.'

'Oh, that. Yes. You… you'll never believe me, I thought you were my husband's lover.'

'You're – my God.'

'Yes. Stupid, isn't it? Where is he now – Steve?'

'I don't know. Out on a job somewhere.'

Annette emitted a brief half-laugh. 'Always the same. Probably with some woman.'

'I wouldn't be at all surprised.'

They were silent.

'How do you like it here?' Annette asked.

'Better than I thought I would.'

'They all say that. Don't want to come here, but then they don't want to go away.'

'I don't know about that.'

Annette looked at her queryingly.

'I'm not sure I should stay,' Jocelyn said.

'Why not? Not because of *this*, surely?'

'Not entirely.'

'But that's ridiculous.'

'Is it?'

'You've got a family, haven't you?'

'I've got a son, yes.'

'Well then. He's your life, isn't he? You can't give it up just because…'

'It's not *just*. There's other things.' Annette waited. 'I'm not sure I love him any more,' Jocelyn added.

'Oh.'

'So we're both in a pickle,' Annette said.

'Looks like it.' Jocelyn's gaze wandered over the framed family photos around the room.

'Must've been Shirley,' Annette said suddenly. 'She's the only one who'd… You know her?'

'I don't know anyone called Shirley.'

'Silly girl. I wonder why.'

'I'd best be going,' Jocelyn said abruptly.

'No… not yet…'

'I have to. I've got to meet Simon.'

'Of course. How old is he?'

'Nine.'

'Nice.'

They faced one another.

'I can't believe I've done this,' Jos said. 'But now...'

'I'm glad too. Really.'

They smiled briefly.

Annette stood in the front doorway as Jos drove away. They fluttered their fingers at each other.

28

T HE SHIP WAS a once-ramshackle pub lately spruced up
to get in tune with the Sixties. Ancient photographs
of the nearby harbour towering with masts of brig, barque
and schooner had given way to posters of rock bands, and a
newly installed jukebox blared out the Beatles and Rolling
Stones. The new landlord, Phil Battersley, contentedly
surveyed his mixed clientele of students – who now put the
pub high on their list of watering holes – and reluctant locals,
whose threats to boycott the place in protest had quickly
been crushed by the sheer weight of habit. Phil, fortyish,
shirt sleeved, knew he was on to a good thing and happily
pocketed the takings.

Few took any notice of the couple sitting at a corner table.
Meurig had on a leather bomber jacket and jeans, Brett a
sports jacket and open-neck shirt. Meurig was downing a pint
of the local brew – Roberts's dark – while Brett had a Scotch
and soda.

'So,' Brett said, 'how goes the job then?'

'So–so.'

'Get all those books on the royals sorted out yet?'

Meurig shot him a glance. 'I'd burn the buggers if I had
my way.'

'Now now. Mr John wouldn't like that.'

'I don't suppose he would. Know him, do you?'

'After a fashion. Good shop though, you must admit.'

'Could be a lot better.' Meurig took out a packet of Senior
Service. 'Like one?'

Brett shook his head. 'Thanks, but I've given them up.'

Meurig lit up, took a deep drag. He looked at Brett reflectively.

'How long you been working there, Meurig?'

'Too long.'

'Could be doing something else, I suppose.'

'Could I?'

'We all could,' Brett said.

'What do *you* do then?'

'Me? I'm a rep.'

'Commercial traveller, you mean.'

'No. I said rep and I meant it.'

'What's the difference?'

'Wouldn't like to be called a flunky, would you?'

Meurig frowned. 'What d'you mean, flunky?'

'You know what a flunky is, don't you?'

'Course I do. I'm not thick.'

'I know that, boy. Coleg Harlech, aren't you?'

'How d'you know *that*?'

Brett smiled thinly, sipped his Scotch.

'I'm no bloody flunky, mate.'

'I know that, don't worry.'

'You know too bloody much, seems to me.' Meurig's eyes were dark, troubled. 'Why'd you ask me out here, anyway?'

'Come on,' Brett said softly. 'Don't have to ask me that, do you?'

'I don't know. If you're a copper...'

Brett smiled. 'You really think that?'

'I don't know. I...'

Feeling Brett's hand on his thigh, he stopped abruptly.

'You're no flunky,' Brett said seductively. 'And I'm no copper.'

Meurig shifted position and looked around him. Nobody was taking the slightest notice.

'Just don't do that,' he said.

'OK then.'

'Not fucking here.'

'Point taken.'

They were alone in the house. Simon was out having tea at a friend's house – he was settling in nicely, after a few weeks of threatening to run away back to London. She'd been on her own for a while and then Steve had come bustling in, full of himself and the people he'd met, the quotes he'd got, how the Chief would be over the moon, he'd actually said that, *over the moon*, and now he'd settled down, reading the papers. And she felt different. Entirely different.

She'd never thought she'd actually *do* it, but she had. She'd actually gone to the house of a complete stranger, knocked the door, confronted her with her own past. Because she had to. She couldn't go on unless she'd done it.

And Annette was in her life now. And so was her dead baby. And she'd discovered a thing or two about herself as well. That she was thinking of leaving Steve. She hadn't known that before.

But was she?

She looked across at him, sitting there reading the papers. Oblivious of her. And her thoughts. Oblivious of everyone but himself.

But he'd always been like that. Hadn't he?

So what was different about now?

The fact that he'd hidden it from her. The most important thing in his life.

The baby he'd fathered. His first love. Annette.

His real reason for coming back to Glanaber. She was sure of it now.

He looked up. 'You're quiet.'

'I've got nothing to say.'

'Oh. Not like you,' he said lightly. But didn't mean it. 'Been anywhere today?'

'Bit of shopping. Nowhere special.'

He shifted uncomfortably. 'You need something to do. Why not write to the education people?'

'What for?'

'They may have something to offer you, part-time.'

'You know that's not on. You can't teach here if you don't speak Welsh.'

'You don't know that for certain. You're only surmising.'

'You've said so yourself. You've told me how wrong it is, keeping good people out, all that.'

'Yes, but I don't *know*. About teaching part-time. There may be exceptions.'

'For me,' she said sarcastically.

'For anyone. Not just you. What the hell's wrong with you, Jos? Why so niggly?'

'I'm not niggly.'

'You certainly sound it.'

He tried to get back to his reading. 'What time do we meet Simon?'

'We don't. They're bringing him back.'

'Oh. That's good of them, isn't it?' he said cheerfully.

She said nothing.

'Good he's making new friends, isn't it?'

'Yes, it is.'

Annette's words came back to her – 'What a pair, eh?'

She left the room suddenly, and went upstairs.

Steve rustled his paper unhappily.

They had sex in Meurig's bedsit, and talked a lot after. Brett was lean, firm-bodied, experienced. He hurt Meurig in just the right way.

Meurig was grateful but not ecstatic. He was guarded about Brett. There was something about him but Meurig was not quite sure what.

Meurig's bedsit was in the basement of a house in the Buarth, an elevated part of town. From the street above there were glimpses of hills and sea, but the only view from the basement window was of a stone wall two yards away. This suited Meurig, who liked to keep well out of sight. He had his own door to the bedsit, at the foot of the flight of battered steps tumbling down from the street.

The room where they sat – the only other was a squashed-in scullery, for he shared a bathroom with the tenant of the flat above – was tidily kept. There was a scattering of books on a shelf and a few leftover paintings from a previous occupancy. A TV past its best squatted on a bamboo table, more care and attention being obviously given to a newish record player and its attendant cabinet of EPs and LPs. The voice of Dafydd Iwan filled the room – strong, macho, and vibrantly patriotic. Brett listened coolly, foot tapping in time with the beat.

The song ended. 'Well,' Brett said, smiling. 'Any more like that?'

'Plenty. You like him?'

'He's OK.'

'Only OK?'

'Bit too crude for my taste. I like something a bit more… subtle.'

'Oh yes? Like what?'

Brett shrugged. 'Ella Fitzgerald maybe – Sarah Vaughan…'

'American,' jeered Meurig.

'Nothing wrong with that, is there?' Brett's smile was smooth, placatory.

Meurig took the record off the turntable, not answering. Brett had a sense of someone not sure of himself.

'What're you giving us next?' he asked quietly.

'Can't tell you. Haven't got any Ella Fitz*gerald* or Doris *Day*,' Meurig said, with jokey emphasis.

'Thank God for that. Don't want to plumb the depths, do we?'

'I wasn't sure. Thought you might…' Meurig slumped on to a black vinyl settee, its back scarred and bruised. He began rolling a cigarette.

'For Christ's sake, love,' Brett said easily. 'What do you take me for?'

'Nothing. Don't know you much, do I?'

'You know *something*.'

'Are you English, Welsh, what?'

'Does it matter?'

'Course it fucking matters. For fuck's sake.'

'I'm Welsh, like you.'

'Like me? Don't think so, *brawd*.'

'Why not?'

'You're middle-class. It's obvious.'

'What are you then?'

'Working class of course. I'm from Ponty.'

'So am I. Well, Cilfynydd anyway.'

'*You're* from Cil?' Meurig scoffed.

'Do you object?'

'Don't believe you, that's all.'

'Why not?'

'I know plenty from Cil. You're not…'

'Don't know everyone though, do you? You know enough, mind.' He gave Meurig a look.

Meurig gave him a look back.

'Where you living now then?'

'London.'

'What part?'

'Tooting Bec.'

'Silly bloody name,' Meurig sneered.

'Only a name. So it's OK then, is it?' Brett added.

'What?'

'You and me.'

Meurig made an O of his mouth and exhaled slowly. A smoke ring, perfectly formed, floated slowly up to the ceiling.

'One thing,' he said. 'Why me?'

'Obvious, isn't it?'

Meurig shook his head.

'Same interests, haven't we?' Brett said.

'What way?'

'Well… Welsh princes. Real ones.'

'How did you know?' Meurig asked, screwing his eyes up.

'Richard Ellis.'

'You know Richard?'

Brett nodded.

29

E VER SINCE SHE'D done it, Shirley had felt a sense of excitement. She remembered every detail – typing out the letter in Ivor's office when he was asleep, putting it in the envelope, addressing it, then posting it – that most of all. She had hesitated before pushing it into the pillar box – it was something so final, so dangerous – like getting married! Only that was so long ago, she couldn't remember *what* her feelings had been like then. But now...

She had gone back home, face flushed – it was evening. Ivor was still sitting there reading the paper, Conrad doing his homework, Josie up in her room with her friend Wendy. Nobody said a word. Ivor hadn't even noticed she'd gone out. How could they not see she was different – that she's done something terrible?

'Cleared up now,' she said defiantly.

'Mm?' Ivor grunted.

'It's stopped raining. They said it would.'

It was as if she hadn't spoken.

Well, bugger the lot of you, she thought.

The excitement was like something hot inside her, a tingling sensation. She felt years younger, separate from them all! It was the first time she'd done anything bad for years, so it was time, wasn't it? But after a few days, she felt worried...

She imagined the woman reading the letter. Would she say anything to Steve? She was bound to, surely! And then what? He deserved it, whatever happened! But did *she*? She didn't know anything about her.

Would she take the letter to the police? Would they go looking for fingerprints?

But what if they did? They didn't know hers from Adam's! And anyway, so what? She wouldn't mind being arrested – it'd be something different. Because she was fed up with everything – the shop, the kids, Ivor, her mother grumbling and whining her way into old age – everything! Tears of self-pity stung her. But then the excitement coursed back. She'd done it – actually done it. To hell with the consequences!

He'd been seeing her again. Annette knew he had. He'd come home late, with the same weary old lies, looking like the cat who'd licked all the cream up. He'd been jovial with her and the kids, cracking jokes, tucking into his food, helping Rob with his homework – oh, he was such a good father! She waited for him to say something utterly stupid, like 'Had a good day, dear?' But he didn't. He didn't really *see* her these days.

She waited till the kids were in bed, and Nigel was nice and relaxed, watching a documentary on telly – one of those wildlife things full of snakes and hippos and tigers stalking their prey. And then, out of the blue she said, 'I had a visitor today.'

'Oh?' he said, hardly hearing her. 'Who was that then?'

'Mrs Lewis.'

'What Mrs Lewis?'

'Steve's wife.'

He looked at her. 'Steve Lewis's wife – here?'

'Yes.'

'What the hell's she doing here – did you ask her?'

'No. She just came. She's very nice. Her name's Jocelyn. They call her Jos.'

'Is this some kind of joke, Annette?'

'Joke? No. Why should it be?'

'What did she want?'

'She'd had a letter. Telling her about Ceri. It was the first she knew about it.'

'But why'd she come here?'

'To talk about it. It came as a shock. You can imagine it, can't you?'

'Who wrote this bloody letter?'

'She doesn't know,' Annette lied. 'Did you, by any chance?'

'Me? Why should I write to the woman, for God's sake? What's it got to do with me?' He was agitated, the TV forgotten, *noticing* her for the first time for days.

'Well, you might have. You were very good about Ceri, weren't you? Wonderful.' She began shaking.

'Annette! What's wrong?' He sprang to her, knelt by her chair. 'Please. *Cariad*. Don't. Don't... cry. Please.'

He took her hand. It was cold. She wanted to thrust him away but could not.

'Coming here like this... she had no right. How did she know where we live? It's disgusting...'

Annette was crying now, crying hard. It was all so unfair – Ceri – Nigel...

'You mean he hadn't *told* her? The swine. The utter swine. I can't believe it.'

He put his arm around her.

'We can't have this, Annette. We simply can't.'

He tried to kiss her. But she turned away.

She stopped crying and simply sat there, elbows on her knees.

He looked at her helplessly. Getting the message.

'I'm sorry, Annette. I'm really sorry.'

He went back to his chair. The programme ended.

Lay the ghost. The phrase kept coming back to him. He had to lay the ghost of yesterday. But how?

He knew he'd done wrong – obviously, he should have told Jos about Annette and the baby long ago. And not to have confessed before bringing her here – that was absolutely stupid! As if any secrets could be kept in a place like Glanaber. Even if you buried them in radioactive waste sixty feet below ground, they'd still emerge – there was no holding them!

But inside, he felt serene. He was *glad* that Jos knew now. It meant his past and present were united. They could put flowers on Ceri's grave – he thought Jos might be up to that, given a decent period of adjustment. She might even agree to meeting Annette and her husband – yes, why not? They could all be friends, couldn't they – a perfect foursome!

Roused to cheerfulness by his basic optimism, Steve took a stroll on the prom on a day when no one at the office was chasing him. There were plenty of days like this – he was more or less left alone. So long as he turned in decent copy for the weekly mag, nobody bothered him. How different if he'd been down in Cardiff with that coterie of news hacks, all chasing the same dreary stories, looking for that elusive fresh angle when the stories went off the boil! He thanked his lucky stars he was out of the rat race, while still earning good Fleet Street money.

It was late September, a time of year when the town was poised between two seasons. The summer visitors had gone, the students not yet returned to begin a new cycle in the life of the university. This quietude was reflected in the natural scene. There was scarcely a breath of wind. The sea, unruffled, idly lapped the gritty sand. The sun, half hidden behind high, diaphanous clouds, cast down a pale yellow light that blurred the edges of rocks and was like music barely heard. It exactly matched Steve's mood, this softness in the outlines of everything – nothing need be too explicit on a day like this, even opposites could be reconciled.

He strolled to the harbour end of the prom, turned about and walked back to the castle ruins. He stood on that grassy knoll, taking in the view over the sea with quiet satisfaction.

'Lovely, isn't it?' came a quiet voice behind him.

Steve turned to meet the dark eyes of an elderly man seated alone on a bench.

'Yes. It is. Beautiful.'

'The sort of view that inspires.' The man smiled. 'Poets especially.'

'Of course,' Steve said vaguely. He felt he knew this man, but could not place him.

'*In the December of my youth I sing,*' the man said softly.

His own words – written long ago – hit Steve like an electric shock. He stared at the stranger.

'You still don't know me, do you?'

'Of course I do. Mr Meredith, isn't it?'

'The very same.' The man stood, shaking his head sadly. 'Oh, why didn't you stick to poetry, my boy? Why didn't you?'

'Meurig! What a surprise. You coming in?'

'If you like.'

'Of course I like. When did I didn't?'

Laughing at her own fractured English, Jenny Briggs opened the door wide. She was in high spirits, bright-eyed, welcoming. Meurig hesitated before stepping in shiftily, as if already regretting the impulse that had brought him here.

'Well, go on up. You know the way.'

'You first,' said Meurig, stepping aside.

'What's wrong with you, *bach*? Bit slow today, aren't you?'

Jenny tripped upstairs, Meurig plodding behind doggedly.

'I haven't seen you for ages. What you been doing, anything special?' she asked, inside the living-room.

'Depends.'

'On what, the weather? Oh, don't mind me, I'm being silly. I've had good news, you see. We're definitely going ahead with the school.'

'Oh. That's good. Got the money then, have you?'

'Money, the premises – the lot. There's no stopping us now, Meurig. Isn't it exciting?'

'*Diawl*, yes. Thrilling.'

'Say it as if you mean it then. What's up with you, boy? Lost a shilling and found sixpence?'

'Nothing so simple. Wouldn't have a beer, would you?'

'Don't stock it. You can have a glass of wine if you like.'

'OK then.'

'Red, white?'

'Anything. So long as it's wet.'

With a déjà-vu feeling – had they really had this conversation before? – she poured him a red from the half-empty bottle.

'Busy, aren't you?' He nodded at a table strewn with papers.

'You could say that. There's a lot to do.'

'Get any help from Heulwen?'

'Of course. She's in it with me.'

'Bet you do most of the work.'

'Now, Meurig. Stop stirring.'

He twitched his nose, looked more relaxed, sitting with legs stretched straight out. But still a tension about him.

'What is it, Meurig?' she asked eventually. 'Something's bugging you, isn't it?'

'Not bugging, no.'

'No?'

'Well.'

'Out with it. Come on, now.'

He took another slurp. 'You heard of someone called Brett? Simon Brett?'

'Sounds like a film star. No, can't say I have. Why?'

'I've met him a couple of times. Don't know what to make of him.'

'Friend of his, are you?'

'Sort of.'

'Oh aye. Like that, is it?'

He shrugged.

'You're a fool. Why don't you go straight?'

'Don't be stupid.'

'Not half as stupid as you.'

He said nothing.

'You people,' she said.

He flinched. 'How's your boyfriend?' he asked coldly.

'I haven't got one.'

'Bugger off.'

'Oh, you mean Nigel?' she said sweetly. 'He's not my boyfriend. He's married.'

'So?'

'It's all over. Didn't amount to much anyway.'

'That's not what I hear.'

'Shouldn't listen to gossip, Meurig.'

'Have you told him?'

'Told him what?'

'It's all over.'

'Not yet.'

He smiled maliciously. 'You people.'

'Touché,' she said delightedly. She lifted her glass of Chardonnay.

'Fed up with him, is it?'

'We're talking about someone called Brett. If you remember.'

'I'm talking about your boyfriend.'

'Well, I'm not so drop it.'

'Don't need him any more – that it?'

'Mind your own business.'

'You people,' he mocked.

'If that's all you can say, fuck off.'

'Oh dear.'

They lapsed into an unhappy silence.

'Oh shit,' he said suddenly.

She was all concern. 'What is it, *cariad*? Who's this Brett then?'

'I don't know. I know fuck-all about him.'

'How d'you meet him then?'

'He came into the shop. I was stacking books.'

He told her about the princes of Wales, their meeting in the pub, their return to his flat.

'You're worried, aren't you? Why?'

'He knows Richard.'

'Does he now,' said Jenny seriously.

'Yes.'

'And?'

'I don't know. Where it's taking me.'

30

S HE WAS STACKING bed linen into cupboards, being the good housewife. If they hadn't moved, she'd have been teaching now. Simon would have been in his old school, while he'd have been – what? Steve pushed the thought aside, spoke eagerly, anything to cheer her up.

'You'll never guess who I saw today.'

'King Kong?'

'Not quite. My old editor – Gwyn Meredith.'

'Fancy.'

'He was very good to me, when I worked under him years ago. He didn't want me to go up to London, you know. He offered me a job in Carmarthen – in charge of the office there.'

She gave him a look. 'Doesn't compare much with the *Comet*, does it?'

'That's not the point. I'd have been a different person then. I'd have got on with my poetry.'

She turned her back, resuming what she was doing. She was growing her hair longer now. It seemed to be changing colour – not merely fair but somehow richer, more succulent. Golden hair, he thought. As in the fairy tales.

'That's what he told me – Gwyn Meredith,' Steve plunged on recklessly. 'I should have stuck to poetry. I had a poem published in London – he remembered it. He even quoted the first line.'

He realized Jocelyn wasn't moving. He willed her to turn around.

'Of course, I could have gone on with it anyway. It was my fault. I just let it drop.'

Jocelyn shut the cupboard door, kept her hand on it for a second.

'You'd have been alright then, wouldn't you?' she said, turning. 'You wouldn't have married me.'

'That's not what I meant,' Steve blustered. 'That's stupid.'

'Is it?'

'You know it is.'

'I don't know anything, Steve. Not a thing.'

She brushed past him. He stayed where he was, thinking.

'You might as well know,' she said downstairs. 'I'm going away for a few days. I'll take Simon with me, of course.'

'You can't do that.'

'Why not?'

'He's in school. It's term time.'

'I'll ask permission. I'm sure they won't refuse me.'

'Where are you going?'

'To Mum and Dad's of course. Where else?'

'What the hell for?'

'There's no need to swear.' She had a book in her lap, pretending to read it.

'But why? What's the idea?'

'I've got to get away. I want to think.'

'About what, Jos?'

'Everything.'

He knew he was playing a part now. He had to get the words right.

'This is crazy. All because of that stupid letter.'

'It's nothing to do with the letter.'

'What is it then?'

'I told you. Everything.'

He sat beside her. 'Please, Jos.'

'Don't pretend,' she said icily.

'I'm not pretending. I want you here, Jos. All the time. I love you.'

'No you don't. You only love yourself.'

'That's a terrible thing to say.'

'It's the truth, and you know it.'

Suddenly he saw Annette again, as she had been on the day they had met in the cemetery. Walking towards him on the path, the black sweater clinging to her throat. The vision caught his breath. Jos didn't notice.

Jocelyn closed the book. 'I'm not leaving you, Steve. But I need time to think.'

He tried to remember his next line, but failed.

Lorna Morris had experienced many ups and downs in her life, but one of the constants in it was her love for her daughter Annette. It was a love which had sometimes been ambiguously expressed – there'd been raging rows in the past, for Annette's teenage uppitiness had grated on her mother – but her stalwart support of her aging parents had made such eruptions a distant memory. Living just up the road from Ted and Lorna – up the hill, more specifically – Annette was a frequent visitor. Son-in-law Nigel was a more elusive presence, a fact which did not escape them. 'Got too big for his boots,' they'd confide in each other wisely. 'Bit different when he was courting her, wasn't he? Couldn't see enough of us then.'

Today, with Ted home early from work – his hours restricted by his increasing age and the lessening demands of the university department where he worked part-time –

Lorna was enjoying a good old chin-wag about rumours she could hardly believe.

'They say the girls in his office knew all about it. Well, why didn't they say something, that's what I'd like to know. All they had to do was pick up the phone and tell Annette, isn't it? Doesn't take much, does it? What they think they were doing?'

'May not be true,' said Ted. 'Could be all lies.'

'There's no smoke without fire. Something's going on, believe you me. That Jenny Briggs! Right little madam, she is. Up to everything with them Welshies, painting pillar boxes and invading offices and the like. Remember the time they all sat down on the road, stopping the traffic? Disgusting, it is. Should've been locked up – or shot.'

'All the same,' Ted said reluctantly. 'Doesn't mean Nigel's been doing something he shouldn't. Can't believe it myself. Not the type, is he? Comes of good farming stock.'

'Good poppycock! All men are the same. See a bit of skirt and they go crackers.'

'Oh. Thank you very much.'

'I don't mean you, Ted. Good God…' She gave him a glance, considered a mild joke at his expense – who'd fancy him now? – thought better of it. 'Always been good to me, you have.'

He looked pleased, in spite of himself. But at heart he too was troubled. He knew what it was to be tempted. Long ago, in his postman days, he could have had his way, sure enough, with a nice little brunette living out in the country. No one would have known. But he hadn't. End of story.

'Look – we'll have a talk with her,' he said. 'When she comes round. Might be here tonight – the *Black and White Minstrel Show* is on telly. She likes them, don't she?'

'She might not *want* to talk about it,' snapped Lorna.

Ted suppressed a sigh. One minute she seemed to be asking his help, the next she was slapping him down. Typical!

Annette *did* call around, not to see the blacked–up 'minstrels' but to ask a favour. She had to see someone at four o'clock next day – could they possibly look after Jo and Rob for an hour or two after school?

'Course we will. You don't have to ask, gel,' said Lorna. 'Who you seeing, anyone I know?'

'No, not really.'

Lorna bit her lip at the snub. Tonight of all nights, she didn't want to quarrel with her daughter. 'You'll have a cup of tea then, will you? Fancy a Welsh cake? I've been doing a bit of baking today.'

'Yes please, Mam. Better than shop cakes any day.'

'I should think so, indeed.'

Reconciled, mother and daughter sat together cosily. Ted was in the way, but didn't see it. After a while, Lorna said: 'Going for a pint tonight then, love?'

'Wasn't thinking of it. Why?'

'Thought you wanted a word with Dewi. About that trip down to Cardiff you were fancying?'

'For the football? That's not for another month yet, mun. He might not…'

Catching her eye, he got the message. 'Suppose I might as well then,' he conceded. 'Need to get the tickets anyway. Don't mind, do you, 'Nette? Only be out for about an hour.'

'You go, Dad. Enjoy yourself,' Annette said, playing her

part to a T. She knew what was coming. The Inquisition. She could sense it as soon as she had stepped inside. It was in the tone of her mother's voice, the way she moved, the very air she breathed. She braced herself for it.

Of course, Lorna didn't raise the subject immediately. It was something that had to be approached obliquely, by an infinite series of ever-diminishing circles. A hint here, a hint there, and then the steady bearing down on it, so that by this time it was utterly surrounded and could not escape.

'Not true though, is it?' said Lorna, with a sniff.

'Oh yes. It's true all right.'

'But why? What's behind it?'

'If I knew that, Mam…'

'Oh, I know, love. Men are so – *ych y fi!*'

'I've known for a long time.'

'Have you talked about it then?'

'Not really. Could you – if it was you?'

'Don't know, bach. Never had to.' Her lips were set, prim-tight. 'But *Nigel*,' she burst out disbelievingly. 'He seemed so…'

'I know, Mam. I thought so too.'

'It's *her*. It must be. All that showing-off. It's not natural.'

Annette gave her an odd look. 'Natural?'

'They want to be like men these days. You know what Gran used to say? They should never have given us the vote. That's what started it. Girls acting like men. Going out making trouble. They'll be fighting wars soon, you mark my words.'

'Don't be silly, Mam. That's got nothing to do with it.'

'Hasn't it? I don't know so much.'

Annette nestled into her mother's knowledge. It was somewhere safe and comforting. Her thoughts went back fourteen years, to the time Lorna had found out she was pregnant with Ceri. She'd imagined her mother would be sharp with her, unforgiving, but instead she'd been all understanding.

'What are you going to do, *bach*? Not divorcing him, are you?'

The word 'divorce' sliced through Annette's soul like a steel shard. She shuddered.

'Don't say it, Mam,' she struck back. 'Please!'

'You've got to face it,' Lorna said stoutly. 'You're entitled.'

'Maybe it's me. Maybe it's my fault. I haven't been a good wife.'

'What? You don't mean you – as well…?'

'Don't be *stupid*, Mam.'

Annette flung herself away from her mother's embrace – a movement not so much physical as mental. 'It must be though, mustn't it? He was so good to me – over Ceri.'

'No excuse,' muttered Lorna. 'No excuse at all.'

'*Excuse*. Who needs an excuse?'

When Ted got home, he thought at first the house was empty. There was no sign of his daughter or wife. Dazed by their absence, befuddled by drink, he stared at the blank TV screen, sat down for a few minutes, went for a pee, looked in the bedroom. And there was Lorna, sitting propped up by pillows in the double bed they had shared all their married life.

'Oh. So that's where you are,' he said.

'Yes. Surprising, isn't it? Bet you thought I'd have run off with the grocer.'

'Don't be daft.'

He took his jacket off, then his tie. Sat on the bed to take his shoes off.

'Pity she didn't, in't it?' she said, after a moment.

'Didn't what?'

'Marry Steve.'

He stopped what he was doing. 'What the hell d'you mean by that then?'

'Well. Would've been far better, wouldn't it?'

'Don't be soft. You're talking rubbish.'

'No I'm not. They were two of a kind.'

'You didn't think so at the time. You couldn't stand him. He was messing about with that woman down the harbour – what's her name now?'

'Poof! That didn't matter.'

'What's the point going all over that, gel? That's all in the past, mun.'

'Not for me, it's not.' She put a hand to her chest. 'It's all inside here.'

'I know, love,' he said quietly. 'I know.'

31

RICHARD ELLIS WAS playing the clarinet when Brett arrived. Brett could hear the sound through the bay window of the house in North Road – cool, controlled, like Ellis himself. When Brett rang the bell, the music stopped immediately. Ellis was a disciplined man.

'You're early,' he remarked after ushering Brett into the front room.

'Am I? I didn't think so.'

'Two minutes.'

'Ah well.'

Ellis's eyes darkened. 'Two minutes is two minutes.'

'No denying that,' Brett said jokily. Ellis did not respond.

The music stand, temporarily abandoned, stood in the centre of a room which exuded an air of high learning. It was furnished by books in as effective a way as in any of Anthony Powell's novels. A writing bureau in a corner spoke of Victorian purpose and self-denial. Richard Ellis belonged to a priesthood, but the nature of his religion was hard to specify.

There was little small talk between these two men. Their relationship was clearly defined – Ellis was clearly the master. Brett acknowledged this without being deferential. They sat side by side, discussing matters in low voices.

Outside, the gloom of a mid-October evening thickened as if in response to the high seriousness of their intent. Ellis left it late before drawing the heavy curtains and switching on the light. By the time Brett left the house, it was already night.

Simon didn't want to go away with his mother – he made that perfectly clear. 'Why can't I stay home with Dad?' he asked plaintively. 'You go on your own, Mum. I don't mind – honest.' He gave her a bright, you-know-you-can-trust-me smile – the good little boy personified. When it didn't work, he tried another tack. 'I'm not ill, Mum – I *ought* to be at school. Mr James wouldn't like it.'

'I told you, I've spoken to Mr James – you don't think I'd go against him, do you?'

Simon knew there was trouble between his Mum and Dad, but there'd been trouble before. He knew it would blow over – it always did. Dad was Dad and Mum was Mum. That's all it amounted to. They fell out over something, and then they patched it up. He got what he could out of it – he knew just how to play one against the other, to his advantage. But it was not what you'd call *serious*. It was just them – the way they were.

Usually he wouldn't have minded a few days out of school – what normal nine-year-old would? – but for Simon, these were unusual times. He'd been in his new school just over a month, and was enjoying it much more than he thought he would. He'd been afraid of being teased because he was English, but there'd been none of that. In fact there were lots of English kids in the school – the town was full of them. He'd quickly learned there were two junior schools in Glanaber, and the other one was the 'Welshier' school. In fact it was *called* Yr Ysgol Gymraeg, the Welsh School, and all the lessons were in Welsh. Here in Parc Junior, English was predominant. Everyone was taught Welsh – there were four lessons a week – but you could get by without it. So he had no real grumbles. Quite the opposite in fact. Because one of the girls in his class was called Mair. And she'd told him – whispering – that he'd be getting an invite to her birthday party next Saturday. Which made him blush a fierce red. Because he liked Mair very much.

He'd said nothing about it at home. How could he, when he hadn't been invited yet? He only had Mair's word for it. Her parents might not want him. They'd said nothing to Mum and Dad, or they would have told him. And Simon felt shy about it all. Painfully shy. Just to mention the *possibility* to Mum and Dad was utterly beyond him.

That was why he felt so miserable, being dragged away with his Mum, leaving Dad behind on his own, missing out on the party, missing out on being with *Mair*.

It made his stomach feel empty. Because he'd never met anyone like her before.

Steve came across them in a corner of the newsagent's, quite by chance. He picked the top one up and skimmed through it. He didn't recognize any of the poets' names – Alison Bielski, David Elias, Bryn Griffiths, Peter Gruffydd… There was a poem called 'Depopulation':

> *They say this is no place for the ambitious.*
> *The young men leave, trailing*
> *A pity for the people left behind,*
> *Nailing the coffin of the town they go,*
> *Finding refreshment in familiar lies…*

Nothing like Dylan Thomas. Or Vernon Watkins. Or Idris Davies, for that matter. The Welsh poets he knew best. Not that he knew very many. Not that there *were* very many. So far as he knew. Writing in English anyway. As for those writing in Welsh... they were a closed book. Not his scene.

He looked at the cover again. Very strange it was too. A squiggly black pen-and-ink drawing – of what? – and above it a human head – male or female? – next to the title: *Poetry Wales*.

No price on the cover. He looked inside. 'Price: Three Shillings.'

He could manage that. He dug a half-crown out of his pocket, plus a shilling piece. 'Thank you,' he said, handing them over.

The man behind the counter was reading a spread-out copy of the local rag. He looked up briefly, checked the money, rung it up on the till, handed Steve sixpence change without a word.

Steve went out of the shop. He felt excited.

She recognized signs that nobody else would notice, leave alone be able to interpret. There was the peculiar half-grunt in the back of his throat now and then, the tap-tapping of his fingers on the table, and – especially this – the paleness at the corners of his mouth, the tiny white circles that denoted intense anxiety over something. It had been there when his firm had been threatened with action over alleged misrepresentation, when his father had suffered a sudden heart attack, and when she – Annette – had skidded into a hedge on an icy road. And it was there now, as they ate supper together as a family – a rare moment these days. He said very little, but did not need to as Rob was full of the visit they'd had at school from the great Trevor Ford, sometime footballer for Wales, who during a business trip to the town had dropped in at the request of the head, a personal friend. 'And he might coach our team! Dad, would you buy me some new boots, I might get in it then. *Dad.*'

He got through to his abstracted parent at last, who made the appropriate promise but could not resist remarking that rugby was a much better game than 'soccer'.

'You need more than new boots to get in the team,' Joanne said cuttingly. 'You're hopeless.'

'No I'm not!'

'Yes you are. You can't kick a ball straight – everyone knows that. Anyway you're only seven. You'll never get in the team yet.'

'Yes I will. Mr Pollard's getting a new team for under-nines so there!'

'Who's Mr Pollard?'

'Our new teacher. He's great. He played for Rotherham United once – he told us.'

'*Rotherham,*' she mocked. 'Who are they then?'

'They're a good team. They're in the Second Division. They're…'

'That's enough, you two,' Annette cut in. 'Now, eat your supper and no more fighting.'

When the children were safely in bed, she waited.

'I just want you to know,' Nigel said eventually. 'I've finished with her.'

'Have you now.'

'I've been a fool.'

'Fancy.'

'I'm sorry.'

'So am I.'

'You knew, of course?'

'I'm not a fool, Nigel.'

'Christ.'

She was half-looking at the telly.

'Did you finish with her,' she asked, 'or did she finish with you?'

He stared at her, puzzled. 'Does it matter?'

'It does to me.'

He took a deep breath. 'She finished with me.'

'I thought so.'

The small white circles stood out clearly.

'Well,' she added. 'It's nice being honest, isn't it?'

32

THERE WAS A wildness in Jocelyn she'd never felt before. It showed itself in her driving, which at times bordered on the reckless. 'Slow down, Mum!' Simon pleaded, as she only just squeezed to safety after overtaking a lorry. The driver of the car coming in the opposite direction flashed his lights and, for good measure, gave her the V–sign. Jocelyn's heart thumped, with the exhilaration of it. She just didn't care. *She didn't care.* But yes, she did. Of course she did. She had Simon to consider. She didn't want to kill him as well as herself, did she?

She was wearing dark glasses, a sure sign that she was out of herself. She wore them to prove she would not be taken for granted, that she'd live life to the full, that she'd do exactly what she wanted. Seeing them, Steve had looked uneasy. 'Are you sure you want to go?' he had asked. 'You can always change your mind. Mum and Dad won't mind.'

Mum and Dad! she'd thought scornfully. They weren't his Mum and Dad. Steve's mother lived near Cardiff. His father was dead. He sounded so false, laying claim to her parents. He didn't really like them, she knew. How could he? He was Welsh, while they were English to the core. Simon – he was English too. He'd been born in London, hadn't he? He'd always lived in London. How could he be anything but English?

She was dimly aware of a 30 m.p.h. sign coming up. Just after passing it she braked sharply, throwing Simon forward in the back seat. '*Mum!*' he shrieked. 'I want to go home. Turn around!'

'We're alright, pet. I'm sorry. I'll slow down. I'm really sorry.'

'I want to go *home, home, home!*' The boy could see Mair plain as anything, she was pleading with him to go back. 'I've got something on, I didn't tell you. I'm going to a birthday party – please Mum, please!'

'What? Whose birthday's that then? When?' Confused, she slowed right down and stopped to let an old woman cross the road. She twisted around in her seat. 'You didn't say anything about this, did you? Whose birthday is it?'

'You don't know them,' Simon said miserably. Already he was regretting his outburst. 'It doesn't matter.'

'Of course it matters.' She drove on slowly through the village. 'It's nice you're making friends. Who is he then, this boy?'

'It doesn't *matter*. I can't go there anyway, can I?'

'I want to *know*, Simon. Did they give you an invite, his parents? I'll have to reply, don't you see that? I can't just ignore it, that's rude. What's his name, did you say? Simon!' she cried peremptorily. '*Please.*'

'It's not a boy,' he said sulkily. 'It's a girl. Her name's Mair.'

'Oh.' She glanced in the driving mirror, tried to conceal a smile – not too successfully. 'I see. When is this party then?'

He mumbled something.

'What's that? I didn't hear you.'

'Saturday,' he bawled.

'Oh. Well, it's only Monday. We can go back by then, I suppose. But I wasn't planning to. When did they ask you then? You didn't tell us.'

From the back seat, silence. And then a sudden, revealing snuffle.

Ah well, she thought. We all have our problems.

They'd only been gone a few hours and he was missing them already. The house felt empty – colder, somehow. There were things that needed doing about the place – a new washer on a tap, the back door jamming unexpectedly – but he wasn't in the mood. Could he, perhaps, write a poem? To pose the question was to provide an instant answer. He was as empty of poetry as a mausoleum was of hope. There may be a spark somewhere, but it would not fly today.

He found himself by an upstairs window, staring out at the sea. There was something about it today that chilled him to the marrow. It was the indifference of it – yet not even that, for the word implied consciousness of a kind. It was dead, sterile, alien. He shivered.

The feeling of loneliness grew. He was at the edge of the world. No one cared for him any more. Jos didn't – she might leave him. The paper didn't – they'd cast him aside. For years he'd been at the heart of things, doing big stories, enjoying the gossip and rough camaraderie of Fleet Street. Who remembered him now? He was finished, utterly finished.

Swamped by depression, he slumped into a chair. And, out of nowhere, came the sound of a voice – that of the tennis club secretary back in Putney, Jack Palmer. 'Do try and make it, old boy,' he was saying. Over and over. 'Do try and make it.' Smiling his sweet smile. Being his most persuasive. It was the way he'd looked and sounded months ago, when trying to get them to go to that special meeting to decide the club's future. But he hadn't gone, because he'd been here in Glanaber, chasing up the story of the college principal who'd hanged himself. Had Jos gone? He hadn't asked. And she hadn't told him, to his knowledge. Why was he thinking of this now? It was weird.

He sprung up impatiently, put on his raincoat, left the house. A light rain dampened his hair, freshened his cheeks. He had no clear idea where he was going, until – of their own volition, it seemed – his legs took him to the cemetery where the body of his daughter lay. He found the little tombstone, stared at it. Children just out of school, taking a short cut home along the cemetery path, passed him by without seeing him. Their loud voices skirled and spun. One voice seemed different from the others. He fancied it was Ceri's voice, trying hard to reach him.

There would always be a welcome for them in her parents' house, but it was soon clear that it was warmer on her father's part than her mother's. 'Why couldn't Steve come with you?' Laura Wiltshire asked, puzzled. 'Is he too busy or something?'

Jos knew she was being deliberately obtuse. She'd already explained on the phone. She was coming just with Simon. She needed time on her own, to think. Space for herself.

The second evening there, with Simon in bed and Dennis Wiltshire pottering around in his den, the two women had a heart-to-heart. Jos told her mother about Steve's betrayal, as she thought of it – his not saying a word about the girl he'd got pregnant and very nearly married. Even though she was bound to find out about it, in a small town like Glanaber. She could have coped with that – she'd had her boyfriends too – it was the cot death of his baby daughter that made it so different. She recalled the shock she'd felt at reading that ill-spelt letter from *A WELL WISHER* – 'aught' for 'ought'! It was all so public on the one hand, and all so sneaky and underhand on the other! 'I felt everyone was looking at me, and laughing at me – I still do. Can't you see, Mum?'

And yes, Laura did see – while wondering at Steve's concern for the child he'd never known. 'It's so unusual, isn't it?' she pondered. 'Young men don't usually care – they don't give a damn who they get into trouble, or the consequences. It says something for him, doesn't it?'

Oh yes, Jos acknowledged, it did say something – but the fact he'd said absolutely nothing about it said even more. Her face was tight, unforgiving. Laura hadn't seen her like this before.

'What's up with her, then?' Dennis asked her in bed. Laura explained. 'H'm,' Dennis said. 'The trouble is, he's Welsh.' And Laura knew what he meant, without any further explanation.

'That job's still open, you know. With the bank. They've postponed an appointment. Couldn't find anyone suitable. Shelved the whole project.'

'Ah well,' Laura sighed. 'That's that.'

'No it's not. It can be taken off the shelf. I think they're keen to revive it.'

It was just gone eight. The supper things were cleared away, the washing-up was done, she could settle down now to look at a bit of telly. (Ivor was in his little office behind the shop, dickering about with something – she didn't quite know what.) Then the doorbell rang. Sighing, Shirley went to answer it.

A tall man stood in the gloom. A very tall man. She knew she'd seen him before, but couldn't place him. He was lean, well-dressed, hair parted in the middle. 'Detective-inspector Jenkins,' he said thinly. 'Mrs Morgan, I take it?'

'Yes,' she replied, dry-mouthed.

'Is your husband in, by any chance?'

'Of course. Do you want him?'

He smiled, chilling the air still further. 'If you please.'

She hurried to the office, noticing things in the hallway that normally escaped her – the wallpaper curling away in the top right-hand corner, that awful frame around the photo of Ivor's grandparents taken in the year dot – why on earth did they keep it there? Short though the walk was, she was out of breath when she got there.

'There's a man at the door wants to see you. A policeman,' she gabbled.

'Policeman? What's he want?'

'He didn't say. He's – he's a detective.'

'Detective? Why didn't you ask him in, woman?'

'I don't know, I...'

She wanted to grab Ivor, plead with him to stand by her – they wouldn't send her to prison right away, would they? Surely not with the children?

'Out of my way then,' he said brusquely. 'I can't get past.'

'Ivor,' she cried out as he made for the door. 'I didn't mean to.'

He seemed not to hear her. Had she really said that, or imagined it? *Oh God! The day of reckoning – it's come. It was her own fault – she shouldn't have done it!*

She stood where she was, hand stuffed in her mouth, biting her finger hard. The rumble of male voices. Then the door closing. Footsteps coming towards her – he was coming to arrest her! She'd make a full confession – she would!

'What're you doing still here then?' asked Ivor, astonished. 'Go back in, mun. And why didn't you say – hey!'

Shirley's legs gave way. Ivor caught her as she fell. Next thing she knew, she was back in the living-room sipping water. She pushed the glass away. 'I'm alright – honest.'

Her daughter Josie was staring at her – big-eyed, disbelieving. And Conrad, school books on his lap, even more worried than his sister.

'You OK then – sure?' asked Ivor, hovering. A long figure behind him – the detective! Smiling now, encouragingly.

'*Diawl!* Didn't half give us a shock. What's up with you then – not sick, are you?' Ivor's eyes were large – bigger even than Josie's. She'd never realized before how big they were – like saucers!

'I'll come back again,' Jenkins said. 'It's not urgent, really. It's just about the stolen paint – as I told you…'

'No, you're not going nowhere. You'll stay and have a cup of tea with us – put the kettle on Josie, good girl.'

Josie gave her mother a look, and disappeared.

'Never known her faint before in my life.' Ivor, full of apologies. 'You must've given her a shock – I don't know why, I'm sure. It's not as if she doesn't know you.'

'Well, I don't suppose she recognized me – that street lighting's dreadful. And I had to be a bit formal – took her by surprise, I suppose. I'm sorry, Shirley.'

'That's OK.' She felt stupid. Of course she knew him – as a customer. But did he have to talk like that – and look so frightening?

The men took their cups of tea into the office. Shirley sipped hers. Hot and sweet – just as she liked it. She'd refused a brandy – she wasn't ill. Just been surprised, that's all – who wouldn't be?

Conrad had gone up to his room, to do his homework. Shirley still caught funny looks from Josie. What was wrong with her – what was she thinking? She didn't know anything about that letter.

'Haven't you got any homework?' Shirley asked her, more sharply than she'd intended.

'No,' the girl said brusquely. 'Have you?'

'What d'you mean by that?'

'Nothing.'

Laughter drifted from the little office. The men were enjoying themselves. Shirley remembered something – they both belonged to the Lodge. Well, that was alright then.

33

THEY DID THE sort of things they usually did together – elevenses in Guildford High Street, a spot of window shopping (sometimes even buying something) – but in no sense was this the normal kind of get-together. Laura kept wondering how long Jos intended to stay, and whether she should mention the fact that the bank job was still available for Steve – if he wanted it. In fact, this business about the dead baby seemed quite ridiculous. Why make such a song and dance about it? Was Jos trying to tell her something else – that Steve was still keen on his old girlfriend? The more she thought about it, the more confused she became. And then, of all things, Jocelyn suddenly asked if she would look after Simon for a few hours while she met up with an old friend!

'You don't mind, Mum, do you?' Jos said, with a bright smile that to Laura (she couldn't help thinking it) looked more than a little false.

'I don't know. I don't suppose so,' replied Laura dubiously. 'Who are you seeing then – anyone I know?'

'No, I don't think so. It's someone I used to teach with – Fay. We're having lunch together on Thursday – if that's OK with you, that is.' Again that quick, brittle smile.

'How can she manage lunch if she's teaching?'

'Oh, she isn't teaching now – she's having a baby. It'd be nice seeing her again – get all the gossip!'

This didn't sound like Jocelyn – nor did it look like her. That new hairstyle of hers – it just didn't suit her. And she'd coloured her hair too, its natural flaxen overlaid by a richer tone that made it look dangerously like the falsely golden sands of seaside resort postcards. Something else was different – something inside her. Laura felt uneasy, but not inclined to argue.

'Well, if it's alright with Simon...'

'Oh, he won't mind – he loves being with you two.'

Jocelyn was there first, in a country pub she'd been to once or twice with Steve. She bought a drink at the bar, and took it to a corner table. There was no one she knew there – she didn't expect there to be. At last he bustled in, full of apologies. 'Sorry I'm late, pet, meeting just dragged on and on – you know what it's like.' Jack Palmer smiled flashily, planted a kiss on her cheek. 'Great to see you – what can I get you?'

'I'm OK thanks, Jack.'

'Nonsense! I'm getting one for myself anyway. Ugh!' He had just spotted her Babycham glass, complete with trademark Bambi. 'Not drinking that vile stuff, are you? Can't have that. I'll get you something decent.'

'This is fine for me, honestly.'

'Not for me it's not. You're with me, remember? Can't sit opposite a woman with Babycham – do my reputation no end of harm.'

She smiled up at him, her spirits rising by the second.

'Alright then – I'll leave it to you.'

Standing at the bar, Jack Palmer looked perfectly at home. He exuded ease and self-confidence – it was like an aura around him, practically visible. Again Jocelyn glanced around. What a risk she was taking! But was she? What was wrong with being an old friend – discussing Tennis Club matters, possibly?

She had amazed herself, when she had summoned up the nerve to ring him from a call box. And she was amazed still, that he had actually kept his promise to join her. Her legs went weak as he returned with the drinks and a menu. This was serious stuff. It was silly pretending otherwise.

He looked cool and unconcerned, as if they did this every day.

'Well, bottoms up.'

'Cheers,' she responded.

As they clinked glasses, he gave her a straight look. She met his gaze candidly, his unspoken question clearly answered. He relaxed, outwardly the old Jack again.

'You like that?' he asked

'Mm, I do. What is it?'

'Oh, just a Sauvignon. Nothing special. But better than that ghastly poison you were drinking. So what brings you to these parts?'

'Oh, nothing much. I just felt like a break.'

'Couldn't Steve come then?'

'No, he's too busy. Up to his eyes at the moment.'

'Really? I thought he'd been put out to grass.'

'Good heavens, no. What gave you that idea?'

Jack shrugged. 'Seems perfectly obvious. Fleet Street reporter dispatched to Welsh wilderness. QED and all that.'

'Well, it's not like that. It's something we both wanted.'

'Really?' he drawled. That straight look again. She glanced away. 'Anyway, what do you fancy? I can recommend the chicken in a basket.'

'I'm not really hungry, Jack.'

'Oh? I thought we were having lunch together.'

'We were. But I'm not very hungry now.'

'I see. So what do we do then?'

'Take me somewhere.'

He said it was only ten minutes away, but it was more than twice that by the time they'd gone through a small town and two sets of road works. It was set back from the road, almost hidden by trees. The woman at reception was very discreet, barely glancing at Jocelyn. Their room overlooked a crescent-shaped pond, with farmland beyond and the Hog's Back in the distance.

They sat on a settee by the window, looking out.

'I never thought I'd see you again,' Jack said.

He was constantly changing. A human chameleon, Jos thought. His eyes kindly now. Concerned.

'I've never seen you unhappy before.'

'You've never really known me, have you?'

'I'm not sure I do now. In fact, I know I don't.'

She nearly said, 'Just as well.'

'You're lovely,' he said.

Her tears surprised her.

'We don't have to, you know,' he said later.

But by then it was too late.

With little to do and nobody else in the house, surely this was the time to get back to writing some poetry? Steve Lewis sat at his desk, frowning at the blank sheet of paper. It frowned back, mocking. He put down words – any old words – scattering them across the page, seeking neither sense nor connection. He varied his handwriting, spoke the words aloud, and intoned them with Dylanesque rotundity, walked around the room declaiming them. And that was all. Poetry eluded him.

He had spoken to Jocelyn every day, except Thursday. She wasn't well that day – she'd gone early to bed, said her mother. 'Nothing to worry about,' Laura assured him. 'Just a little tired – she saw an old friend today.' They'd be home on Sunday. He hadn't realized he'd miss her so much.

He decided to surprise her by buying her flowers – something he rarely did, even on her birthday. He felt it effete, even corny, and it embarrassed him also, walking out of a shop clutching blooms to his bosom. But today, he felt cheerful just thinking about it. And proud of himself, too. The things he would do for her!

The florist he had in mind kept a corner shop in Water Street, not far from the ironmonger's run by Ivor Morgan and Shirley – ghosts from his past he had so far avoided. He stepped inside, filled with a sense of virtue. He'd come early and no one else was there, apart from the woman behind the counter.

'*Bore da*,' he began, thinking she might have been a Welsh speaker.

'Good morning,' she responded, with a faint smile.

'I'd like a nice bunch of flowers, please. For my wife. Or two bunches. Depends what you've got.'

'Well,' she said slowly, 'it depends what you're looking for, doesn't it?'

The smile was more obvious now. A slow smile, suggesting hidden meaning. 'Would it be her birthday now, that it?'

'No,' said Steve shortly. 'It's not her birthday. I just want some flowers for her, that's all.' The woman was smartly dressed. Deep brown eyes. Auburn hair. Fiftyish, perhaps? It was hard to tell with women. 'Can you suggest something?' he asked impatiently. 'I don't know much about flowers.'

'Well, lots of men don't. But they know about other things, surely.'

It was the accent that alerted him – the slow, spacious speech of the Welsh border country, Montgomery and Shropshire intermingled. That, and her eyes. The hint of mockery in them.

'I know you, don't I?' he ventured.

'You could say that, Gerry.'

Gerry! He stared at her disbelievingly.

'Didn't recognize me, did you? Must be my hair.'

'What are you doing here?'

'What am I? I live here, remember?'

'No, I mean – all this.' His sweeping gesture took in the shop, the flowers and, by implication, her success.

'It's my shop, Gerry. Do you like it?'

'Don't call me that.'

'Sorry – Stephen then, is it? Or should I call you Mr Lewis, now you've gone up in the world?'

'Don't be silly. I'm just surprised to see you, that's all. Somehow I thought…'

'What?' she asked teasingly.

He remembered that tone of voice. It all came back to him in a rush. That hot summer morning, fifteen years ago. Back Row, the run-down cottages by the harbour. Smells of decay and neglect. The woman slipping her shoes off, saying 'Who's to know then, eh?' Sara Baker, standing before him now.

'I thought you'd have left here long ago.'

'Why should I? You're the one that left, Steve.'

Her teeth gleamed.

'Well,' he said coolly, recovering. 'I'm glad to see you doing so well. So how about those flowers then?'

The shop door opened. He chose the flowers and she wrapped them. The couple who had just entered waited politely.

'There you are then, sir,' Sara said. 'I hope your wife likes them.'

'I'm sure she will.' Their eyes met.

Ivor surveyed his shop proudly, eyes settling with satisfaction on the neatly-stacked tins of paint. 'Thank goodness that's settled then. Never dreamt it would be young Dai Tomos nicking them though. *Daro!* When you think what a good family he comes from.'

Shirley, back turned, silently got on with the job he'd assigned her.

'Fair play to Ben Jenkins and his boys though – did their job alright then, mm?' He glanced across the aisle at Shirley, seeking a response.

'Yes, I suppose they did.'

'Suppose! There's no suppose about it. They did, mun. No question about it.'

His wife's contemptuous 'H'm!' was so faint, Ivor didn't notice. The fact that Inspector Jenkins had pretended not to know her – '*Mrs Morgan, I take it?*' – still rankled. But then, that was typical of this town. Give anyone a bit of authority, and it went to their head good and proper. If they'd seen a bit more of the world, it'd be different. But why had she fainted like that? Could have aroused his suspicions. Should be alright now though – hadn't asked to see their typewriter...

'Pity about the boy, mind,' Ivor was saying. 'Don't like to see anyone in trouble.'

Shirley half-turned. 'Does it have to go to court, Ivor? I mean...'

''Course it does! Got no choice in the matter. There's too much of this thing going on…'

Shirley gave him a look. He knew what she was thinking. His young brother Lennie had often sees the inside of a magistrate's court. If it had been him…

'It's got to be put a stop to!' Ivor cried, semi–coherently.

'Of course it has, love,' Shirley said pacifically.

34

'WHY ARE YOU only writing these nice little pieces about pooftas and painters and that? Why don't you give us something solid for a change?'

Gerwyn Hopkins confronted Steve belligerently at the bar of the Boar's Head, colloquially known as the Whore's Bed. His eyes glinted behind steel-rimmed glasses that appeared to be leftovers from the early days of the NHS.

'I've got to look for off-beat stories. That's my brief,' Steve replied.

'Brief! You sound like a bleeding solicitor. What's happened to you, man? You used to be shit-hot once. I wouldn't give tuppence for the stuff you're writing now.'

'Oh, thanks very much. That's nice to know.'

'I call a spade a spade, Steve. You know that. I think you're wasting your time. If that's all you can do, you may as well go back to London.'

'They like what I'm doing up there.'

'Oh, do they now. Well, that surprises me. All I can say is, they must be easily satisfied.'

In spite of himself, Steve smiled. He knew Gerwyn of old. He was the stirrer-in-chief of Glanaber, a man who saw conspiracies in every corner and spoke his mind with all the tact of a JCB excavator. But he knew his stuff. By rights, Steve mused, Gerwyn should be doing *his* job.

'You should be doing my job,' Steve said out loud, without thinking.

'Too right I should.' Gerwyn tapped ash from his

hand-rolled fag, plucked stray bits of tobacco from lips. 'I can't talk to you here,' he went on, sotto-voce. 'Let's move.'

They migrated to a beer-slopped corner table.

'Now then,' Gerwyn resumed, pale face ghostly in the shadows. 'What I'm going to tell you now – right? It's between you and me – right? No passing it on, OK?'

'Scout's honour,' promised Steve, making the appropriate sign.

Gerwyn faced him sternly. 'I mean that. I know your sort, Lewis. Say one thing and do another. But this could get me in a lot of trouble. You too, if you start messing round.' He dragged smoke down to his leathered lungs. 'Now then. What d'you know about the Nats?'

'Gnats? Flying insects?'

'No, you stupid bugger. Nationalists. Fascists. Because that's what they are, every one of them.'

'Are they?' Steve asked, surprised.

''Course they are. Everyone knows that. Well, look what they do. Seal up pillar boxes. Paint 'em green. Attack banks – tearing up forms and that because they're in English. They even stopped the traffic on the bridge once – did you know that?'

'Yes, I've heard something about it.'

'Sat down on the road, they did. Silly buggers. I'd have run over the lot of 'em.'

'Bit drastic that, isn't it?' Steve teased.

'No laughing matter, boy. Think what it would be like if they took over. They'd have us all speaking Welsh by order. No English allowed. Believe me.'

Steve wondered where this was leading. He thought he'd be enjoying a sociable pint or two with his old mate. He should have known better.

Gerwyn leaned forward conspiratorially. 'There's something afoot,' he murmured. 'Something big. You've got to do something about it.'

'What is it?' Steve prompted, as the silence lengthened.

'New movement. Violence. They're going to start attacking property. People too, probably.'

'Who are?'

'I told you. The Welsh Nats. Don't you listen to me?'

'Plaid Cymru?' said Steve dubiously. 'Doesn't seem very likely. They're pacifists, aren't they?'

'No, not them. The new crowd. They'll stop at nothing. Like the Irish.'

'Who are they then? Give me some names.'

'Don't be stupid. How do I know? It's up to you to find out. You're the newshound, aren't you?'

'Oh, sure.' Steve felt a stab of frustration. Gerwyn was right. These so-called 'colour pieces' he was writing now: what did they amount to? Bugger all. When he thought of what he'd been doing a couple of years back...

'Doesn't seem very likely to me,' he said abruptly. 'Sure it's not your imagination?'

Gerwyn shook his head sadly. 'You've changed, boy. Shouldn't have come back here. Just want the easy life now, don't you?'

'No replies at all?' said Rachael Miles.

'No, nothing,' Annette said.

It was coming up to noon in the Pelican Café. The mid-morning coffee crowd had drifted away, the lunchtime sandwich-and-roll rush not yet begun. All the same, the two women kept their voices low. It did not do to be overheard in the Pelican, or indeed any coffee house in Glanaber. A snatch of conversation, half heard, could be magnified into a major scandal.

The coffee machine spluttered and hissed, plates clattered together, Italianate voices behind the counter injected spasmodic urgency into the indolent air.

'I suppose people take their time to reply to these box numbers,' Rachael ventured.

'It's been in two weeks running now. Not a sniff of anything. Waste of money, waste of time.'

'What did your ad say, exactly?'

'I thought you knew.'

'Remind me.'

Annette sighed. 'Experienced shorthand-typist seeks part-time work. Refs provided,' she chanted jokily. 'Box so-and-so.'

Sitting opposite, Rachael considered this. Her middle finger flicked her thumb, the unconscious habit which, at this moment, Annette found unbearable. She cupped her hands around her raised cup, to blot out the sight of it.

'Why didn't you give your phone number?' Rachael asked.

'What? And have every Tom, Dick and Harry ringing up? You must be joking.'

'Might have been better. Some people can't be bothered to write to box numbers, I don't suppose.'

'If they can't be bothered, they're not worth bothering with.'

Annette's voice sounded brittle, as if it might split any second, spraying the café with fractured syllables.

'Maybe Gethin can find you something. Shall I ask him?'

'No thank you.'

'Don't make it easy, do you? But I've been asking around.

There's absolutely zilch.' The word, the accent, that habit of finger-flicking – *why doesn't she stop it?* – were all pure Rachael: touches of exotica. Even her olive skin – that Levantine inheritance – seemed deliberately provoking.

Seemingly unaware of her friend's irritation, Rachael puffed out smoke from her Silk Cut cigarette with a backward jerk of her small head.

'And how are other matters?' she ambiguously asked.

'Pretty hellish.'

'He's still seeing her?'

'No, I don't think so. I don't care though, frankly.'

'Oh. That eez bad.'

A quick smile accompanied the self-mocking mispronunciation. Annette did not respond.

'You need to get away together – just you two,' said Rachael.

'I don't think so.'

'He wouldn't want it?'

'*I* wouldn't.'

'And Steve?' Rachael asked, after a pause. 'How does he fit into all this?'

'He doesn't. Why bring him into it?'

'Well, he's a factor, surely – if only in a negative sense.'

'I don't know what you mean, Rachael. You talk in riddles.'

Rachael gave her a long look. 'You mean you have no interest in him?'

'No. None whatsoever.'

'I find that hard to believe.'

'Tough.'

'He's been writing some good pieces lately. Have you seen them?'

'No. We never buy the rag. I'm surprised you do.'

'It's amusing. Makes a change from the *Guardian*.'

'You sound as though you fancy him yourself.'

'Perhaps I do.' Her smile glinted.

35

WHEN GLANABER HAD a home match, Meurig usually went to watch them. It wasn't the kind of rugby he was used to – the scrummaging was poor, the lineouts pathetic – but allowances had to be made. There was no rugby tradition in this part of Wales – soccer was the game here – but gradually the team was improving. It had a steady full-back, a pacy winger or two, and a fly-half with the right sort of cunning. Give him a decent sidestep and he might go places. Standing on the touchline, Meurig sometimes felt the old sensation of the ball in his hands, the exhilaration of a dummy successfully delivered and a way clear down the middle, if only he could outpace the bastard at his heels.

He had played one or two games for the stiffs on first going to Glanaber, but had suffered on the pitch and after. He'd been too long away, couldn't be bothered any more.

In the pale light of this late autumn afternoon, he was now nowhere near a rugby field. Another game was on his mind – a far crueller game.

'It was near here,' Brett said quietly. 'Mynydd Hyddgen. We could walk there easily if we had the time, but it's getting dark. You can't take risks with these mountains.'

A breeze shivered the steely waters of Nant-y-moch reservoir, a little way down the slope from where they sat in Brett's car near the summit of Plynlimon, the rounded mass of moorland high in the Cambrian Mountains that stood sentinel between the Welsh border and the sea. It seemed to invade the car itself, chilling the air with the breath of an old hatred. Meurig felt the thrill of something akin to sex, a compulsion that stirred the blood, yet was life-denying, not enhancing. He tried to picture Owain's warriors marching up here, half a millennium ago. What would they have been wearing? What weapons would they have carried? And then their wild whoops as they descended on the English, the savagery of the fight, the screams of the wounded...

'Oh yes, they've marked the spot alright,' Brett was saying, answering an unspoken question. 'There's two big blocks of stone there, roughly on the battlefield. He was outnumbered you know, Owain – nearly three to one. He got 'em sorted alright.' He laughed briefly.

Meurig had a weird sense that they had fallen through a cleft in time, down through the centuries of disillusion and defeat.

'So,' Brett said softly, 'what's it to be then? Yea or nay?'

'I told you,' Meurig replied. 'Count me in.'

'You sure now?'

'Positive.'

Brett took a deep breath. 'That's it then. Good man.'

'So what happens next?'

'You'll be hearing. Soon enough.'

Steve was perplexed. What was it about Jocelyn? She had come back in a good mood, thanked him for the flowers – they were indeed a pleasant surprise – was no longer the cold, resentful wife she had been when she went away. Could everything be sorted out so easily? Simon, on the other hand, seemed thoroughly out of sorts. He barely spoke to his father, went early to bed with no fuss. 'What's up with him?' Steve asked. 'He looks as if he's lost a shilling and found sixpence.' 'Oh, it's nothing,' said Jos. 'Don't worry about him. Just got a crush on one of his little friends at school, that's all. It'll soon pass.'

'You mean – he's in love? I'd no idea. Who is she then – did he say?'

'I don't know – Mary something – no, Mair. She had a party and he wasn't invited.'

'Poor little sod. Didn't know anything about it, did you?'

'No, not a clue. Pass me those clothes, darling, will you?'

She stood by the washing machine, hand held out imperiously. And this too was strange, her apparent indifference to Simon's let-down. He could sympathise with the boy, having had his share of pre-pubescent heartaches.

Steve lingered in the kitchen doorway, seeing her – as he had seen her before – as a woman out of her time, her long-lashed, downcast eyes having something medieval about them. Suddenly he was filled with a sense of the strangeness of her, and something else – a remoteness in her that set her apart, disturbingly.

'You enjoyed yourself then, did you?' he said, probing.

'Yes, very much. It made a nice change.'

'Change from me,' he said heavily. 'Can't say I blame you.'

'Now, don't start that.' She shut the door of the machine, set it going.

'See anyone you knew there?'

'You know I did. I told you.'

'Ah yes. You had a bar meal. What was her name now?'

'Fay.'

'Fay,' he mused, pretending. 'Can't say I remember her.'

'Why should you? You never met her.'

'You never mentioned her,' he retorted, nettled. 'That's what I mean.'

'How do you know? You don't remember everything I tell you, do you? 'Scuse me, darling.' She gave him a quick, febrile smile.

He followed her into the living-room. She had placed his flowers in vases. They lit up the gloomy morning. He thought of the woman in the flower shop, the slow smile of her, the earthy brown of her eyes. Jos had picked up a woman's magazine and was flicking through it, unconcerned.

'See anyone else you knew?'

'No. Except mum and dad, of course. Oh – Bill next door. He sends you his regards.'

'How is he, OK?'

'I think so. Seems to be.'

He lounged in an easy chair, looking at her reflectively. Again he heard a voice from their recent past, saw the face of the man, smiling.

'Did you go to that tennis club meeting after?' he asked suddenly.

Just for a second, her eyes flickered with surprise and uncertainty. 'What meeting?'

'You know. That special meeting they called, to talk about the future. Jack was keen for us to go, but I couldn't. I was here, covering the principal story.'

'Good heavens, Steve,' she said lightly. 'That was light years ago. How am I supposed to remember that?'

'You would have if you'd gone to it, surely. Jack Palmer was so keen. He practically made it a three-line whip.'

'Well, it's a bit late to ask about it now, isn't it? I haven't got a clue whether I went or not.'

'Strange.' And stranger still was the delicate pink that touched her cheeks.

'I wouldn't worry about it, darling,' she said reassuringly. 'I'm sure they survived without us. Coffee?'

'No, I don't think so. I'm seeing someone at twelve.'

'Oh? Who's that then?'

'Some farmer out in Llanilar. Judges horse shows and stuff. Bit of a character, so they say.'

'You've got time for a coffee, surely?'

He shook his head. 'Nah. Got to think what I'm going to ask him.'

He went to his 'office' upstairs. She stared thoughtfully at nothing.

Nigel was seeing her again. How could he not? Their separation had been merely token; they had not believed in it, not for a moment. The only difference was that now he approached her flat by means of an alleyway that had once led to a stinking 'court' of slum houses. The slums had long been swept away but the alleyway remained, furtive and constrained, a physical expression of the use to which it was put by such as Nigel Allan, solicitor and adulterer. He had gone beyond shame now, and concealment. He wanted the young body of Jenny Briggs, but something else too, far more dangerous to his marriage: the idea of her, the rebel caught up by a cause with which he increasingly identified. Gone now was that acute sense of the righteousness of the law, the sense of orderliness that had existed alongside his devotion to wife and children. Liberated from one, he was free too of the other. He did not know where it might lead. He did not care.

What had begun in pure lust was now consumed by love: such love as he had not felt since his teenage years, when he had fallen for Gaenor Charles, daughter of a college professor. She had been tall, black-haired, slim, a lissome girl with proud eyes and a kind of sweeping movement as she breezed through life with something like contempt for those around her. She had friends, yes, but only of a certain kind, the offspring of such parents as hers, consciously middle-class and superior – *so* superior – to the hoi-polloi of the market town and its surroundings. A farm boy such as himself was decidedly below the salt. It was not so much a question of money as of rank, so-called 'breeding' and a proper sense of the natural order of things: an essentially *English* order that put some occupations above others, some values above others, and naturally, the English language above the Welsh. Gaenor Charles had gone out with him a few times but only out of curiosity. There'd been some kissing and fumbling that had proved far more satisfying to him than to her, and she had dismissed him in a way that bruised his ego as well as his heart. He had suffered for it, this intense adolescent passion that had left its mark in the defences he had built around himself afterwards. Annette had pierced them, certainly, but his love for her was less unconditional than his feeling for Gaenor had been. It was rooted partly – and, it seemed now, fatally – in the comradeship of the office where they had worked together, and his admiration for the way she had coped with the 'shame' of having an illegitimate baby and, even more, with the tragedy of losing it.

His feeling for Jenny was of a different kind. There was the allure of her: those come-to-bed grey eyes, the heavy breasts, the physical recklessness of her – the way she'd splayed her legs out as she sat on that wooden crate, so excitingly and provocatively – and something else, that could not be adequately explained. It was in the assumptions they shared, as vital as those that held the 'toffs' together, assumptions interwoven with the language they always spoke together, the old Welsh tongue of their ancestors. It had swallowed him up, and he no longer tried to resist.

The coming of Christmas aided and abetted them. There was something in the air, an emotionalism you could almost touch. A small Sally Army band oompahed bravely in the streets, accompanied by bonneted collectors holding out tins with bright, trusting smiles. Nigel pressed money into them fervently, advance payment on future happiness. He and Annette did some token shopping together, but she knew he was betraying her again and that this was a mere lull in the storm that had engulfed them. The children were embroiled in it, for the effect on them was obvious. Joanna had turned against her father, while Robert clung to him with a kind of wordless pleading. For their sake, an outward pretence was maintained: Nigel and Annette still slept together, but there was no warmth in the house and disillusion seemed to drain everything of its colour.

The effect was felt, too, in the offices of Richards and James, Solicitors. The secretaries, Glenys and Delyth, treated Nigel with thinly veiled contempt. Stella, back from maternity leave, made up for lost time by making a great show of her dedication to her work, while – Nigel suspected – creeping to the boss, Edgar Richards. Prim, upright and essentially one for the easy option, Edgar had none of the charisma of his late father, who had run the practice with fierce moral authority. He knew of Nigel's goings-on – who didn't? – but turned a blind eye while his progenitor presumably turned in his grave. And in the privacy of Jenny's flat, the erring couple planned their future together.

36

STEVE MADE SEVERAL more half-hearted attempts at writing poetry, then gave it up. All that was behind him. And so, he now realised, was much else. His pride in himself as a journalist, for one thing. Gerwyn Hopkins had struck home. All this flimsy-flamsy stuff was so much garbage.

But he was stuck with it. Wasn't he? He had settled for it by bringing Jocelyn all the way here, to a place she detested. No wonder she had gone away without him for a few days. And come back a changed person? It certainly seemed so. Something had happened, but he would never know what.

He found himself thinking of the woman in the florist's. He couldn't remember her name now, but he'd had sex with her – it could hardly be called an affair – as a young reporter on the *County Dispatch*.

The woman in Back Row! That's how he remembered her. She'd taught him a lot, sexy bitch! It had been weird, seeing her again.

He walked the streets of the town with a strange sense of detachment. The Christmas lights had gone up, but he didn't feel at all Christmassy. The old restlessness was upon him.

Mooching around, popping in the pubs for the odd pint, he got wind of a rumour doing the rounds. A man called Meurig Owen had been arrested for possession of explosives with intent. Seems he had been set up by an M15 agent posing as a friend. A whole nest of Welsh Nats was under suspicion. All this was no concern of Steve's, as he had been told by head office that the *Comet*'s hard-news man in Wales, Tudor

Powell, would be coming up from Cardiff to cover it. The final humiliation.

He decided to put a wreath on Ceri's grave. A holly wreath for Christmas. He found another florist, near the cemetery, and took it to the grave one dreary morning. He hoped that Annette might be there, but she was not. He placed the wreath on the grave, read the simple inscription, and stood there for a long moment, saying goodbye.

Also by Herbert Williams

Novels
A Severe Case of Dandruff
The Woman in Back Row
Punters
The Marionettes

Poetry
The Trophy
A Lethal Kind of Love
Ghost Country
Looking Through Time
Wrestling in Mud

Short Stories
Stories of King Arthur
The Stars in their Courses
Tiger in the Park

Biography
Davies the Ocean: Railway King and Coal Tycoon
John Cowper Powys

History
Stage Coaches in Wales
Railways in Wales
Battles in Wales
Come Out, Wherever You Are

TELERI BEVAN

The Ladies of Blaenwern

The story of The Dorian Trio
and the Llanarth Welsh Cob Stud

yLolfa

£8.95

The Vagabond's Breakfast
Richard Gwyn

£9.99

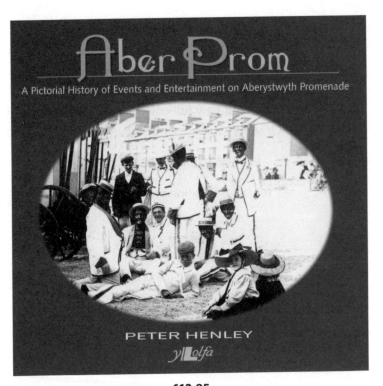

Aber Prom

A Pictorial History of Events and Entertainment on Aberystwyth Promenade

PETER HENLEY

y Lolfa

£12.95

Love Child is just one of a whole range of publications from Y Lolfa. For a full list of books currently in print, send now for your free copy of our new full-colour catalogue. Or simply surf into our website

www.ylolfa.com

for secure on-line ordering.

TALYBONT CEREDIGION CYMRU SY24 5HE
e-mail ylolfa@ylolfa.com
website www.ylolfa.com
phone (01970) 832 304
fax 832 782